DEATH
SERVES
AN ACE

HELEN WILLS

(Champion Tennis Player in the 1920s-1930s)

DEATH SERVES AN ACE

HELEN WILLS AND ROBERT W. MURPHY

COACHWHIP PUBLICATIONS
Greenville, Ohio

Death Serves an Ace, by Helen Wills and Robert W. Murphy
© 2018 Coachwhip Publications

Published 1939.
No claims made on public domain material.
Cover: Tennis ball © Mikael Damkier

CoachwhipBooks.com

ISBN 1-61646-453-4
ISBN-13 978-1-61646-453-0

CHAPTER ONE

I hadn't, in the first place, booked passage on the *Princess Victoria* to meet tennis celebrities, although for a long time afterwards a great number of my friends insisted that I had. Tennis was an afterthought. My trip was a business one primarily and happened to fall at the same time as the matches at Wimbledon. I liked tennis and I'd always wanted to see it at its peak on the famous Center Court. By pulling a few strings I'd got myself a ticket and hoped I'd have time to use it. As it turned out, I had the time and plenty of trouble along with it; for I saw too much of Wimbledon, and too much of Scotland Yard.

Very few of those same friends are convinced even yet that I didn't get mixed up in it on purpose. I'd always liked—from a great distance, of course, and mostly through the papers—Betty Dwight. I liked her style of play and the way she looked, I liked everything about her, and I'd been very vocal about it. "She's been Women's Singles Champion for five years," they'd say, "and that ought to be enough for her." Or "She plays as though nothing else in the world mattered to her. It's sport, isn't it? What's she so intent about?" It never failed to start me off. For she was a natural champion and proud of it, she didn't want to quit with her abilities at their peak; and if she played with an intensity that hadn't time for gestures toward the gallery it was because it was necessary, against the world's best competition, to concentrate utterly on the game and do her damnedest. I didn't know anything about her private life; it was none of my business; and there was little in the papers about her private life anyhow. She kept that in a different compartment, despite the fact that she was a public figure and fair game for editors in need of something to fill up a column or two every so often.

We sailed at noon and for the first day and a half out I hadn't even known she was on the boat. I hadn't looked at the passenger list, and I didn't go out of my cabin.

Work interested me now. After a somewhat carefree existence for twenty years, on an income that had made me very comfortable through school and college and the first two years at the Massachusetts Institute of Technology, I'd suddenly discovered at the beginning of the third year that I had ambition and a handy way in the designing of airplane motors. Thereafter the gilded stamping grounds of my youth grew accustomed to getting along without me. I still took a little time off for duck and quail shooting, but that was all. I'd gone the last two years at the Institute full out, and then started a sort of experimental factory which had grown in six years to be of great importance to me and the forty-two hand-picked men I'd gathered together. We had at last happened on something that looked revolutionary; it had looked so good that I'd set off for Europe to talk to as many experts as I could find; but on the day before I sailed a mistake had turned up in the calculations. My appointments were all made, however, so there was nothing to do but sail and try to straighten things out on the way.

Besides that, there was Wimbledon; and Captain Brererton of the *Princess Victoria*, an old family friend, and I wanted to sail with him.

So I was innocent of pushing myself forward with the Champion. Captain Brererton did that, for he'd held a place for me at the Captain's table, where Miss Dwight was sitting, and on the third night—a little bored with my warfare with the sliderule—I showed up and was introduced. Miss Dwight was very gracious; her aunt, a Mrs. Cosgrove, was also very pleasant. Mrs. Cosgrove—Aunt Bea, she was called—was a very nice old lady, small, silvery-haired, lively and chic; but I soon found out that the world hadn't changed much for Aunt Bea since her twenty-first birthday. Now, at sixty, she was phenomenally innocent. Her legs were more agile than her comprehension of the evil in the world; for she skipped rope in her cabin one hundred times daily before breakfast, but talked to drunks without realizing their happy condition. She read innocuous romances by the hundreds and talked a great deal about them, so I steered clear of her whenever possible. I didn't steer clear of Betty Dwight.

After dinner we went into the lounge for coffee, and as we were talking, I had an increasing consciousness that someone was watching me. I looked up and saw a pretty girl sitting with a group of people some distance away; she bowed. I returned the greeting but could not make out who it was. At that moment someone Betty knew asked her to dance. When Betty left me, the girl got up and came over to where I was sitting and sat down in Betty's chair. I noticed, curiously enough, that she was about the same height and build as Betty, but nowhere near as pretty.

"You're puzzled," she said. "Do you always dance with so many people that you can't remember the lucky ones? I'm Cynthia Blythe. I was at Freida Clark's party in Chicago."

I remembered her then; I'd had two dances with her and the suspicion returned that she'd engineered the second one herself. She telephoned my hotel the next evening and made a great to-do about my meeting her at a cocktail party— with more than faint suggestions of dinner afterwards—and a generally hysterical air that got my back up. Then business called me out of Chicago and I forgot all about the girl. And now I found that my first impression had lasted—she was pretty, in a petulant fashion, but over-effusive and insistent. I wished she'd go away before Betty came back.

"Are you dancing this evening?" she asked.

I was determined not to dance with her. I said, "No, I am waiting for Miss Dwight to finish this dance."

Her eyes darkened swiftly, and she glanced quickly out towards the floor. I could see Betty on the far side, her back towards us. The music had just stopped. Miss Blythe got up suddenly and said with a forced smile, "Well, I hope you have a nice dance with Miss Dwight." Before I could get up she was on the way back to her own group. The orchestra began playing again, and I watched Betty. She looked as if she were floating on air. I forgot I had told Miss Blythe I was not dancing, and Betty and I had several dances before she went to her cabin. She was retiring early because of Wimbledon.

That evening left me with the feeling that I'd better be a little careful. There had been something in Betty's clean-lined, cameolike face, in her candid brown eyes, which held for me an instant seduction. I couldn't define what it was, although I frequently caught myself thereafter, holding the sliderule and staring into space, trying. It might have been a quality of life in her, a vitality secret, grave and personal, which made her a little remote, a little mysterious, despite her quick friendliness. Provocative might have been a word to describe it, except that it was inadequate; for she was provocative in a special sense, beyond mere attraction. It had been somewhat upsetting, after all the talk about intentness, iron self-control, coldness, all the things I'd been reading in newspapers for years. There had been a lot of it, a lot of talk about her being a "killer" in sport and what not. It didn't tie up.

Maybe that was the thing which interested me at first, the seeming incongruity. I wanted to find out. Or maybe that was the excuse I gave myself. At any rate, I spent part of the next day with her. We got on wonderfully, despite the frequent interruptions; for there were candid camera nuts and autograph hunters all over the place, and everyone wanted to talk to her and be photographed with her and hear what she had to say about the coming matches or anything else. She was very generous with her time with them, she liked the excitement of it and had a great interest in people; but I wished them all to the devil.

By late afternoon of that day I knew I'd have to be more than a little careful, for strange things were happening to me. I wanted to be with her all the time; and when I went below and looked at the sliderule I had an impulse to throw it out the porthole. I had, in a remarkably short time, got myself into a bad way, and decided that it had to stop. It had to stop right there, I told myself, and after somewhat of a battle took off my coat, rolled up my sleeves, and sat down to the table with the sliderule. I didn't get very far; after an indeterminate time I suddenly discovered myself staring at the wall, recalling her profile against the dancing glitter of the sea as I had seen it earlier that afternoon, when, with all the other things in the world to talk about, we had been talking about star sapphires. A stone worn by one of the passengers, a man named Andrews with whom I'd

talked several times, had started it off; and as I had always
been a little cracked about star sapphires I'd launched off
on a windy dissertation. It seemed that she liked them too,
and I'd told her that she should wear one. They had always
been rather mysterious stones to me, with their dark depths
and color and star in them, and somehow I connected them
with the mystery that I'd chosen to find in her.

When I reached this point I got up and went into the
bathroom and held my head under the cold water tap for a
while, then returned to the desk and went to work. I worked
until dinner, had a tray sent in, and worked again; about
ten a storm blew up and rolled the *Princess Victoria* about
so violently that I gave it up and went to bed.

I didn't go on deck the next morning. I went to work
again and worked all day. It was an overcast day, chilly and
gusty, and a very long one; but I'd decided that I wasn't
going to make a fool of myself and stuck to it. Also, I felt
sorry for myself. She knew everyone, she was a well-known
figure in the world, there was nothing to it, no chance at
all, and wasn't I unfortunate? About nine-thirty the Captain
rang me up.

"What is it?" I asked him crossly.

"David," he said, "I'm a little concerned about Miss
Dwight. She hasn't been out all day. She should be enjoying
herself, and the Line wants her to think well of it."

"So what?" I said.

"You got on with her," he said. "She liked you. The
moon's come out, David. Listen now: run along up to the
boat deck and see if there aren't a few flying fish. Very handsome they are with the moon on them. Run up, now, and
see, and we'll send her a little note."

I put up a protest at that, a protest that wasn't as strong
as it might have been, and finally I went. He knew if there

were flying fish, they could be seen from the bridge or any of the crew on duty could be asked about them, but that was all right. There were no flying fish, as I discovered after I'd walked the prodigious length of the boat deck three times. But the moon on the ocean was beautiful, riding a wrack of clouds. I knew on the first lap that I was going to ask her to come up, but a lingering sense of discretion did its best to dissuade me. I fought with it, and presently paused in the dense shadow of a lifeboat, out of the wind, before I finally beat the sense of discretion down.

I hadn't been there very long before a movement forward caught my eye, and at the same time someone came from the stern, walking toward me. I got back into the shadow a little farther and stood still, and a woman walked past, sharply defined by the moonlight. She was tall and powerful, without a hat; she looked Scandinavian, there was a touch of the Viking about her. She was a striking figure with her upright carriage and pale hair, her predatory yet secretive face, but the thing which stood out more than anything else was her hands. I saw them for only an instant, but they seemed to be highlighted by the moon; they were the strongest woman's hands I had ever seen. She didn't look at me; all her attention was forward, where another figure was, and it was an attention with something inimical in it. As soon as she was past I stepped out a little, feeling that something was up, and then I saw the other figure plainly. Although it was pretty well down the deck and had its back to me, there wasn't any doubt in my mind that it was Betty Dwight. The shape was hers and the carriage, the beautifully coordinated way of moving, the same long white dinner dress and short marten jacket. She moved in a little toward a boat and stood still, and the other figure walked toward her, came even, and stopped. They met, stood for a moment talking; the tall, fair woman looked up and down the deck, then they got back into the shadow of the boat.

There was something that seemed so conspiratorial in their actions that it gave me a strange feeling. I didn't know who the Scandinavian was; I had never seen her before; but her bearing, her glance along the deck, and the retreat into the shadows hardly seemed like a usual thing. Wimbledon wasn't far off and Betty was defending her title. It was rumored that this was her last year. She naturally wanted to retire a champion, and anything hinting at skullduggery looked bad.

I stood very still, wondering uneasily about all the "killer" propaganda the sports writers had been busy on for years. Presently Betty emerged from the shadows, crossed the deck quickly and went below. The Scandinavian walked on around the curve of the bow.

I left the lifeboat's shadow and made my way to the Captain's quarters. He was there, reading, puffing clouds of stinking smoke out of a pipe as big as his fist. His weather-beaten, kindly face turned toward me and he grinned, and as usual his eyelids dropped a bit and showed their pale, untanned surfaces. "Well," he said, putting the book down, "you found a few flying fish, didn't you?"

"You knew I wouldn't," I said.

He rubbed his chin meditatively. "I wanted you to find them," he said, after a moment. "You've got to find a few."

"Let your third officer do it," I said. "That's what the Line pays him for. I don't want any of it."

He squinted a little. "No, no, he hasn't enough weight. David, Marie Azarin's aboard."

"Marie Azarin!" I said. She was the girl who would, in all probability, face Betty in the Center Court at Wimbledon for the title, a girl who had come on so rapidly in the last two years that she filled all the sports pages; she and Betty had never played each other, and the reporters had been making great capital out of what would happen when they did. It was an upsetting thing for Captain Brererton. "How did she get aboard in the middle of the ocean?" I asked.

"Ah," the Captain said, gloomily. "It's that damned uncle of hers. It's one of his damned sculpin's tricks. He got the three of them aboard under assumed names, and they lie low until the last night out. Then when Miss Dwight was coming in to dinner with her aunt, Marie walks up to her in the middle of the dining saloon and tries to get her to shake hands and talks in a voice loud enough to knock the port-holes out about how well she—Miss Dwight, I mean—*used* to play tennis. To upset her."

"Nice," I said. "What happened?"

"Miss Dwight wouldn't see her hand, and told her that she had always understood tennis was a *polite* game. It looked very cold-blooded, David, and now the passengers are sure the newspapers were always right."

"Weren't they?" I asked.

"Damn it!" he said, in an exasperated tone. "They weren't. Marie Azarin held a gun on her. Miss Dwight's a nice girl. You thought so yourself. I could see it in your eye. Now she's gone to her cabin and won't come out, and by God, David, you've got to help me. Walk her up and down and smooth things over."

"She's been smoothing things over for herself," I said, and told him what I'd seen.

He gave me a long stare. "You're dreaming," he said. "This ham-fisted blonde you're talking about is with Aza-rin. She's a sort of secretary and masseuse, and her name's Helga. No, no, I don't believe it. You saw somebody else. The stewardess insists she hasn't come out and won't. I sent her a note myself."

I didn't say anything. There was always the chance that I could have been mistaken. It was a long deck and marten capes usually looked alike, but I thought I knew the way Betty walked. I regretted I'd been busy and dined in my cabin, missing the famous meeting. I could have got some feeling about her out of it, some intuition maybe, to go on. I didn't believe in the newspaper twaddle about all this coldness; it had been trumped up to make her more dramatic and sell more papers. Secretly I sided with the Captain; but the cynicism about top-flight tennis which had been growing within me for the past several years, combined with what I had just seen, started a feeling of uncertainty.

The telephone rang. He got up and answered it. His eyes moved toward me and his brow drew down. "Yes," he said. "I'll investigate immediately. I'll let you know." He hung up. "Betty Dwight's cape's gone," he said. "It's gone from her cabin, and she says she had hung it up near the window and went into the bathroom and when she came out it was gone. The window opens onto a little-used deck. She doesn't say exactly when. Maybe you saw Betty in that cape on deck and maybe you didn't!" He called the officer on duty, gave some instructions, hung the phone up with a scowl, and sat down again. "Nobody saw you up on the boat deck?" he asked.

I raised my eyebrows. "You wouldn't suspect Betty Dwight of lying?" I asked, with fitting irony.

"I wouldn't," he said. "But what's this all about? They say this is Miss Dwight's last year, and she's set on winning. And I'll tell you one thing more: she had the doctor in this morning, although he wouldn't tell me why. She wasn't seasick from the blow last night, although nearly everybody else was. I got that much out of him. What the hell's wrong with her? Or is she afraid of this Marie Azarin? I don't like it. All at once I don't like it. The uncle, Azarin, is as crooked as a snake. He'd do anything for money."

"Betty hasn't any money," I said. "Her aunt has it."

"The hell with her aunt's money. There's going to be enough talk about this. If an ordinary passenger lost a cape nobody would hear of it; but the Lady Champion gets the devil's own amount of publicity whether she wants it or not. I'll be keel-hauled by the office. For the last time, David, will you take her for a walk and cast everything else out of her mind by your insistent and manly charm? Anything short of assault and battery. I don't want the anchor shoved down my throat because of the complaints of the Lady Champion."

I stood up. "I'll think it over," I said. "I'm getting curious myself."

I went back to my cabin and sat down on the bed to think a moment. If Azarin had stolen Betty's cape and sent someone to the boat deck in it, why had that been done when nobody was about? If it was Betty herself on deck, had she seen me and raised a row over a supposedly stolen cape to protect herself? Did that have anything to do with the doctor's visit, and why had she suddenly (before she knew of Azarin) decided to stay in her cabin? Something, I estimated, was liable to happen now that Azarin had mixed himself up in the situation. I knew little enough of him, but that little was not reassuring. The day before I'd been talking to Horace Andrews (the wearer of the sapphire), who was going over to see the tennis, and who had let drop a mysterious hint or two about Azarin. I decided to hunt Andrews up, and went to the lounge.

It was an expensive room, done in the best modern manner, and there were plenty of people in it. There was a concert of sorts going on, discreetly subdued in order to avoid interference with conversation. I wandered about and finally found Andrews sitting by himself. He was a rather distinguished-looking man, touched with gray at the temples, tanned and fit. He had mentioned that he had retired from the brokerage business, and amused himself by collecting paintings and serving on the boards of several charities. He nodded and indicated the empty chair beside him; I sat down.

"I haven't seen Miss Dwight about," he said. "Is she ill?"

He had talked to her quite a little himself, and noticed the attention I'd paid to her; but why would he ask me about her the first thing? The scene on the boat deck was fresh in my mind, and I even began to suspect him of something. "She *was* rather ill," I said, to see what would come of it, "but she's much better. Didn't you see her in the dining saloon?"

"Oh, that? No, I dined late. I've heard about it, though. Everybody on board's heard about it. Quite characteristic of Azarin, I should say."

"Do you know Azarin?" I asked.

"Good Heavens, no! But I became interested in him when this niece of his came into the limelight. He went from the Riviera to California, where he suddenly discovered this surprisingly proficient niece. I don't think she's any more his niece than you are."

The newspapers hadn't got around to that, which was surprising if there were any grounds for it. "Why?" I asked.

"Well, I think he's a gambler. He had a villa in Cannes, on the Croisette, for a number of years. He played about with the gayer set and spent a good deal of money, but nobody seems to know where it came from. That Swedish woman was with him there, in a somewhat anomalous position. She wasn't a servant, she was a sort of secretary and what not. But there was never any mention of Marie."

"But the sports writers—" I began, deciding to stay away from the subject of Helga.

"If the sports writers have anything on him they're keeping it for some reason. I understand there's proof of relationship and adoption. I wouldn't put it past him to forge the papers."

"You don't seem to like him much," I said.

His nose wrinkled slightly. "Mr. Cameron," he said, "he is, to me, the logical result of the changed viewpoint regarding tennis. Tennis was a gentleman's game, a matter of pure sportsmanship. It was not like baseball and wrestling, games for the masses, without subtlety. One expected shady characters in them. But tennis—the things happening to it have a philosophical significance, indicating the spread of an all-pervading cynicism. As a last stronghold, it has fallen; it is not played for sport anymore, but to make money. It is an expression of national policy, a playground for gamblers, a refuge for dumb-bell athletes. I see this with great regret. The only reason I became so interested in Azarin was because he is, to me, a symbol of decay in a game I have always loved."

"But a smart one," I said, to keep things going.

"Indeed, a smart one. A redoubtable fellow; his rather theatrical name is well chosen. There is an air of curling black moustaches and chicanery about it."

I didn't reply at once. His remarks may have been exaggerated, but there was more information in them than I'd expected. The music had become louder as we talked, and he had raised his voice several times. He was beginning to attract attention, so I asked him if he'd join me for a Scotch and soda in the bar. I wanted to hear more.

"A Scotch and soda?" he asked, turning toward me. His tanned, urbane face took on a strange expression. There was at once something frightened and reckless in it, a sort of spasm which was gone almost at once. I didn't know what to make of it, and while I was searching my mind for a recollection of seeing him mentioned as a temperance crusader he said, as though to himself: "Why not? Why not? Yes, let's get a drink."

We got up and went off to the subdued leather-and-gold-and-lapis splendor of the bar, sat down and ordered. When the drinks came he got half of his into himself as though he was thirsting to death. His eyes shone, in a manner which made him look much less urbane. "Ah," he said, licking his upper lip quickly. "Don't make the mistake of talking to Azarin," he said suddenly. "If he finds out you've been friendly with Miss Dwight . . . No, I wouldn't become entangled with him. It might be unfortunate later on."

It was, in my opinion, a very strange thing for him to say. I began to wonder if he had an ax to grind himself, how he knew so much about Azarin that hadn't seen the light of print, why he wanted to keep me away from Azarin. I wondered if what he had told me about himself was true. He was busy swallowing the rest of the whiskey, and his manner of doing it suited neither his high-flown sentiments about tennis nor his appearance. It had the unpicturesque haste of a hog getting into a trough. He drained the glass and signaled for the waiter.

"Miss Dwight's illness, as I understand it, is not very serious?" he asked.

"It might be," I said, carrying on. "All streptococcic infections, no matter how minor, are liable to be serious."

"Dear me!" he exclaimed, and knocked his empty glass over. "Who will defend us against the powers of darkness? This is most unsettling." He stared at me in a manner that might have been described as aghast, reached down for the glass, put it back on the table, and drummed his fingers on the tabletop. The waiter came up with another whiskey. He stared at that too, then stood up. "Excuse me," he said. "I should like to go to the washroom. I'll be right back."

He went out, and after several minutes I went after him. I didn't believe the washroom story and my lack of belief was soon vindicated, for the boy on duty said he hadn't been there. I thought of going to the radio room, but decided there wasn't time. I returned to the bar, and after a few minutes he returned.

He began to talk about Art. "It is rather exciting," he said. "In Italy, the most wretched hovel holds possibilities which are tremendous. I . . . ah . . . tremendous!" He leaned forward slightly. "That Azarin should have been an art dealer. It is just the trade for his peculiar talents."

I began to feel that there was something mad in all this, that possibly I was having a mad interval myself. If he was a gambler, his appearance and manner (with the exception of his drinking) indicated that he was a good one; and if he was a good one he would do nothing so crude as rush to the radio room on the instant of hearing my talk about infections. He began to drink the second Scotch and soda, but in a much more civilized manner, and to talk about Leonardo da Vinci. He talked very well, entertainingly and with knowledge, but there seemed to be a tension in him. His eyes grew too bright; his beautifully manicured fingers drummed soundlessly and continually on the table; and as I was more interested in Azarin than in Leonardo I tried several times to swing the conversation back to him.

"Azarin," he said finally, and with apparent reluctance, "intends to have this match. The rewards of tennis these days are large, and he is not the man to take Marie to Wimbledon for the purpose of furnishing an easy victory for

Miss Dwight. He doesn't work like that. There has been talk in some circles that he is taking Marie to Wimbledon to give everyone the impression that she is ready, and putting his money on Miss Dwight. I do not believe it. I have seen Marie play. She is a valuable property, and I do not think he will take the chance of discouraging her. He has never been a man for long shots. And because he wants to win, I consider him dangerous."

I wondered what circles he meant, but before I had a chance to ask him he finished the whiskey, signaled for another, and began on Leonardo again. I'd had enough of Leonardo; at the first break in his monologue I stood up, excused myself on the pretext of an engagement, and left. It was beginning to sound like a good idea to ask Betty Dwight to look at the flying fish after all. I went through the lounge, where Marie Azarin, sitting with a sleek, dark young man, looked up and saw me. She smiled faintly, a smile at once non-committal and encouraging, carrying a hint that I might consider making her acquaintance if I was so minded. She was a tall and handsome girl, with blue-black hair and cheekbones as high as an Indian's, very decorative; but there was an arrogance in her face, perhaps because of the cheekbones, which hinted at a savage and vindictive temper. I smiled back, and kept on going; I had other fish to fry at the moment. I went through all the multitudinous public rooms on the ship, a weary succession of minor masterpieces in *l'art moderne*, and Betty wasn't in any of them; I started back to my cabin to write her a note.

I was going through a transverse corridor on my own deck when Andrews passed the end of it. He was walking with the suggestion of a stagger, which was to be expected; what interested me was what he was after. I knew his own cabin was on the deck above; I hurried to the end of the corridor and peeped around. He went on, weaving a little, looking at the numbers on the doors; when he came to a cabin almost opposite the one I was in on the other side of the ship he paused, rubbed his chin, moved up to the door and knocked. He glanced up and down the corridor. The door opened, he made a quick gesture, and went in.

When the door was closed I walked past it, got the number, and went to my own cabin. I called Captain Brererton, and asked who occupied the cabin Andrews had gone into. He said he'd call me back; in a few minutes the phone rang.

"Captain Brererton?" I asked. "Whose cabin is it?"

"Azarin's," he said. "Listen, David, what have you got?"

"No marten jackets," I said. "I'm leaving them for you."

Before he could say anything more I hung up, wrote a note to Betty, and rang for the steward to deliver it.

CHAPTER TWO

Either my luck was in or Captain Brererton had made a convincing job of talking me up as a trustworthy young man, for the steward came back with a note: "Thank you. I would like to go out for a little while. Could you come by for me? B. D." I put on my topcoat and went along to her cabin, hoping that her Aunt Bea wouldn't be about. I didn't feel quite up to Aunt Bea, so when Betty came out alone at my knock I heaved an inward sigh of relief.

We stood looking at each other for a moment. She was smiling slightly, very self-contained, probably trying to estimate what I was thinking about her, about the affair at dinner. If so, it was an impossible job, for I didn't know myself. For the first time I had her away from the autograph hunters, the candid camera nuts, the curious, and it gave me a strange feeling. The sense of pleasure I had while looking at her, the seduction, was there as always—badly confused by the memory of the scene on the moonlit boat deck. That scene was entangled in the legend that had been built up in my mind for years by the printed word—a rather mysterious girl who played with a concentration which shut out everything. We started to walk slowly down the corridor.

"It's practically deserted on the boat deck," I said, "and nice for walking. Shall we go up?"

"Yes," she said. "I'd rather not see many people. You were in the dining saloon?"

Her voice had a light, appealing timbre. It was, I thought a little sardonically, a wonderful voice to put a man off his guard. It couldn't have been better. "No," I said, and waited for her to justify herself.

She didn't. "It was very unpleasant," she said. We came to the stairs, passed several people who stared, then we stepped out into the moonlight and the wind caught at us. We walked the length of the deck once without speaking. The ship rose and fell slowly and regularly, as though breathing in its sleep; the moonlight gleamed on the superstructure and followed the long seas in a running glitter, and the fresh breeze was just strong enough to give one the lively, pleasant feeling of fighting against it. The light, clean scent that she used—some field-flower or other—came to me now and then. Despite the suspicions that were on me, the uncertainties arising from what I had heard and the strange things that had gone on, I began to feel a sort of exultation at being with her. I couldn't help it. I had been predisposed toward her from the beginning; at that moment I didn't care what she did to win tennis tournaments, what means she might employ to combat Azarin or anybody else. She wanted to win, and had to fight Azarin with Azarin's tactics. I wouldn't have cared if she had told me that she privately sacrificed her small nieces and nephews to Moloch. It was a typical example of moonlight-and-pretty-girl logic, and amidships it inspired me to swing over to the rail between two boats and stop. We leaned on the rail side by side, looking at the sea.

After a short space I turned toward her. She was looking out, toward the horizon; her cameo-like profile, clear against the luminous water, was intent and still. She seemed to have forgotten me.

"What are you thinking about?" I asked.

She didn't turn. "Nothing," she said, in a low tone. "Nothing at all."

"That's not so," I said.

"What do you think I ought to say?"

"You don't have to say anything," I said. "But I should like us to be friends for the moment, that's all. We may never look at an ocean like this again. I'll watch you win at Wimbledon and go on, and never see you again, probably." She turned and looked at me, her eyes dark. "Let's stop the clock for a little while," I went on. "It's perfectly simple."

"It's not so simple as that," she said. Her voice had a note of surprise in it, as though she had been recalled by something completely unexpected from deep thought about herself—about her troubles or plans, perhaps. "No," she began again. "There is a . . ." She suddenly caught herself, as on the edge of a confidence; a defensive look crossed her face. People had probably tried to get information out of her that way before.

"Forget about it," I said.

"No, no," she said quickly. "Not about stopping the clock! Why did you say that?"

"Ah," I said, still thinking of the defensive look. "Out of a full heart, or to be amusing."

"It's you who are not telling me what you are thinking," she said, in that same low tone.

Maybe, I thought, she really did want a moment's friendliness, wanted to shut out for a short time all the currents of suspicion and antagonism, her plans and the plans of others, the entire welter of maneuverings and ambitions. "Ever since I met you," I said, "I have wanted to tell you what was in my thoughts."

It sounded silly as I said it, like something an adolescent boy would get off, and yet I meant it. Not in that phraseology, perhaps; that had popped out; even her eyebrows went up slightly at it. She seemed to lean towards me a little. "You don't know me," she said. "You don't know anything about me. Everyone you talk to, now—"

It didn't sound like a leading question; not then. "It doesn't make any difference," I interrupted. Then, before I knew how it happened, I kissed her lightly where the end of her eyebrow winged up in such a beguiling way. I was surprised at myself. It was a mistake, and definitely finished the moonlight-and-pretty-girl side of the affair. It was marvelous and unfortunate.

We both drew back a little. She stood looking at me, her hands at her sides. "David," she said. "You are very foolish."

"I want to be!" I said. I took a step, but her hands came up and I stopped. "Why don't you give up the idea of Wimbledon?" I said urgently. "Don't go any further with it. You're out of your class with that man."

Her head came up quickly. "What do you know?" she said. "What have you found out?"

"What were you doing an hour ago?" I asked. I didn't say it as a reproach, not the way I was feeling then; it was a sort of lever to urge her to drop Wimbledon. It was the first thing that came into my mind. "Don't play," I went on. "Say that you're ill, say anything. The ship's doctor can certify you aren't fit to play." There was some idea in my mind of fixing it up with Captain Brererton; he'd put a little pressure on the doctor for me.

It seemed to me that her face had got paler in the moon-light; her eyes, fixed on me, were very dark. There was a moment of silence. "I am very upset," she said suddenly.

"Can't you let this tournament go?" I asked. "You've been on top long enough, longer than anyone ever was before. Things have changed a lot. Betty, please let it go."

"No," she said, without moving, in a stronger tone. "No! This is my last one. You can't make me stop, David. Nobody can."

Her tone was defiant, but she seemed to linger an instant on my name. "Good Lord!" I said, thunderstruck. "Do you think I came up here with an ulterior motive? Do you think I'm in with the rest of them?" I took a step toward her, but she moved quickly back. "You can't go on this way," I said heatedly. "Suspecting everyone, dodging about."

"Can I, I wonder?" she asked. It sounded as though she was questioning herself, not talking to me. She was silent for a moment; we stared at each other; then she said: "Come see me in London, David. We'll be at the Dorchester."

Before I could answer she turned, practically ran across the deck, and vanished. I was too surprised to move; I stood and watched her go, then looked quickly up and down the deck. I was on the edge of anger, mostly at myself, and badly bewildered. Before this evening I had possessed a little detachment. I had been interested in her. But now the detachment had evaporated, and the interest had blazed up into an emotion of sufficient proportions to confound me. That was bad enough, and her anomalous position made it worse. She hadn't denied being on deck earlier, and she had implied complete confidence in being able to take care of herself with Azarin. A pretty affair, I thought to myself, and took a few turns up and down the deck to calm down.

Half an hour later I went by Captain Brererton's cabin, knocked, and went in. He was still smoking the tremendous pipe, but he wasn't reading. He gave me a somewhat sardonic stare, and gestured toward a seat.

"So," I said. "You're speechless. Haven't you found the cape yet?"

"You're still interested in that?"

"Why wouldn't I be?" I asked.

"I thought she'd changed your mind, up there in the moonlight."

That had a nasty sound to it. "You've been peeping?" I asked. "You, after egging me into this for your own perverted enjoyment, turn and rend me."

"David—"

"Sentimental David," I said.

"Anything you like. Of course, I've kept a bit of a watch on her. I've got a bit of a watch on everybody. After she left you she went back to her own cabin for about twenty minutes then to C deck and into an alley that two cabins open out on. One of the stewards saw her standing in front of the cabin door, with her hand up. She'd just knocked, then went in. After a bit she came back to her own cabin."

"Who was in the cabin on C deck?" I asked.

"A woman named Cynthia Blythe, by the records. Ever hear of her?"

"Yes, I met her a couple of months ago in Chicago," I said. "But she wouldn't have anything to do with the cape."

"Maybe not. The stewardess says she's very quiet, and hardly ever goes out." He took his pipe from his mouth, blew out a great cloud, and said suddenly: "Damnation! I'm a quiet man, I can handle most devilment on my own ship, but what the countersunk hell's all this about? First Betty Dwight has a pow-wow with Azarin's masseuse; then her cape disappears, then she takes you into camp; then she talks to Cynthia Blythe. Who the devil's Cynthia Blythe? What did Miss Dwight say to you?"

"She said she was nervous and upset, but that she was going to win the tournament. Nobody's going to stop her."

"You seem to like her better than ever!"

"Listen, Captain Brererton—"

"I won't listen. Did you sign anything? Besides having this monkey business on my ship I've got you to watch out for." He stood up, and just as he did it the phone rang. He turned toward it with a curse. "Hello!" he said furiously. "What? Oh, has it?" he asked, sarcastically. "And what about Miss Dwight?" There was an interval of talk, which he interrupted with another curse. "If you let her out of your sight for five minutes more I'll have your job, you . . . you . . ." He failed to find a word, smacked the receiver down, and turned to me. "Miss Helga Lindstrom's cabin has been ransacked," he said, mimicking the first officer's voice. "After Miss Dwight returned from C deck and went into her cabin they relaxed their watch for a moment. The next time they saw her she was walking calmly down the corridor, and went into her cabin again. Ah!" he said, in inarticulate fury, and walked up and down for a moment. "The bloody lunkheads! Excursion boat sailors!"

"Who reported Miss Lindstrom's cabin?" I asked.

He stalked to the phone and talked some more. "Azarin," he said, when he hung up. "And don't tell me he fixed it so Miss Dwight was out of her cabin at the time. Don't tell me anything. In five minutes I'll have such a watch on the lot of them . . . Damn it, I wish I had twenty more in the crew. Get out! Leave me in peace. I've got some work to do."

"With pleasure," I said. "If you're coming up to London tomorrow, look me up at the Mayfair. You might be able to

tell me something." I left, and he slammed the door behind
me. I was glad enough to go. He'd roar about for ten minutes, have everybody's job, then calm down and go to work.
That was the way he went at it; an explosion, and then cool
and complete efficiency. Nothing more would go on that
night, but that was beside the point. What had gone on
was enough for me. Thinking about it as I walked down the
corridor I suddenly noticed several petty officers grouped
around an open door; when I pulled even with them I saw
that the cabin was Andrews', for he was standing in it. He
was singing low, somewhat alcoholically, and a chair came
out. One of the petty officers caught it, then Andrews saw
me. He had been lifting another chair; he put it down, stared
at me, and said: "Well, well. It's the friend of the champion.
My lad, does your mother know you're out?"

I hesitated. One of the petty officers very politely requested me to keep moving. Andrews took this amiss. "I
want to tell him," he remarked, "to take a hitch on himself.
He's so young." He began to sing again, loudly. The two
men looked at each other and started for him; he picked up
the chair; then the men had him, pulling the door closed as
they went. There was a series of thumps, and I continued
on my way.

I would have given a good deal for ten minutes' talk with
him, for he was apparently in the condition to be informa-
tive. I wanted information badly, particularly about Betty,
and from his remarks he was the man to give it. Probably
he would have said a number of things I wouldn't have believed; but at least he would have given me some indication of what to look for. I'd always admired Betty from a
distance, and that had been enough. But now, suddenly, it
wasn't enough anymore. Captain Brererton and the moonlight had finished that; I wanted to know all I could, the

good and the bad. And what part, if any, she was playing in this rather extraordinary picture.

There was nothing priggish in my interest. I knew no one who accomplished anything got through the world in the spotless robes of a Methodist hymn angel, and her life had been more active than most; besides that, I hadn't been looking for an angel to fall in love with. I was ready to accept any explanation within reason, if I could only get one.

I was thinking about this when I reached the bottom of the stairs giving on to the B deck corridor, so preoccupied that I nearly ran into Azarin. He had, apparently, been coming from the stern, seen me, and stopped. I'd often seen pictures of him and once glimpsed him at a distance; I'd never been so close to him before. He was a rather heavyset man, dark, with a skin that was almost olive and seemed to have a faint, greasy shine on it; he had a sly, sleepy-looking face, like some of the long dead ancestors of the Dutch House of Orange. His eyes were coolly blue when they opened a little, accentuated by the dark brows and lashes; there was a sort of Continental urbanity or sophistication about him, an impermeable surface—like armor, without openings, giving the impression that it concealed something so slippery that if you ever got inside the armor you'd be no better off than you had been before. Despite this he had a presence, a finish, and such a good one that you wondered if you weren't doing him an injustice to think ill of him. He was very confusing.

"Good evening, Mr. Cameron," he said. "I was looking for you."

For a moment I was too surprised to say anything. Then I did manage to get out: "Indeed?"

"Yes," he said. "My niece noticed you passing through the lounge. There are few interesting-looking people on the ship, and she wanted to talk with you. An unconventional wish, I must admit, but at such a time I try to indulge her in these little matters. Her nerves are somewhat on edge, as you may judge."

He got this rigmarole off very smoothly, and at any other time I would have gone with him just to see what it was all about. But the day had been enough for me. I bowed slightly and said: "I'm sorry, but I must ask to be excused." It sounded very stilted. "The fact is," I went on, "I'm tired as the devil. I wouldn't do justice to your niece's flattering impression. Some other time, perhaps."

His head nodded but his eyes remained fixed on mine, and there was something inimical in them—or there seemed to be. I couldn't be sure. His very proximity seemed inimical. My head was full of thoughts of Betty, of all the mysterious things that had gone on, of his trumped-up excuse to take me to meet Marie Azarin. It struck me that I had somehow got involved in something I knew nothing about, or that someone had involved me. "Yes," he said. "Some other time, perhaps." There was a sort of submerged, mocking irony in his tone which implied that he knew more of my position than I knew myself. It was disconcerting. "I have taken a cottage on Wimbledon Common. You must visit us there."

He bowed and took himself off, walking up the stairs with his toes pointing out. I went to my cabin, undressed and got into bed, but I couldn't sleep. Faint reminiscences of Betty's perfume came to me, the texture of her skin, Azarin's eyes, the scene on the boat deck, the image of the Scandinavian with the great hands in the moonlight; I finally got up and rang for some allonal. That knocked me out finally, but not even that could keep dreams away from me. I spent a wretched night, had breakfast in my cabin, and let the steward pack my things. When I finally dressed and went on deck they were docking the ship.

The world was full of watery morning sunlight and smoke and whistles and waterfront smells; gulls swooped overhead and people milled about. England was all around me and I didn't want to look at it; I went inside, and sat in the lounge until the time came to go ashore. Betty and her aunt had apparently got through the customs early and left, for I saw nothing of either of them.

As the man went through my luggage I walked over to a place from which I could see the "A" division. Andrews and Azarin were there, paying no attention to each other, and as I watched there was a stir at the gate and a woman came through, hesitated for an instant, and looked about. Poised against the grubby barrier, she was strikingly beautiful: tall and fair, in features and complexion she was the ideal type of English beauty. She was obviously the product of generations of breeding and privilege, and if you'd had any doubts about the system you forgot them looking at her. She spoke to the chauffeur behind her and started for "A" section, and as I followed her progress I saw Andrews turn, look at her, smile and take off his hat. She waved gaily; they met with great warmth, like very old friends, and began to talk animatedly.

That was the first jolt my romancing about her received. The second followed closely upon it; for suddenly she stopped talking to stare over Andrews' shoulder at Azarin, who had just straightened up from his bags. Her color changed a little; her face took on a mask of concentration, as though she was exerting her will to the utmost to make him look at her. He turned, and for an instant forgot himself and seemed to have tasted something sour. The expression was gone at once and he came forward, well under control, affable, wary and

polished. She was obviously excited at seeing him, so excited
as to forget Andrews, but Azarin brought him to her attention and was introduced. The two men acted as though they
had never seen each other before, as though Andrews had
never secretly visited Azarin in his cabin. The Englishwoman
seemed to forget Andrews again; her attention and her
glance were concentrated entirely on Azarin.

While this was going on Marie Azarin came up. She gave
the woman an unpleasant look and got as good in return; I
felt if there had been knives handy they'd have gone for each
other without more ado.

It was surely a happy little scene, and Azarin must have
liked it. He towered above them all like Jove in his cloud,
and only intervened when the women began to glare a bit
too pointedly at each other. I wished I'd been closer. Things
apparently became warm, for Azarin unbent enough to
speak a few words to Marie with a sort of detached politeness. Azarin and Andrews shook hands and spoke briefly;
the Englishwoman said something to Azarin urgently, looking into his face. Then he took Marie's arm and drew her
away. I had the feeling that I'd see them all again, including
the Englishwoman, and that it wouldn't be for the better
either. A porter came up and told me my bags were ready,
and I asked him who she was.

"Lady Irene Wrexford-Bond, sir," he said. "An angel if
there ever was one, sir."

I nodded and followed him, thinking that she might
have been an angel indeed with the exception of the company she kept. A sense of impending trouble for both Betty
and myself descended upon me as I walked after the porter,
a sense of loneliness; for Azarin and Andrews, secretly allied
and up to something, would surely utilize the established
order in the person of Lady Irene as far as they were able.

CHAPTER THREE

Arriving in London I got comfortably settled by lunch time, ate alone, wasted an hour or so, and went to the Dorchester to see Betty. Having achieved an enviable eminence as the best hotel in London, the Dorchester lived up to it; I waded through enough leisurely British formality to suit anybody, and ascended in the "lift." A man with whose face I was vaguely familiar opened the door of Betty's suite and smiled upon me. He was pleasantly drunk; not in the staggering stage, but carrying it in that cheerful fashion which indicated that such a condition was a retreat for him, and that his retreats were long ones. It was impossible, somehow, not to like him at sight. There was a sort of kindliness in his face, a sweetness which was underlaid by melancholy. But I wondered how he happened to be around.

"Come in," he said. "Come right in. Betty's here somewhere." I stepped in and introduced myself. "Glad to know you," he said. "My name's Gasden. You want to see Aunt Bea, I take it?"

I remembered him then. He'd been on the Davis cup team six or seven years before, a tower of strength until arthritis had suddenly finished him; and as tennis was all that he knew, all he had ever been interested in, he had

turned into a sort of barfly and tennis hanger-on. He followed players around, living mostly in England and France.

"Good to see another American," he went on. "I'm one
myself." He suddenly shouted: "Aunt Bea!"

While this went on I collected myself. We were in the
sitting room, spacious and expensive; Gasden began to talk
again, moving beside me with a hobbling walk, and before
we reached the middle of the room Mrs. Cosgrove came in.
It was evident she didn't realize Gasden was drunk; it never
occurred to her; she laughed at him while shaking hands
with me.

"Charley's *so* amusing," she said. "And so clever. He came
to see Betty, of course. I suppose you did too?" I nodded.
"Well, Charley insists she's here, but she's not. She went out
with the strangest-looking man right after lunch. I think
she shouldn't have done it, but of course the English police
are so nice. I'm sure she won't get into trouble. Really, the
strangest person."

I swallowed this in silence. She glanced at Gasden, and
leaning toward me whispered: "He looked like a gangster."

"Secrets?" Gasden asked, with great good humor. "I knew
Betty before he did. Fatherly interest. I did, too," he said,
turning toward me confidentially. "Wonderful girl. Fun."

"She said she was coming right back," Mrs. Cosgrove
said. "And that's been two hours ago."

"Did he give his name?" I asked. I was beginning to feel
that something funny was going on.

"Oh, no," she said. "Betty called him up. I don't see how
he got into the hotel. Oh, his clothes were nice, but . . ."
She forgot about him. "Betty's always disappearing, so I'm
used to it. Do you remember two years ago, in Melbourne,
Charley?"

"Sure," Gasden said. "When she said she was going to the photographer's. That was the year that Australian girl got ptomaine poisoning."

They both laughed, and Mrs. Cosgrove said: "You see? He remembers everything. We joked about it. We told Betty that she'd done it, because we found out she didn't go to the photographer's at all."

I recalled the Australian girl; she had been a formidable opponent. The pair of them laughed again.

I decided I'd had enough of it. "Will you tell Betty I stopped in?" I asked. "I'll try again tomorrow."

The pair of them walked with me to the door. "In the afternoon," she said. "Betty will be practicing all morning. The time was so short this year. We wanted to come much earlier, but every boat we reserved passage on that horrid Marie Azarin reserved passage on too. I told them at the tourist agency to let me know."

I was in the hall by then, and got to the elevator as quickly as I could. I wondered apprehensively if they talked like that where people could hear them. I devoutly hoped they didn't, and fell to thinking of what Mrs. Cosgrove had said about Azarin booking passage on all the boats they had booked passage on. That was a new angle, and took Azarin's campaign much farther back. It was true that he had crowded Betty, for there were only three days until the matches began. It wasn't long enough, particularly when I thought of the Captain's story of the doctor being to see her. And then, who could the man be who "looked like a gangster"? I decided to call upon Azarin. There wouldn't, I was sure, be any trouble about that. He wanted to see me as much as I wanted to see him. As soon as I got back to my hotel I put through a call to him, and was promptly invited to come to Wimbledon after dinner. In fact, he'd send a car for me; it was only about forty-five minutes. I thanked him and accepted.

The car that came for me that evening was one of those miniature affairs that put your knees into your chin. We went off toward Chelsea, over Battersea Bridge, and through the very poor part of London in a gathering fog. The chauffeur struggled with it, telling me in an aggrieved tone that London didn't have such fogs at that time of year. But it grew thicker by the moment; we were reduced to crawling, and if the chauffeur hadn't known his way by instinct we would have had to camp for the night. As it was, we were very late. Some people were already there. Even as the maid took my hat in the hall I could feel an atmosphere in the place that made a sort of prickle along my scalp. I hesitated in the doorway and saw a large room, rectangular, and predominantly gray in tone. There was a fireplace with a fire in it halfway down one wall and the furniture was gray too, a wood I didn't know. Azarin must have rented it from some Colonial administrator who had enough money to own a house in that somewhat expensive neighborhood. It was liberally sprinkled with African native sculpture, gleaming black masks and a figure or two. It was these things which gave the room a strange air; for they stared at you with empty eyes and. their outlandish, stylized features seemed full of a secret and ancient mockery. At the far end of the room a gray mask nearly three feet high hung on the wall above the built-in bookcases. It had long straw hair and red teeth; the eyes were slits in swollen sockets, the forehead bulged, and the cheeks swelled like two boils; it had a look of weary, savage ennui and broken hopelessness. Beneath it, on a divan in front of the bookcases, Lady Irene sat talking without apparent interest to a cropped, mightily muscled

young man who looked like a Prussian. A small table was
before them, with drinks on it. Not far off Andrews stood
holding a glass, watching Lady Irene with covert attention.
Marie, with her back to me, was moving toward the divan
as I came around the frame of the door; she was extremely
décolleté, and carrying herself as though she meant to make
the most of it; as she neared the divan the blond young man
stood up, brought his heels together, and put one large hand
caressingly on her arm. She half turned, smiling at him with
an obvious backward motion of her head. Lady Irene said
something to which no one paid any attention, stood up,
and walked over to Andrews. It was, for some reason, a curious scene.

The atmosphere I had felt in the hall grew more pronounced, yet there seemed no particular reason for it. No
one was doing anything extraordinary; the blond young
man wanted to paw Marie, Marie wanted to encourage him,
Andrews was thinking some secret thought about Lady
Irene—who looked as though she was controlling herself
with difficulty. It appeared commonplace enough to the
eye; I was just about to go in and see if I could find some
basis for my feeling when a hand fell on my shoulder and I
turned to see Azarin behind me. His face shone dully; his
eyes, half veiled by the lids, looked at me with a sort of cool
and measuring mockery.

"Delighted to see you," he said smoothly. "I am glad that
you got here."

"It was a little difficult," I said, and caught a movement
behind his shoulder out of the corner of my eye. It was the
Scandinavian, Helga Lindstrom, dressed in a severe dark
blue frock. She stared at me coldly and a little sullenly;
her eyes were light blue and piercing, and she seemed big
enough to pick Azarin up and walk off with him. Her eyes

moved to him as soon as I looked at her, and she nodded slightly.

"Pardon me," Azarin said. "I will be back shortly. Andrews will introduce you."

He left with Helga, and I stepped into the room. Lady Irene saw me first. She had been watching Azarin, I took it, and when he left she started across the room. I might as well not have been there; she looked through me stonily and walked rudely by. Andrews saw me next. He had started to follow Lady Irene, still talking, then stared at me. He came up to me and shook hands. It was not what you would call a pleasant welcome.

"I didn't expect to see you here," he said. His features seemed to have sharpened since I saw him last; his eyes had an avid look in them, but the incongruity of his presence didn't seem to bother him at all. "I thought that you were genuinely in the other . . . ah . . . camp."

"I didn't expect to see you here either," I said. "It seems that neither of us took your advice as to the company we kept."

"Ah," he remarked, and his eyes narrowed. "Then it's tennis you're interested in?" His head moved forward, jerkily.

"Of course," I said.

"You'll learn nothing here," he said. Even his intonation had changed; there was something nervous in it. "Take my advice and get out." His voice suddenly took an accent of hostility. "Yes, get out. Don't make a fool of yourself."

"Thanks," I said, wondering at the hostility.

He gave me a blank sort of stare, and a sudden air of agitation took hold of him. "What's that you say?" he asked sharply. "Very well, my young friend, but look out! Azarin will squeeze you dry!" And with that he turned on his heel and marched out the door.

I couldn't make anything of it. His actions, abrupt and nervous, were so different from the way he'd acted on the ship that he seemed like another person. I glanced at Marie and the young man. They were still so preoccupied with each other that they had noticed nothing, so I followed Andrews.

No one was in the hall. I started cautiously for the rear of the house, and after passing a turn in the hall came to the door of another room. Voices were coming out of it; I flattened myself against the wall at the edge of the jamb.

"You should have stayed in the other room," the voice of Helga said. It was deep and blurred by an accent. "There was a man here, that was all."

"I don't want to be left alone all the evening," Lady Irene said, in the clipped voice I'd expected of her. "It is very dull, and that damned African sculpture is enough to drive one mad. Who is there for me to talk to? No one but your niece, who is half sa—"

"Please," Azarin said hastily, "do not allow her to hear you say that." He sounded strangely apprehensive, I thought. Whatever his niece was (or whatever half of her was) must have been pretty bad. "You must be patient," he went on, his tone becoming so surprisingly conciliating that it struck me she had something of the first magnitude on him. "My dear Irene, you do not realize how much you will help me by being patient."

"No, you do not," Helga said, and there was venom in her tone.

"But you do, I daresay?" Lady Irene asked, with equal venom. "You've had more opportunity to observe, is that it? How a man can live for years under the same roof with such a creature as you are—!"

"Irene!" Andrews exclaimed, and there was a moment of crawling silence. I wished fervently that I had the key for all this: the mutual hatred of the women, why Azarin was so conciliating to Lady Irene, what she had on him, what Andrews was doing in it.

"If you and Andrews will go back," Azarin said, "we will soon come in. Do you know what this David Cameron is doing? Marie will pay little attention to him unless Betty Dwight is mentioned to her. She—"

"She wants to catch your eye with that weightlifter," Lady Irene cut in acidly.

A chair scraped. "Come, Irene," Andrews said.

"Yes, yes," Azarin said. "We will do nothing without you, Andrews, you may be sure of that. How can we? You must be patient too. My God, isn't it worth a little patience?"

Someone took a step, and I started to move off quickly. I caught the first part of a phrase: "The odds changed to-day—" in Andrews' voice, then I was out of earshot. I didn't go back into the living room, but upstairs, into a bathroom near the head of the stairs. I turned the water on, let it run, and considered. Andrews, it appeared, after going to Azarin in the first place, was now afraid to trust the man out of his sight, particularly with Lady Irene; Marie, for the good of the cause, was to be set to work on me; Lady Irene and Helga hated each other and possibly every other woman who came near Azarin, and there was something wrong with Marie which might be valuable to know about.

This wasn't much, but it was a starter; I wanted more. I racked my brain as to how to get out of the house; finally I walked to the window. A heavy trellis came from the ground on one side of it, so I eased the window open, got out, and descended to the ground. The fog was thicker than ever, and after stumbling about I came to the window of the small room where they all had been sitting. The curtains were drawn, but there was a crack between them.

Azarin and Helga were alone now, sitting close together, talking; the door was shut. I couldn't hear what they said, but Azarin gestured with his thumb toward the living room, pointed the forefinger of his other hand at Helga, shook his head and spoke with the utmost seriousness. Helga made a sneering face; her head went back, and she laughed. Azarin scowled, then leaned toward her; he put his hands on hers, then lifted one after the other and kissed them. Helga made a pose of being distant and scornful, but it was only a pose; she leaned toward him, then suddenly they sprang violently apart and jumped up. Azarin made a quick motion, picked up a round, flat box such as medicine comes in, which I hadn't noticed on the table until that moment, fairly threw it at Helga, and went to the door. Helga slid the box into the bosom of her dress, and Azarin let the maid in.

There was some conversation between the three of them, and Helga followed the maid out; Azarin waited until they had gone, then went out himself. My suspicions caught at the little box. What was in it? The more I tried to think sensibly about it the more I tried to laugh at myself, but somehow it didn't quite come off. There might be something in that box to upset Betty, to interfere with her co-ordination or her vitality; it might be a sedative, it might . . . "The devil!" I said aloud, and jumped at the sound of my voice. I knew I couldn't go away now, so I began to move around the house.

I came to a corner and crept around it. Nothing could be seen in the fog; even the two windows in the range of my vision made little headway against it, the light coming from them being reduced to a dull and short-ranged glow. I made for the first one, but it was too high to see into; and as I was feeling about for something to stand on I thought I heard a subdued voice from somewhere near the other window. I made toward it, and the vague shape of what I

took to be the rear entrance began to loom up. I was sure of
the voice by that time: a sort of monotonous voice, a man's,
but I couldn't distinguish what it said. It stopped suddenly,
and a woman's voice, Helga's I was sure, made a quick reply.
I couldn't distinguish what she said either, and in a flash of
irritation I forgot to look where I was going on my next step
and kicked what must have been a bucket.

There was a muffled, tinny thump and the thing began
to roll noisily away from me; a flashlight made a sort of
useless halo on the porch, to be flung down with a curse,
and the man made a dive for me. Almost before the door
slammed he was on me. He had calculated my location to
a nicety, and hit me with a terrific thump. I swung wildly
and missed him; his arms went around me like steel bands,
and we went down. For a moment we fought like devils,
rolling about. He was short and wiry, extraordinarily quick,
and even in my desperation to break away from him I recognized clearly the smell of garlic on him. We crashed into
a bush; the thick branches were suddenly all about me, and
a faint scent of lilacs penetrated the virulent odor of garlic.
The man must have caught one of the branches for my arm,
because one of his hands vanished; I bit the other one viciously, and he turned me loose with a yell.

Knowing where he was I kicked out, caught him in the
ribs, rolled clear and crawled swiftly for ten yards or so. I
took off my shoes, tied the laces together and hung them
around my neck, and started out. He was groaning and
cursing in Spanish not far away, and someone came to the
back door and shouted. He answered with another curse;
there was a blasphemous stir at the door, and I cleared out.
I could just about see the lights of the house, and not wanting to chance running into anyone coming out the front I
went directly away from it. It wasn't long before the lights
faded out altogether.

CHAPTER FOUR

Waking up the next morning, very late, was no pleasure to me. I was bone tired from wandering about in the fog most of the night, I had a slight but annoying cold in the head, a black eye and a great number of stiff muscles. I took a hot bath and had breakfast sent up, and after I ate it asked them to get me a masseur. He came along presently, and while he worked on me I tried to pull my wits together. I had, it appeared, gone a long way to mess things up; for Azarin, not knowing what I had discovered in my peregrinations, was more than likely to do something to counteract possibilities; and it wasn't unlikely that I would come in for some attention.

I didn't mind that particularly, for as long as I stayed in sight very little could happen to me; England wasn't the United States. There was the little flat box, of course; and after the masseur had gone I had the assistant manager up and talked a little about my food. Said I had reason to be alarmed about something, and would they watch it. He looked at me as though I was mad—which I might have been—assured me in an embarrassed manner that care would be taken, then went out with a faintly outraged air. That was all right; I called Betty, and was finally connected with Mrs. Cosgrove.

"Why, David!" she said. "How nice to talk to you! I'm afraid Betty's not here."

"I really didn't expect her," I said. "I thought she'd be practicing. But I'd like to see her this afternoon if you could prevail on her to hold an hour or so open."

"Oh!" she said. "David, I'm *so* sorry. She said she was going out with that Spanish man again."

"Spanish man?" I asked, and my voice must have gone up two octaves.

"You know," she said, and dropped her voice to a mysterious whisper. "That . . . *gangster.*"

I groaned to myself, wishing that someone had strangled her in the cradle. "Ask her to call me, anyhow," I said. "It's very important. The most important thing you could think of."

"How exciting!" she said. "I'll be *sure* to do it. Goodbye."

That was that, and left me the rest of the afternoon. I looked at the paper—full of the Spanish War and its cruelties—and went back to bed. I felt dispirited and low, and after a while fell into an uneasy sleep. It was nearly dinner time when I awoke, with a very bad taste in my mouth; I had dinner sent up and waited the rest of the evening in my pajamas, but the phone didn't ring. Finally, in desperation, I called Betty again, but they were all out. I left a message for her to call me, and that ended the day.

The next morning my cold was nearly gone, and I felt better. I was shaving when a cable was brought up. In all the pother I'd forgotten that there might be cables, and the sight of it recalled to me the fact that I had come to Europe for more reasons than to climb down trellises and go to Wimbledon. I had a premonition that I didn't want to read it, which was more than justified; for it said things which made it imperative for me to be in Paris that afternoon.

That put me in a fine spot. A great deal of my future interest in life and the incomes of the forty-two men I had working back at the plant depended on the trip, and I couldn't dodge it. I called Betty again, and couldn't even get Mrs. Cosgrove; and then, after a lot of messing about, Scotland Yard. They must have thought I was mad too, but in twenty minutes there was a knock at the door and a very quiet-looking man in a blue suit came in. He introduced himself as Sergeant Portrush; he was of medium height, strongly built, with a pink and white complexion and a square, friendly face. He stood still just inside the door, and in standing still became more remarkably quiet looking than before. He was, I felt sure, an extraordinary fellow; for he managed to seem at once alert and as steadfast and immovable as an oak. I asked him to sit down, which he passed off with a "Thank you, sir"; and as he remained where he was I gathered that my ill-considered Yankee democracy was being gently rebuked.

"It's about Miss Dwight, Sergeant," I said. "The ladies' singles tennis champion. She will probably play a Miss Marie Azarin this year. Miss Azarin travels with an uncle, James Azarin, who, from what I can gather, is a gambler, a rather mysterious man. I may be wrong; but we all came over on the same ship, and from several things which occurred I feel that this Azarin may do something to interfere with Miss Dwight's game."

The Sergeant had got out his little black book, and wrote in it. "Would you care to detail the occurrences, sir?" he asked.

"I . . ." I began, and stopped. To recount what had gone on to the quiet Sergeant, it struck me suddenly, would be like telling him something out of the Arabian Nights. I hadn't the courage to do it; for while the things had a very present reality to me, they would, I felt sure, take on a quality of fantastic nonsense if described aloud to him. "I don't think it necessary," I said. "Only I am going away, and I want to be sure that everything is all right."

"Quite so, sir. We will see that no unpleasantness occurs, sir." He asked me a few details as to where they all were staying and so on, shut the little black book, took up his hat, gave me the most reassuring bow I had ever received, and departed. It was a wonderful performance to one accustomed to the "Oh yeah?" school of policemen, but it left me confused; I didn't know whether I'd been a fool not to tell him everything. In this frame of mind I packed a bag and started for Croydon.

The flight over the Channel was uneventful enough, and I wasn't much interested in it. My meditations weren't very cheerful, and by the time the plane landed at Le Bourget a feeling of anxiety had taken possession of me and I couldn't get rid of it. I did all I could to cut the trip short, but things piled up. I had to go to Berlin and then to Prague; I ate endless dinners and talked endlessly with men who seemed inspired by the devil to long-windedness and procrastination. The tennis started, and got into the semi-finals; I sent Betty telegrams every day and spent my spare time reading the papers. Betty was having three-set matches, which was unusual and disturbing; Marie Azarin was having two-set matches, and that was more disturbing still. The final match between them became inevitable; and finally, by the grace of God, I managed to get back to London the night before they were to play each other, too late to call Betty.

I called her the next morning, and got Mrs. Cosgrove.

"Oh, David!" she said. "I'm *so* glad to hear from you. I wanted to tell you how sorry I am. I forgot to tell Betty that you wanted her to call you. Please, I'd like *so* much for you to forgive me. There was a message from you, too, and I've been carrying it around in my pocket until this minute. I . . . I thought I still had it, but it's gone. Oh, David—"

"Don't give it a moment's thought," I said sweetly. "Don't bother your pretty head about it. If you let me speak to Betty, I'll forgive anything."

There was a long pause. "Oh, David!" she said. "I'd like to more than anything, but I can't. She just won't do it. She's *concentrating*. She's not here, anyhow. She's gone out."

"Gone out?" I asked hollowly.

"Yes. I think she's concentrating in the Park, or maybe she had to see someone. I don't know. But David, please be a good boy and not try to see her. Not until after the game. Why, she won't even talk to me."

"Can't I come by for both of you in a car?" I asked, as a last ditch offense. "I'd like to take you to Wimbledon."

"Please, David, don't do it. We're going in a car. Oh, David, pray that she wins. She wants to so much. Come see us after the game. Goodbye, David."

I stood for a moment admiring my self-control because I didn't break up the furniture, then looked through my mail. There was a note from Captain Brererton: "Sorry I missed you. The cape never showed up, even in the customs." The rest of the mail was about what I expected.

That left me the rest of the morning on my hands, and I was too jumpy to sit in my room. I wandered about until it got too much for me, then went out and walked down Berkeley Street to Piccadilly. I knew then where I was going, but I pretended that I didn't. I was going to Hyde Park to see Betty; not to speak to her, not to bother her in any way, but just to look at her from a distance. But I didn't admit it; maintaining the pretense, I told myself that I'd walk a bit in Green Park and go back to the hotel. Accordingly I crossed

over into Green Park and admired from a distance the two
palaces, Buckingham and St. James; but as I admired them
I kept walking toward Hyde Park all the time.

Finally I found myself at the Park Lane end of Green
Park, and an urge to walk more came over me. It was such
splendid exercise. I was easily convinced, and it wasn't long
before I was walking along the edge of Hyde Park, searching
among the dogs and children and other lovers of nature for
Betty. I was almost across from the entrance to the Dorchester before I saw her sitting in one of the chairs they rent for
a penny or so. She was quite a way off, sitting quietly; but
she got up almost at once and turned toward the Dorchester. There was a man leaning against a tree not far from her;
as she passed him the man took off his hat and spoke. She
stopped; they talked for a moment; then she looked at her
watch, spoke to the man again and went on, crossing Park
Lane and vanishing into the Dorchester's side door.

The man came toward me, limping a little, and because
he had talked to her I had a sort of companion feeling for
him. I stood waiting for him to come by. He was a tall man,
and as he came close and passed by I saw that he had a long
scar, like the scar of a sabre cut, across his cheek.

Any fugitive impulse I may have felt to speak to him
because he had talked to Betty passed when I saw that scar.
It put me off; I let him go by, and knowing that Betty probably wouldn't come out again I wandered back to my hotel.

I wasn't much interested in lunch, but got through it
and went out to the car. I was in no hurry. The first match
of the afternoon was one of the men's singles semi-finals,
and I didn't care whether I saw all of it or not. It was a fine
day, and the first few minutes of the ride were enjoyable.
We went along Green Park, past the Marble Arch and Hyde
Park. We crawled across Putney Bridge, and I noticed that

the Thames didn't look very attractive. The tide was out and the mudbanks at its sides were glistening in a way peculiarly tropical, as if there should have been a few crocodiles about.

I asked the driver where we were as I had not been out there before and he said, "We are going up Putney Hill, sir." It was a narrow street, bordered by the same kind of shops as on the other side of the River, and I felt more cheerful when we reached the top of the hill where there were trees, and villas which were not unpleasing with their air of suburban rusticity. My driver volunteered that that was Wimbledon Common on the right. It had the look of the country with its open space and trees. We took a turn to the left, opposite, and drove down a road so closely bordered by trees that they met overhead, forming a green tunnel. The cars were nose to end; half of England seemed headed towards Wimbledon. Abruptly, we dipped down into an easy hollow, and turned the corner onto a road I noticed was called Wimbledon Church Road.

All the London newspapers, except *The Times*, it seemed, had been employing players at Wimbledon to write articles for them. Posters with big red letters announced this fact on either side of the road. "See Wimbledon with Kay Bodgett," "Stories of the Stars, by Derek Blount," "My Biggest Thrill, Mlle. Simon." Shades of the Amateur Rule! How did they get away with it?

To the right, ahead, I saw a large, gray building among trees. It must be, I thought, the Center Court Grandstand. It was a strange-looking edifice, with a slit or opening, running like a band, just under the slightly sloping roof all the way round. This gave it a dark accent that seemed rather sinister. There were no other openings visible, at least from this side. It looked like some kind of stronghold from Mars, built for defense, and had a curious uninhabited air, which couldn't have been further from the truth, as I was soon to discover, for there were already 14,000 people inside and more arriving all the time. As we came nearer, I saw that the building was not rectangular in shape, but hexagonal. A modern edifice for a modern sport. From a flag pole flew the purple and green Wimbledon colors.

While I meditated on what a world-wide and important game tennis had become, we reached the gate. A tall, blue-clad London Bobby stood in the center of the road waving cars sharp right. We followed between tall wooden fences and stopped alongside the stadium. Glancing up I saw that it was much higher than I thought. About equal in height to a three- or four-story building. I told my driver to be back at five-thirty.

"We aren't permitted to park here, sir. I'll wait by this entrance myself till you come out. It will save you time if you walk across the road to the car park. It's very difficult here, sir."

"So it seems," I answered. "All right."

There was an intent look on people's faces as they hurried through the gates presenting their pink tickets, and they weren't saying much either, no doubt being considerably upset that they had missed at least half of the first match. I'd have been rather sorry myself if I hadn't been thinking so intently of Betty, because the match was between the new, red-haired American champion, popularly called "The Comet," and an English boy, who much to the pleasure of the feminine fans was supposed to look like Robert Taylor, and to the satisfaction of England's sporting element, was credited with the forehand drive and all-around style of Reginald Doherty. I wasn't interested at all in this match, or the niceties of style of any other player besides Betty.

However, in spite of my concern about her, I felt picked up by something in the atmosphere of the place. The crowds, the buzz, like in a bee-hive, a kind of spirit in the air. There was a burst of clapping, like crockery falling downstairs. I sprang up a couple of steps, and stood looking down onto the Center Court.

My eye swept the entire sea of faces, the Royal Box at the end of the court in its key position, the velvet-green turf with its markings of white chalk. Everything was centered on what was going on on this patch of emerald carpet. Every move of Leigh-Jones, and of the American, Wallop, was being followed with utmost attention.

Soon it would be Betty and Marie Azarin on that same court. My feeling of anxiety returned. Where was Betty now? Somewhere behind those packed stands, nervous perhaps. Probably looking quite calm on the surface, with that impenetrable coldness she could throw over herself at command.

But on the Center Court at that moment, Leigh-Jones, in spite of having the English crowd solidly behind him, was surely going down to defeat before our red-headed Comet. It was almost over. Wallop eased up to the net, stretched himself lazily, as if waking up in the morning, and put a lob to sleep at point set, thereby moving into the finals, and if I were any judge, from there into Wimbledon's famous list of champions.

That might all well be, I thought, breathing a sigh of relief as they extracted their racquets from a welter of towels under the umpire's stand, and made their way through the crowd of photographers and radio men towards the exit, but what about Betty? Where was Azarin? Where were those people I would like to have been keeping my eye on?

I began to squirm in my seat, and inadvertently poked the lady next to me with my elbow. I looked at her with uncalled-for alarm wondering if she had caught me talking to myself, but her eyes were glued on the end of the court where Betty and Marie Azarin would appear first.

Something was going to happen. I looked at my hands which had little rivers of cold sweat in their palms, then wiped them on my handkerchief. Why didn't the girls come out? What had happened to delay them?

The umpire, who looked as if he had wooden legs, was stalking around measuring the net with something like a yardstick. It was exactly the length of a racquet, plus the width across the widest part, or was it? That's the way we used to measure the net at home, but perhaps that was not exact enough for Wimbledon, where everything had to be quite perfect. Too perfect, that was it, too awesome. The silence was dead silence, the sudden bursts of applause primitive and cruel—but polite, of course.

A half-moon of camera-men formed near the net, but off the sacred turf bounded by the lines. Several officials stood with bowed heads, as if in prayer, while they studied the grass. The umpire laid his measuring stick to rest under a doormat, yes, an honest-to-goodness doormat, brown, with bristles, which for some reason had been placed across the cord that led from the umpire's microphone to whatever intricate machine would soon begin to spread his voice throughout the stands.

The audience had become a bit restless. If the delay went on any longer, it would turn into the serious offense of "keeping the Queen waiting." A good deal of buzzing filled the air. What were all the things being said in that monotone of sound? Betty was the defending champion; she was a great player. Everyone knew that. Marie Azarin was an unknown quantity, at least on British courts, but her prowess had been played up in the press, one would have thought, to the point of exaggeration—her grace, speed, the surprise element in her game, the subtlety of her tactics. Sports writers had watched Marie in practice when she first arrived, they had followed her progress as she advanced round after round in the tournament up to the finals. They had predicted a great match between Betty and this dark-skinned, hawk-faced girl, whose game was built upon a series of birdlike swoops. There had been no disappointments en route. Marie Azarin had won all her preliminary matches in straight sets. For once, it seemed that the sports writers, in their hope for a sensational final, had not been carried away by their enthusiasm for a newcomer.

Here was a dish for the most exacting tennis epicurean. All the elements were there. Even the players were contrasting types, one blonde and cool, reserved, the other dark, fiery and possibly (onlookers hoped) temperamental. Ice against fire. One played a steady calculating game that rolled on no matter what happened. The other relied more on bursts of speed, and unexpected tricks. They both could play net, but each did it in a different way. Betty with a pre-conceived logical plan, Azarin with a sudden swoop, which hadn't as much thought behind it, but which was often effective because of its suddenness. There was a kind of savagery in the latter's play that writers called "colorful," but it was to me a quality that hinted of jungle ancestors. No, she was not a pleasant person. And there was the story of their tiff on the boat that had got into the papers somehow or other, possibly with malice aforethought on the part of Marie and Azarin themselves. The audience had the pleasure of contemplating a match in which there existed a certain enmity. This made it lick its chops. Betty must have hated the whole thing at heart, but she had had it thrust upon her. It was the penalty of being a champion.

There was a stir in the audience, as the two girls came suddenly onto the court from behind the backstop below the Royal Box. They walked side by side, each carrying an armful of racquets. Both appeared quite cool, with set smiles on their faces.

Betty looked like a goddess. Venus, Aphrodite, mixed a bit with the Victory of Samothrace (with arms, of course) and a few pounds lopped off. Sun glinted on her fair hair which was tied with a blue ribbon. That matched her sweater. Her shorts were longer than Azarin's, who seemed to think she was in the front row of a chorus and obliged to show as much bare leg as possible. Betty's waist—what a waist! And honey-colored skin. Nothing of the hefty female athlete about her. She was the best proof that a woman doesn't have to look like a weight-lifter to be good in sport. If I hadn't disliked Marie Azarin so violently, I'd have had to admit that she wasn't unattractive to the eye either, but her appeal was all animal—probably her eyes would shine in the dark like those things you see at night along the road in the glare of the headlights.

She wore a yellow band around her hair and a sweater of the same color with long sleeves. The girls stood for a few seconds before the cameras, then laid their extra racquets on the shelf under the umpire's stand. At least Marie did. There was not room for all the racquets, and Betty tossed hers under the stand alongside some towels. The cameramen had gone out. There were, near the umpire's stand, only the umpire, the two girls, and two ball-boys who held in their hands six snow-white tennis balls just taken out of the ice-box at one side. The umpire watched while Betty spun her racquet. Marie had "called"—but did not watch for the result. With almost affected indifference she stood apart, took off her sweater, and threw it under the umpire's stand on top of Betty's racquets.

As Marie removed her sweater, I was surprised to see a bandage midway on her right forearm. I heard comments about it on either side of me. Evidently Betty had won the toss, for she chose to serve, which she always did if she could start a match that way. She looked very pale, and seemed to be in a dream. I felt that she was as remote from the audience as if she had been a hundred miles away. Marie Azarin, on the other hand, made her personality felt. She appeared pushing and aggressive, bold, almost belligerent.

I had often seen Betty play in America, long before I knew her. Always very controlled, she had been, but with a fluid ease and grace beautiful to see. Today there was a wooden quality about her movements that was unlike her. She walked at times with a slight limp. I watched with dismay a hesitancy, an almost imperceptible absence of coordination which nevertheless was sufficient to interfere with her usual perfect timing of racquet on ball. Something was wrong somewhere. I thought of the things that had happened on the boat; and of other things I had half seen. Her conduct since landing had been most unlike her, and her goings and comings had confused us all, even her aunt Mrs. Cosgrove. Betty wanted to win this match more than anything in the world.

But why had she behaved so strangely towards me? She knew that I cared for her. Even if this meant nothing to her, she still could realize surely that I was another human being who wanted to help. I was face to face with the fact that there was the suspicion in my mind—that she was

capable of doing one or two things not quite on the books.
I recalled very plainly my reaction that night in the moonlight on the ship, when I conceded that even if she fought
Azarin's tactics with Azarin's own weapons, Betty would still
mean as much to me as if she ignored him entirely, and
played fairly. But now there was no moonlight, the witchery
of her nearness did not influence me, the sun shone down
with intense clarity upon the two white-clad figures on the
Center Court, as if it were bent upon revealing everything.
I could judge now, for myself, where I had not been able to
before.

As I watched the two girls in the preliminary rally, I
wondered, with a sort of detached self-irony, what would
happen to my feeling for Betty, if I knew, beyond doubt, the
complete tale of her actions since I had met her on the boat.

The warm-up was over. All the balls were being rolled
and tossed by the ball-boys to the north end of the court,
where Betty was going to serve first. The umpire eased himself more comfortably into his elevated chair; the audience
rustled expectantly like birds going to roost.

In spite of the outward show of calm on Betty's part, I
sensed that Marie was the calmer of the two. She was still
smiling, but not very pleasantly, and if her arm bothered
her she gave no indication of it.

Betty went to the baseline three balls in hand. Marie
Azarin stood ready to receive on the right side of the court.
Betty threw the ball well up into the air directly above her
head, and served. All eyes followed the ball, the first shot
of the match. My feeling of anxiety was forgotten for the
moment as I fastened my attention on the rally that ensued.
There was a long exchange of shots with the ball travelling
fast and low. Marie stepped right out, probably as she had
been told to by Azarin. He knew her game depended on the

direct attack, and not so much upon brains. Marie managed her feet like a dancer, placing them with precision for each stroke. If she had any Latin blood, it showed up here. Her movements were like those of a bull-fighter. Azarin must have been quick to notice this. That same agility enabled Marie to take the ball "on the rise"—which meant she was hitting it very soon after the bounce. It took skill, but was hard to maintain throughout a match, because it took absolute co-ordination. Fatigue would make a great difference; I wondered how long she would be able to sustain that pace.

Betty started deliberately. I could see she was going to try to tire Azarin by running her. Betty was the less colorful at the start, taking the ball carefully, playing a safer game, and making a special effort to place the ball first on one side, then on the other. She soon had the other girl on the run, and won several important points down her backhand line. In between bursts of applause, there was dead silence in the stands. Here was a match whose outcome seemed unpredictable. It was fascinating to see the control and mastery of the two girls' strokes. It all looked easy, but the Wimbledon audience knew its tennis well enough to know that it was watching the beginning of what was going to be a great match. I breathed a long sigh—I knew I would never care again as much about the outcome of any tennis game. As the balls flew back and forth, and those of Betty came dangerously near the baseline—she was playing all her shots deep—I leaned on my neighbors, right and left. I needed the space of three seats.

After the score reached thirty-all, Betty won an outright service **ace** to make it forty-thirty, and then won the game by a sharply angled crosscourt shot from her backhand. All the rallies in this game were long, and closely fought. In one of them the ball must have crossed the net twenty times. It was a very unusual game for the first one in a match, when players usually make more mistakes than later on when they have thoroughly warmed up to the action.

Even though it was first-class tennis, I could see that Betty was not in her best form. She had not yet overcome that certain tenseness either in her movements or in her attitude that was noticeable to me, who had seen her play so often. She had not relaxed, and I wondered if she were going to. She would tire much more quickly, if she took the match hard like this. Marie Azarin was out to make hay while the sun shone, no doubt about that. I made a survey around the audience with my glasses while Betty and Marie were changing courts after that first game. To my astonishment they fell upon Azarin himself down in the very front row in one of the seats they sold by the day. These seats were down on the level of the court in a section not considered as good as the elevated parts of the stand, where he might have been expected to sit. He was directly behind the umpire's stand—not the best place for viewing the match, as it hid the net. But he was as near as possible to the spot where the players passed each time they changed courts on the odd games. He was about twenty feet away, too far for conversation, but quite near enough for any signs, and even lip-reading. I was sure it was he, because the rounded side of his head was unmistakable, and I would have known the slope of his shoulders anywhere. I thought it stupid of him to be there for purposes of the game, because there was a strict rule against players being coached during a match. But then, I asked myself, was he there for "purposes of the game"—it looked pretty strange to me. I continued watching him. Then I realized that the woman he was sitting next to, was with him. He was speaking to her. She had on a white hat and a black and white printed dress. It wasn't

Helga, as it was too slight a person for her, and I doubted very much if it was Lady Irene, who would have refused to sit in such an uncomfortable seat with the sun beating down on her shoulders. As the girls were changing courts after that first game, I caught a flash of movement from Azarin. He whipped out a white handkerchief and mopped his forehead violently.

Marie turned slightly in his direction and looked at him. Betty happened to glance up, saw the direction of Marie's attention and turned her head to stare at Azarin so pointedly that the woman next to me said, "She sees someone she knows in the front row." Marie took a sip of water from a glass on the shelf. Betty did not drink at all.

Betty then crossed over to the end of the court nearest the Royal Box. The King and the Queen, in her large blue hat and blue lace dress, were sitting there serene, evidently enjoying the play. They were reassuring personages—but, an involuntary shiver chased down my spine. They did not know, nor did the 16,000 spectators, what was going on behind the match.

It was Marie's turn to serve. Betty sent the return into the net. She seemed disturbed, shaken. I knew it was the episode of the moment before. The audience thought that it was Marie's wonderful serve that had won her the point. It showed how deceiving appearances are in a game. Betty seemed to slow down in the following rallies; Marie instead of trying to hit the cover off every ball, had eased off on speed, and was trying more spin, and some tricky drop shots. Evidently Azarin had seen she was starting off at a pace she could not maintain. These softer shots would have ordinarily been smothered by Betty, but now they seemed to be just wrong for her—they seemed to give her time to think about something else. Her concentration, famous as it was, had deserted her. I stirred around in my seat, and was definitely an annoyance to the woman on my right and to the elderly man on my left. Evidently Azarin's handkerchief had meant something!

The miserable Marie was making Betty run now, and Betty didn't want to. I would have thought that Marie had put a sleeping potion or some depressant in Betty's glass—I wouldn't have put it past her—but I knew for sure that Betty had not touched her glass. A look of satisfaction could be seen in Marie's expression, and her whole attitude was one of smug confidence. Well—pride cometh and so on—we'll wait, I thought, and not get too excited. Betty looked tired, tired unto death, as if there was some invisible pressure upon her.

That game went to Marie, hands down. She looked miles too clever. But I knew that there was nothing in her repertoire that Betty couldn't cope with—provided she was herself and on her game. Why, she should have been walking right through Marie! I ground the stub of my cigarette into the concrete with my heel. The woman next me turned with a curious glance, "I don't think she likes the Azarin girl, do you? I do not like her either."

It was Betty's turn to serve in the third game. Already this match had a flavor of its own. It was unlike any other sporting event I had ever seen. The audience evinced its intense interest by dead silence, except when it broke out into applause. Even the Queen leaned forward a little in her comfortable armchair. All eyes were on the ball. Marie still wore that self-satisfied half-smile; Betty's face was expressionless, but white, and it had a drawn look which was most unnatural for her. She seemed to be gathering herself together though, and was less uncertain in her movements than in the game preceding. Then on the second point both girls stayed in the backcourt and had a long rally, hitting at high speed. Back and forth, back and forth, all the balls deep, and well-placed in both corners. At least fifty times the ball went over the net—I doubted if such a rally at such a speed had been seen before at Wimbledon in a women's match. Betty was rising to the occasion in spite of her bad start. Just as it looked as if Betty had her on the run, though, Marie's ball nicked the net cord and dribbled over as a let ball, falling so short that Betty made no try for it. It would have been useless. Luck had entered in, where skill could not decide the point. The score now stood at fifteen all, and one game apiece—absolutely even.

The pace that marked this rally was continued for two more games. It must have been the fastest women's match ever seen. It was as if each point were the crucial point. Both girls played beyond themselves. I couldn't see how they stood it, for say what you will, tennis is one of the most strenuous sports. They were both keyed up to top-most pitch. To me it was evident that their nerves, minds and muscles were sustained by something more than a mere desire to win an athletic contest. They seemed superhuman, one with an indomitable will to become champion, the other with an indomitable will to remain champion. Marie actually changed in looks, her cheekbones became more prominent, her face sharper; it became more hawk-like and savage looking. It struck me that there was terrible ambition in it, exaggerated far beyond the point of reason, as if the entire course of her life depended upon victory.

Betty had regained her look of composure, but her shots were hardly restrained anymore. She took long chances, hit for the lines, for the difficult angle. I don't know whether from choice or necessity, probably the latter, as she still was not moving about or covering court in her usual fashion

and she had to make up for this lack somehow. I groaned
inwardly every time one of her balls came near the line; sometimes they sent up a little plume of white chalk when they
made a direct hit. She had Marie on the go—not much—
but a little, even though the score had now reached two
games all. It was now Betty's turn to serve. Marie reached
her receiving position on the court and leaned heavily on her
racquet for a moment, Betty dabbed the perspiration from
her forehead with her handkerchief. This gave them a brief
pause. Both girls were glad to have a chance to catch their
breath. Then Betty looked over at Azarin intently. Marie
saw her, and turned her head in his direction too. I looked
at him through my glasses and saw him shift uneasily but he
did nothing. The woman in black and white said something
to him. I don't think anyone noticed, but if it happened any
more it would begin to attract attention. It was not a pleasant sort of thing, and if he signaled to Marie, it would have
been quite off the books at Wimbledon, where the last letter
of court conduct was supposed to be obeyed. There was the
rule that players should absolutely not communicate with
anyone while play was under way.

Betty's face had a strange unreadable expression on it
now. She was disturbed again. Damn Azarin! It looked like
a put up job on his part to throw Betty off her game. I knew
she wouldn't ordinarily have paid any attention to him. She
would simply have risen above it. But these weren't ordinary
circumstances.

Then Betty served and the battle started anew. The audience was fascinated, with applause about evenly divided. It
did not seem possible that such a pace could be continued
throughout the match—it was sure to turn eventually into
pat-ball between two exhausted players. But that time was
far off, it appeared, as they began again, hammer and tongs.

The woman on my left gave little exclamations of dismay, and we leaned on each other when it looked as if Betty was in a tight spot. We had become buddies. It was deuce in the fifth game—two games all and deuce—exactly even again. Betty walked back to the baseline slowly and deliberately and the ball-boy gravely placed three balls on her extended racquet. She took them in her left hand, stepped forward, and placed the toe of her left foot just behind the baseline. It seemed ages, but she was in motion all the time; that was a curious thing about Betty, she seemed to be able to do the same motions at the same speed, but in different lengths of time. She swung her racquet around in a beautiful arc, and brought it crashing down upon the ball. The ball streaked towards Marie, who took a step sideways, and hesitated for an instant, perfectly still, as the ball went past her. Then, with a terrible expression on her face, she dropped her racquet, threw her arms into the air, and fell to the ground. She moved spasmodically a couple of times, then lay absolutely inert.

For a moment the silence held, a shocked and unbelieving silence. You could have heard a pin drop. Then a woman in the audience screamed hysterically. Some people stood up. By the time the umpire could climb down from his stand, the linesmen had run forward. Already a groundsman had called the first-aid nurse. Two first-aid men came onto the court carrying a stretcher. Committee men rushed forward to hold back the photographers. Police ran down the aisles to restrain the curious, and I must say, in tribute to the English crowd, only two or three people from the standing room section tried to get onto the court. I saw Betty standing by the net, as if she were paralyzed, looking towards Marie Azarin and the rapidly growing crowd about her. Betty made no move to go any nearer. I noticed that Azarin leaped over the low barrier onto the court, and hurried to the stricken girl. He pushed himself officiously through the people around her. Then I looked to see what Betty was doing, but she was no longer there. In the face of all the turmoil and excitement she had left the court—using that moment when all attention was on Marie Azarin, to, literally, melt from sight.

CHAPTER FIVE

Back at my hotel I hung up the phone and sat staring at it, then got up and walked about the room. I couldn't get through to Betty; the desk at the Dorchester politely but firmly declined to connect me.

At Wimbledon, after Marie Azarin's collapse and the abrupt termination of the match, my first thought had been to get to Betty. I was out of my seat and running down the steps before hardly anyone in the astounded audience began to move; I turned left and ran in the direction where I judged the Members' Dressing Room would be. There was no one under the stands, but as I turned a corner I collided with two men who were also running. Their hands were full of papers, and one was holding a pencil between his teeth. They both swore as we disentangled ourselves.

"Where's the Members' Dressing Room?" I asked, and then wished I hadn't said it. They were both obviously reporters.

"There's an idea, Eric," one of them said, ignoring me. "You go to the Dressing Room and get the first interview with Betty Dwight while I send this off."

The one called Eric began to run again, and I ran after him. He bounded up some steps, and rang a bell, dancing around with impatience because no one came. The attendant, probably, had heard about Marie and gone to look on. The reporter swore and shoved the door open.

I grabbed him. "You can't go in there!" I said. "The girl's entitled to some privacy, even—"

He shoved me and made a dash for it. By the time I got into the room he was running about, looking everywhere—in the dressing cubicles, in the shower, in the rooms where the tubs were. It wouldn't have made any difference to him whether Betty was dressed or not. She was nowhere about, no one was about, and he ran out again, headed for the cable office.

I went out and closed the door, more upset than I cared to admit. It would have been better if she had been there, for now the cables would go out, to the United States, to every place under the sun: "Sudden collapse on Center Court. Marie Azarin overcome in grudge match, Betty Dwight disappears" . . . and much more of it. They'd play it up as far as they could; they'd make a sensation of it.

By the time I'd got back to London—and it was tiresome and difficult, because another fog had started to come up and grew thicker as the sun went down—the news posters were everywhere on the streets, in great black letters a foot high: "DEATH AT WIMBLEDON," "AZARIN DEAD," "BETTY DWIGHT VANISHES."

So Marie Azarin was dead! They were already making extras of it, hinting at dark things. They said Marie had been dead by the time they got her into the locker room, and the doctors they'd been able to get from the stands could do nothing about it. Acute appendicitis, peritonitis they said, and so on, aggravated by the strain of the game. Boardlike rigidity of the abdominal wall, and so on and so on. Several of the doctors had apparently been surprised by the quickness of her taking off but they agreed with the general diagnosis. The visible symptoms were the symptoms of acute peritonitis and nothing else. There was a good deal of learned talk, garbled for popular consumption, about the unusual strain of the game and the girl's exhausted condition, and quite a little space given to Betty's mysterious manner of getting out of sight.

The next edition, which they brought up about that time, began to mention Azarin. They pictured him stunned at the suddenness of the death of his niece and stricken with grief; but at the same time he had managed to get in a few well-chosen words as to the state of her health. Her health was perfect; she had been thoroughly examined in Harley Street the day before the match. It had undoubtedly been a very hard match, the hardest he had ever seen; but . . .

It had a nasty sound to it, and seemed to promise more. London was boiling with excitement; a little of that sort of thing would go a long way. There had been mention of how the champion walked off the court, looking neither to the right nor to the left; and although it wasn't said in so many words, what they were getting at was callousness . . . a genteel accusation, but there just the same.

The champion hadn't been interviewed, hadn't given out any statement. No one could see the champion. They piled it on politely enough to make me swear. Didn't they consider, I asked myself, that Betty had been exhausted too, and bewildered? Something had been wrong with her; she hadn't been able to get over the court; Marie had attacked her weakness; she had been engaged in standing Marie off with all she had in her, and suddenly Marie had collapsed. Couldn't they, by a wild stretch of imagination, put themselves in Betty's place at that moment? They couldn't; they mentioned her famous control on the courts, her meeting

with Marie Azarin on the boat and everything else that had
ever been said before. It began to look as though the press
was preparing to enjoy a Roman holiday.

I tried to get Betty again, and failed. She was doing herself no good by her silence, and it had occurred to me that
she needed someone to speak for her. The thought of what
Mrs. Cosgrove would do if any reporters got to her disturbed me more than I cared to admit. I stewed around and
swore, and I suddenly became aware that a little thread of
suspicion was going through my own thought. Betty had
known on the boat that she wouldn't be in form; she had
talked to Helga; she had been out on mysterious errands
ever since coming to London. A lot of things came out of
the back of my mind: Mrs. Cosgrove's mention of the Australian girl with ptomaine, for instance. And—this was the
thing that bothered me most—why had she looked so intently at Azarin a little while before Marie fell?

The suspicions which that brought up were silly; they
were monstrous. I found myself thinking that it was impossible to kill a player from the stands. Such things happened
only in mystery tales, which had an airy way with reality;
outside of a book, it was somewhat difficult to give a girl
a super-acute peritonitis by shooting her with a gun concealed in a candid camera or a pair of binoculars.

I had them send a dinner tray up. It took a lot of reso-
lution to eat what the tray had on it, but I managed. Some
time after that I decided to go to the Dorchester and see if
I could possibly bluff my way into Betty's suite; and just as
I was picking up my hat there was a knock at the door and
Sergeant Portrush came in, followed by a tall, blue-eyed,
red-faced man who looked Irish. He was a lean fellow, and
fit, somewhat bushy as to eyebrows, and there was a deliber-

ate air about him; nothing judicial or stuffy, but he looked as though he liked to take his time.

"Good evening, sir," the Sergeant said. "This is Chief Detective Inspector MacMasters. Mr. Cameron, sir."

"Glad to know you," I said, and put down the hat. Chief Inspectors, it seemed to me, didn't come to call merely to pass the time of day. Wondering what tack he was going to take, I asked them to sit down.

The Chief Inspector, meanwhile, had been quietly look-ing me over. He didn't miss much. "I don't want to be a bore," he said finally, strangely enough with an American accent, "but the Sergeant had a tale that I thought might bear a little talking over. There's a hullaballoo going on."

"So I judged," I said. The American accent seemed to help a little; it made the Inspector less of an abstraction. "The Azarin girl seems to have died at a very unfortunate time."

He nodded, keeping his eyes on me. He was, I had to admit, a rather friendly looking man; I am sure he would have made a pleasant companion; but under it all there was a waiting quality in him that I compared at the moment to the Tar Baby's. Why I thought of the Tar Baby I have no idea. Not to be humorous, at any rate. I didn't feel in the least humorous. "What," he asked, "made you suspicious of this Azarin fellow in the first place?"

Something, I felt, was wrapped up in that one. It seemed to me that he should have asked about Betty first. My first impulse was to shield Betty, to lie a little if necessary, but a quick discretion got the better of that. I had a short struggle with myself, and then and there decided that the truth—at least the evident part of it—was mighty and should pre-vail. "He began on Miss Dwight long ago," I said, and ran through the story of the passenger lists according to Mrs. Cosgrove, then the story of the meeting on the boat. "He engineered that, of course. I purposely got rather friendly with him, and went to see him at Wimbledon. Things were very strange out there. I climbed out the bathroom window and saw Azarin and that Swedish woman of his in a room alone, doing suspicious things with a little round box. They hid it very quickly when a maid knocked at the door. From what I'd heard of Azarin I thought it might be something to put Miss Dwight off her game."

"You thought they might give *you* some of it, too?" he asked.

"I thought they might," I said. "After all, when I skipped out I thought they might be worried about me."

"So that's what the manager was getting at," he said.

He'd even talked to the manager of my hotel, and heard about my conversation with him regarding my food. There wasn't, I conceded, any grass growing under his feet. "That was it," I said, and a thought struck me. "You've talked to Azarin?" I asked.

He nodded, and I congratulated myself for that moment of discretion. He'd been waiting for me to say something about my visit to Azarin's, he'd even given me the lead. "How long have you known Miss Dwight?" he asked.

"I met her on the boat," I said. "The Captain was an old friend of mine and introduced me. I liked her."

"That's evident enough," he remarked, with a faint touch of amused irony.

It was at that moment that there was a knock at the door; I went over to it and a bellboy handed me a cable. I excused myself and tore it open. It read: "Gent named Mac-Masters inquiring about you stop have given you clean bill stop what goes on stop." It was signed "Bret." I swallowed that and turned to the Inspector. "Do you know Captain Brererton?" I asked.

"I've known him for years," he said. "Knew him before I went to the States."

I stared at him for a moment, and then the significance of it struck me: it was probable that he had got from the Captain the full particulars of the lost marten cape and all the rest of it; and if he hadn't he'd get them on the Captain's next trip. I didn't know what to say; and he sat there more like the Tar Baby than ever, saying nothing, with a sort of quizzical look on him, apparently enjoying himself in a quiet way.

"Tell me all of it," he said, and stretched his long legs out while I ran through the entire affair as I'd seen it, adding when I'd finished that I was very uncertain as to the girl on the boat deck being Betty. "Naturally," he remarked, with the suspicion of a drawl.

"I see now," I said, "that I should have gone up and asked her. It would have saved a lot of trouble."

"Undoubtedly," the Inspector said. "Particularly in that it was Miss Azarin who died on the court."

So they were suspicious of Betty. That was the focus of the entire situation, and I knew that I might as well face it. I'd get nowhere trying to bandy words with the Inspector. "Listen," I said. "I think the girl's innocent and I'll try to prove it, but while I'm trying I'll work with you all the way. You can discount some of the things I say if you want to, but the basis I work on is this: you've got me outweighed horse, foot and guns, and I wasn't born a fool. I'd like to go with you as often as you'll take me. I'd like to see this business worked out."

He studied me for a moment or so, then turned to the Sergeant. "What do you think of that, Sergeant?" he asked. "Do you think the young man's trying to lead us on?"

"It's a bit unusual, if I may say so, sir," the Sergeant said, after deep consideration.

The Inspector crossed his legs. "I like Mr. Cameron. I've decided to trust him. It would give me a good deal of pleasure if you'd trust him too. His antecedents are quite all right. I've looked them up."

The Sergeant murmured "Yes, sir" in a tone which he endeavored to keep from sounding extremely dubious. I didn't blame him.

"Many thanks, Inspector," I said.

"Think nothing of it," he said.

"I'd like to know what goes on," I said. "And if you really think there's been a murder. All the best doctors at the tennis court, according to the papers, failed to mention poison as a remote possibility. Have you decided to do a post-mortem on the body? Have you anything to go on, outside of the events I thought too silly to tell the Sergeant?"

"The papers," the Inspector said, "are making so much noise that we have to hold an investigation. There wasn't any talk of an investigation until Azarin began to kick up a row. Arrangements were made to take the body to a burial parlor in London, and it's probably there by now. Scotland Yard is going to pick it up there and let a Home Office expert conduct a post-mortem. We'll have a report by morning."

"Then why did you take it into your head to bedevil me before you knew anything?" I asked. "Not that I haven't enjoyed your visit. But have you seen Miss Dwight? Have you frightened the life out of her too? She must be feeling pretty rocky after a match like that."

"Miss Dwight hasn't been bothered. In fact, it was Miss Dwight who bothered us. After your little pow-wow with the Sergeant we assigned a man to keep an eye on her, but his eyesight wasn't good enough. He followed her over into Stepney one afternoon and saw her go into a sort of shop. She was in there the devil of a while, so the man finally looked in. She wasn't there. He went in; there was an old woman there and no one else, and she claimed she hadn't seen Miss Dwight. She said nobody had been in the place all afternoon."

That was a nice one. A nice one right over the inside corner. I looked at the Inspector and he looked back at me; those blue eyes of his were quizzical, and even seemed to be a little amused. "Something I thought you'd like to know," he murmured.

"Damn it!" I said. "I . . . Where the devil's Stepney?"

"This part of it's near the River. Around Limehouse. You've heard of Limehouse, I take it? You couldn't be an American and not hear of Limehouse."

I didn't say anything. The silence seemed to come creeping in on me like something animate, and I almost jumped out of my chair when the phone rang. The Sergeant answered it, in a very low tone, but the tone didn't stay low long.

"Yes, sir," he said, as his tone went up. "We'll report back, sir. Goodbye." He turned to us, losing his air of being constructed of cathedral oak. "The body, sir," he said. "It never got to the parlor, sir. That extraordinary fog had come up, and the driver of the hearse stopped near Putney Station for a pint of bitters. When he got to the parlor the rear doors of the hearse were open, the lid was off the basket, and it was gone, sir."

The Inspector uncrossed his legs and stood up. "Ungrammatical, Sergeant," he said, "but interesting. Our little vacation's about over, by the look of it. Work, eh?"

"Inspector—" I began.

He gave me a sidewise look. "If the Sergeant can stand it," he said, "you'd better call me Mac while the three of us are playing around together. We might see a lot of each other for awhile." The hint of amused irony was still in his tone. He turned to the Sergeant. "Call them back," he said, "and tell them to send out a general call for surveillance of all cemeteries. I want reports from all local offices in England. They'll have to view every body if necessary." The Sergeant went to the phone. "Do you have any idea why Miss Azarin was wearing that bandage?" the Inspector asked me."

"No," I said. "Nobody seemed to know. They were asking about it in the stands at Wimbledon."

The Sergeant finished with the telephone and stood waiting. MacMasters looked at him inquiringly. He said: "The locker room attendant's been brought in, sir. She's at the district police station." "Good," the Inspector said. "Little steps for little feet," he went on, turning to me. "We didn't have any case before the body disappeared, and maybe we haven't got one now. But it won't hurt to look around a bit. Get your hat. You asked for this, so you might as well lose a little sleep."

CHAPTER SIX

It was still foggy when we went out, so it took us a little time to get to the district police station. It upheld the honored tradition of such places all over the world and was dingy enough to suit anybody. Inspector MacMasters had a rather long talk with the Yard by telephone while the Sergeant and I waited; then we were ushered into an office in the rear of the building. The dressing room attendant—a woman well past middle age, rather stout, Cockney, looking faintly bewildered and more than faintly bedraggled, as though she'd got out of bed and dressed in the dark—was sitting there. She stood up nervously when we came in and straightened the grandfather of all queer hats; then Mac-Masters in a soothing tone, told her to sit down and asked her name.

"Mrs. Tyburn, sir," she said. "It's about the young lydy, sir? I wouldn't know nothin' about it, sir. I was that shocked that I went home and got into me bed with a ragin' headache, sir, and then the busies came—"'

"Quite so," MacMasters said, cutting her off. "Tell me, now, were these two girls in your dressing room?"

"Oh, no, sir. Miss Dwight was in the Members' Dressing Room, the same as she always is, sir, quite a distance away, and Miss Azarin, the one with that 'orrid foreign woman, called "Elga' was in mine, sir. I didn't see much of her, sir, because of the foreign woman. There was little for me to do, sir, with her about. I went to me little corner and I sat in it, sir, and kept meself to meself."

"Good," Mac said. "They can go from one dressing room to the other? From your room to the Members' Dressing Room?"

"Only around by the outside, sir. What with the steps and the passages and the locked doors with constables at them, sir, no one could do it. They'd have to go outside in the drive, sir, the one as runs past for the motors to come up."

"You wouldn't know, then, if the foreign woman left Miss Azarin for a moment, or if anyone else saw her?"

"I didn't see, sir. Unless they called me out I stayed in me plyce."

"You saw Miss Azarin when they brought her in, though?"

"Oh, yes, sir. All the people and the doctors and the fair shock of it myde me 'eart turn over in me, sir. But she was dead, sir. They all said that, and then the ambulance came—"

"What ambulance?"

"From the 'ospital, sir, the one near the cemetry."

"The Wimbledon Hospital, sir," the Sergeant put in. "They took her there. That's where the hearse got her, sir."

MacMasters paid little attention to this. "Did you notice her when she first came in?" he asked. "Did she have the bandage around her arm?"

"I couldn't say, sir. She might 'ave 'ad a cardigan on."

"Very well," MacMasters said. "That will do. Sergeant, take Mrs. Tyburn out, and ask them to see her home." When they had gone out he whistled a bar or two of "D'Ye Ken John Peel?" stared at the ceiling for a moment, and remarked: "Nice start, eh? That's the way it'll be. Nobody saw anything. They all sat in their cubicles, being genteel. Very genteel race, the British."

"Why did you leave the United States?" I asked.

"Hay fever," he said. "I was having a good time, too." He wasn't thinking of the question; he'd answered me automatically, and while his eyes were on me they were focused somewhere beyond, as though I wasn't there. The Sergeant came in again, looked at him, and quietly sat down; presently MacMasters stared at him and said: "Tell them we're going to the Dorchester." The Sergeant went out, and Mac-Masters stood up.

I stood up too, but hesitantly; I didn't want to go crashing in on Betty at that time of night, along with two men from Scotland Yard. "I think I'll go back to the hotel," I began.

"No," MacMasters said. "It would be a mistake. We're going to see a gambler named Hajos."

The Sergeant was waiting, and the three of us went out of the station and to the Dorchester. The begilded doorman drew the Sergeant aside and spoke a few words to him; I went with MacMasters and waited while he went to the desk. The Sergeant joined me, then MacMasters came along and we walked through the lobby to the elevators. I was liking it less all the time. We got out of the elevator, walked silently up a long corridor, and were met at the door of a room by a somewhat Oriental-looking man with glasses and a bald head. MacMasters introduced him as Hajos; he gave me a soft, dry hand and a veiled, heavy-lidded and speculative look. We went inside. It was another suite, all pale green walls and mirrors, with a faint smell of Turkish tobacco and incense. Hajos called down for brandy and soda;

his movements were a little precious, and his eye seemed always edging toward MacMasters. We all sat down, and the Sergeant took out his book.

"I had a notion," MacMasters said, "to ask you about the betting on the Azarin-Dwight match."

Hajos looked a little more Oriental; a strange and under-the-surface air of placating and defiance took hold of him. "Yes, Inspector," he said. "Anything I may do, of course. It was very unfortunate. Is there any implication of . . . ah . . . interference? I have glanced at the newspapers, to be sure."

"To be sure," MacMasters said. "Why did the betting go toward Miss Azarin until the last day? Why did it go toward her at all?"

Hajos didn't shrug, but there was a suggestion of it in his pose. "If you mean the odds on Miss Dwight went down," he said, "that is correct. The odds were very heavy on her at first. She is experienced and a fine player. But she began to have three-set matches. It wasn't like her to have three-set matches. She was out of form. Naturally the odds came down."

"She was still out of form on the day of the finals, I take it? And the odds went up again."

"There might have been a lot of money put on her," Hajos said, with a suggestion of weariness, "all at once."

"You wouldn't have an idea who did it?" MacMasters asked.

The brandy came in then, and there was the business of pouring it out and putting the soda into it. It was handed around, and the waiter went out. Hajos sat staring at his shoes for a moment. He had a detached air, but it was plain to be seen that he didn't quite like the way the questions were headed. He was, I think, considering whether to uphold the bluff of knowing nothing definite; he didn't know what MacMasters wanted him for. Without raising his head he lit a Turkish cigarette.

"I don't want to put in a lot of time on this," MacMasters said, conversationally. "Get it out of your mind that I'm after you, and don't hold me up."

Hajos nodded, and in that under-the-surface manner of his looked relieved. "Very frank," he said. "There has been some talk that I knew a great deal about Marie Azarin's death. I am not such a fool."

"You've never been before," MacMasters said.

"There has been that talk because Azarin put, day by day, large sums on his niece—unconditionally. That is what brought the odds down. When they came down more money went on her. It began to look bad for me, it looked as though there was something about the Dwight girl I didn't know. So on the last day the Dwight odds went up. I had to cover."

"So Azarin lost his money?"

"Of course. The wagers were unconditional."

"He made the bets publicly?" MacMasters asked.

"Yes, he made them as publicly as possible. It is in your mind that he did it for effect? That he had much larger wagers on Dwight in private?" He was leaning forward now.

"You're too far ahead of me," MacMasters said. "He didn't come to you in any of this? You didn't make a deal with him?"

"No, no, Inspector. I don't want him in England. I will take his money, but I will not see him. Even in this, it may be, he has used me to advantage."

"Cheer up," MacMasters said. "You made money. You came out clear all around except for him. You didn't hear of any illness of Miss Dwight's?" Hajos shook his head. "You haven't any information to volunteer on Azarin?"

Hajos smiled slightly; it was a smooth smile. "Information?" he asked. "Ah, no, I am sorry. I only know him for a very clever man."

"So are *you,*" MacMasters said. "Peace at any price, eh? Did you ever hear that this girl wasn't his niece?"

Hajos really shrugged at that one. "One hears a great number of things," he murmured. "I never inquired." It was pretty obvious that he was going to say nothing about Azarin. He took a sip of his brandy and soda, and his heavy lids dropped a little. He was feeling a lot more comfortable than when we had come in.

"You didn't hear of a Spaniard hanging about the entrance to the dressing room?" MacMasters asked suddenly.

"No, no, Inspector. How would I—"

"Rubbish!" MacMasters interrupted him. "Don't lie so clumsily. One of my men saw one of your men watching him!"

Hajos' eyes widened slightly during this speech. He swallowed. "Ah," he said. "Now that I recall, one of my men did say something to me about a Spaniard, or a Mexican. I'd quite forgotten it. This person attracted his attention by asking questions about the Azarin girl. He was still there when the ambulance came up." MacMasters didn't say anything; he merely sat and looked at Hajos a little absently, then whistled a bar of two of "John Peel." It must have been a great favorite with him. Hajos didn't like this much, but MacMasters let him stew for a few minutes.

The time drew out; Hajos moved slightly; and MacMasters shot at him: "How did Miss Azarin get that injured arm?"

Hajos jumped, controlling himself a little too late. "I don't know!" he said quickly, in too loud a tone. "I don't know," he repeated, lower. "I didn't know she was injured until she came onto the court." MacMasters looked at the Sergeant, a very obvious look; I think he intended it to be obvious. Hajos didn't miss it. He said, "You're wrong if you think I did know. You said awhile back I'd never been a fool,

Inspector. You can check it anywhere that I wouldn't deal with Azarin. Maybe my boys get into trouble with razors once in a while, but they stay in the . . . ah . . . reservation. You know that. I didn't like the look of this when I first heard that Azarin was bringing a girl over. I don't like anything about him. I don't like these damned Americans."

"Didn't you say she wasn't his niece?" MacMasters asked.

"No, she's not!" Hajos said at once, then looked down his nose. His jaw stiffened, he stiffened all over, and suddenly decided he'd been on the run long enough. He belatedly remembered, apparently, that MacMasters had nothing on him, that he'd been taken for a ride because of a momentary nervousness, and an expression flitted across his face that wasn't pleasant to see. That he'd been on the run at all surprised me, for he looked like a pretty cool article. Apparently, however, he was very much worried over the entire affair. He didn't want any part in it nor any suspicion thrown on him; he wanted to keep as far away from Scotland Yard—and Azarin too—as possible. He'd about reached the mulish stage, and MacMasters stood up.

"Many thanks," he said, "for the brandy. You can report me for drinking on duty if the idea strikes you." Hajos looked as though nothing would suit him better, but he made an attempt at a deprecating smile. "Remember," MacMasters said suddenly, staring at him, "that you've told me you weren't mixed up with Azarin in any way on this. This is a serious case. If we find later that you've lied about these bets I'll put all the pressure of the Yard on you. That'd finish you for good." Hajos shook his head with uncharacteristic vigor, staring; we turned and walked down the hall. "A cheap crook," MacMasters said, "who stays where he is because he's afraid of anything spectacular. Somebody who's not will come along and upset him one of these days, and then our troubles will begin." He rang for the elevator. "He knows plenty."

"He knows enough to steer clear of Azarin," I said.

"Don't prejudice the investigator," he said. "What is it, Sergeant?"

"The doorman told me two of our men have been around here already, sir. Lady Irene Wrexford-Bond and Andrews were in the dining room watching the floor show, sir. But they've left. And begging your pardon, could you tell me how you found out about Hajos' man being at Wimbledon? There's no report on it."

MacMasters grinned. He had a very likable grin. "Pure bluff," he said. "One of Hajos' men is always at Wimbledon, and there was a chance he'd be near the dressing room. Hajos was in a sweat about Miss Dwight, and when Hajos is in a sweat his men are on the job. A wild stretch of the imagination, Sergeant. Avoid such things."

"Yes, sir. Admirable, sir."

"At any rate it knocked Hajos off his perch, eh? He thought we were closer to him than we ever have been in this weary world." He mimicked the gambler. "'I don't like these damned Americans.' You think he was telling the truth about Miss Azarin not being Azarin's niece, Sergeant?"

"Yes, sir. Also about Miss Azarin's arm injury, sir."

"Remember that one," MacMasters said, as the elevator door opened. We got into it, and he gave the boy another floor number—which wasn't Betty's. This time it was a single room, furnished like an office with a large desk and several filing cabinets; a rather heavy, fair-haired man sat behind the desk. He looked up, smiled, and said: "Hello, Inspector. Hello, Sergeant."

"Hello, George," MacMasters said, and in an aside to me: "The house dick." He introduced me to him, and we sat down; George retreated behind the desk again.

"Anything queer happening on Miss Dwight's floor?" MacMasters asked.

A faint pompousness descended upon George. "Miss Dwight? You're on that, what?" His brow drew down in concentration. "I think nothing extraordinary," he announced at length. "The aunt, Mrs. Cosgrove, is out a good bit with an American. A rather drunken American."

"Most Americans are drunk. Many other visitors?"

"Very few, very few indeed."

"Any Spaniards or Mexicans?"

"I haven't noticed, Inspector. No special instructions, to keep an eye on Miss Dwight, you know." He seemed a little hurt. "None whatever."

"Keep an eye on her from now on," MacMasters said. "Get me a list of all her phone calls and a list of who's been there if you can." He seemed to lose interest in George; he got out a small pad and began to make strange characters in it. George watched him for a moment, then began to talk in a low voice to the Sergeant. The Sergeant seemed somewhat non-committal until MacMasters raised his head, looked at the pair of them, and remarked: "Take your hair down for awhile, Sergeant. It'll loosen you up." He bent to his pad again, and George and the Sergeant began to swap reminiscences in low tones.

As they droned on I thought of Hajos. Behind him, I gathered, there was a good deal of dreary viciousness; and he, an unremarkable man with an unreliable nervous system and a flair for organization, possessed a lot of information we couldn't get. It was maddening that he couldn't be strung up by the thumbs until he talked, particularly about Azarin. I doubted if MacMasters would be able to trick much more out of him; for although Hajos feared Scotland Yard much, he seemed to fear Azarin even more. The three bits of information MacMasters had got out of him—the presence of a Spaniard or Mexican at Wimbledon; the fact of Marie not being Azarin's niece; and the fact that Hajos, who "knew everything," didn't know of Marie's injury—would, I hoped, carry things toward Azarin for awhile. As this round of visits with MacMasters piled up, I became increasingly uncomfortable; I was getting the feeling that he was taking me on these preliminary visits to give me the illusion that I was in on everything and was going to leave me out when he called on Betty. He was checking on the things I'd told him, too, like asking the house detective if any Spaniards had been seen around. That had come from my mentioning to him Mrs. Cosgrove's remark.

At this juncture he closed his little book quietly and said: "Had enough, Sergeant? Feel like a trip to Stepney?"

The Sergeant swam up out of his reminiscences, somewhat flushed with simple joy. "Do you have to go, sir? I fancy routine could handle it and save you the trouble, sir."

"Have to show Mr. Cameron the town," MacMasters said, and stood up. "He might not like it, but we had to stop being Pollyannas several hours ago. Ever hear of Pollyanna, Sergeant?"

"No, sir," the Sergeant said. "Not that I recall, sir."

"Delectable character. Almost as bad as some of Dickens'." He nodded to George, and we went out. There was a new doorman, who also spoke a few words to the Sergeant, then MacMasters called a cab, gave the driver directions, and climbed in after us.

"Don't be distressed, Sergeant," he said, as we started off. "I'm paying for this party myself. What did the doorman have to say?"

"He said that Lady Irene and Andrews had gone, in different cabs, sir."

"Fair enough. Remind me to get the report in the morning where they went." We rode for a long time, but I didn't pay much attention to where we were going. I fell to watching MacMasters' profile against the passing lights, and after awhile he looked around and caught my eye. "This man Andrews you met on the boat," he began, without preamble, "is a damned anomalous fellow. He has no criminal record in the States, so far as I can find out. What he told you about himself seems to be more or less true. He's retired and collects paintings and serves on charity boards. He's never been mixed up with shady characters except once, and that was right after he retired, about four years ago. He went to New Orleans and tried to organize all the bordellos in the city."

"That was a funny thing to do," I said.

"Believe it or not, he was trying to make working conditions better. He went about with a few of the ringleaders and spent a lot of money. A sort of Galahad stunt. He gave dinners and talked a lot of rubbish. His mother finally sent for him and put him in a psychiatric hospital for awhile. It must have been amusing for New Orleans."

"What hospital," I asked, "did they send him to?"

"To Bellevue first, then to a sanatorium. Didn't you say that he changed after he took a drink?"

"He changed a lot," I said. "It was after he took the drink that he sneaked off to Azarin's cabin. But what's that got to do with it?"

"Maybe a lot, maybe nothing. Ask a psychiatrist."

I didn't reply, and the conversation languished. I fell to wondering why he'd brought Andrews up, so finally I asked him.

"A notion," he said. "It seemed to me, from what you said, that you are still on speaking terms with him. You can still see him and talk to him, so long as you don't let the rest of them catch you at it. You might find out something useful, for if he's mixed up in a deal with Azarin, I'm sure it's not murder. You can find out more from him than a policeman could."

I stared out the cab window, nonplussed for the moment. I saw that MacMasters was playing a game with me in which he held every high card there was. "How would I go about it?" I asked. "What reason could I give him for looking him up now?"

"You could think one up," he said imperturbably.

It was getting more fantastic all the time. No Scotland Yard man I had ever heard about acted like that. "It's you who should be in Bellevue," I said, "and I think the Sergeant would agree with me." There was a dense silence from the Sergeant. "I won't do it," I said.

"Come, come," he said genially. "That's putting it too strongly. You wanted to see this thing through, and this is your chance. Did you ever read *Cyrano de Bergerac?*"

"Yes," I said shortly. "And if he's a hero of yours I can see the reason why."

"It's not that. Cyrano and Christian set out together to make a hero of romance. We'll make a hero of crime detection between us."

"I won't—" I began, but he interrupted me.

"You can't help it. You're elected. You'll make your reports to me. I'll even put you on an expense account and give you a badge."

His voice sounded as though he were enjoying himself a great deal. I wasn't; I was getting into a fine rage, and as I sat there trying to hold myself down I became conscious of the dismal and badly lighted district around us—a combination of the waterfront, gas and poverty. The Sergeant

was sitting forward; apparently we were almost at our destination—which, according to MacMasters, had been Betty's
destination several days before.

"After all," MacMasters' voice came out of his corner,
"you'd be more in your own circle. You don't want to spend
all your time in town among house detectives and gamblers.
Lady Irene does things up in style, and you'd be at her place
a good deal. Find out why Andrews got mixed up with Azarin in the first place. Find out what was in that box. Find
out all you can—and this is important—about Marie Azarin. It's a nice little assignment."

I couldn't think of anything to say. A sort of inertia
had descended on me. MacMasters and his jokes, practical
or grim, were suddenly too much for me. We were jolting
along a gloomy, cobbled street. The cab slowed down and
stopped before a tall, narrow building squeezed in between
other narrow, dark buildings. There was a dimly lighted show window in the front of it. Two cabs stood at the
curb, and while I waited for MacMasters and the Sergeant
to get out I saw three people come from the building with
the show window and stop on the sidewalk. I recognized
Andrews, the drunken ex-tennis player, Gasden, and Mrs.
Cosgrove. Some sort of argument seemed to be going on
between Gasden and Andrews—Gasden seemed quite voci-
ferous. Andrews with an abrupt gesture left him and got
into the cab in front; Gasden made as if to follow, but Mrs.
Cosgrove restrained him. These two held a short colloquy,
then got into the other cab and pulled away. None of them
had even turned toward us.

I was so startled at seeing this ill-assorted trio, that I
forgot to get out. I sat and stared. After a moment MacMasters said, "Who would have thought it of Aunt Bea! Come
along, let's see what they've been up to."

CHAPTER SEVEN

It was, without a doubt, the most littered and disorderly shop I'd ever been in. Long and narrow, very poorly lighted and smelling of drains, it held everything from portions of suits of armor to floor mops. Everything was covered with a thick layer of dust. A stairway ran from the front to a dirty door in the side wall, and part way up the stairs a man was standing staring down at us. He had been on his way up; he was short and dark, surprisingly well dressed, a hang-dog looking fellow with a bony construction of face that was unmistakably Spanish, and his cheeks bore the blue shadow of the day's unshaved beard. His hands, resting on the stair-rail, were small and white. They hadn't been bitten as I had bitten the man at Azarin's.

"Shutting up," he said, with a faint accent. "No more sell tonight."

"We're not buying anything," MacMasters said. "We just feel conversational. Come on down, there's a good fellow."

"No," the man said. "No sell, no talk, no nothing."

He turned to go on up, but MacMasters checked him. "You might as well talk here," he said. "It will save you the trouble of a trip to Scotland Yard."

The man stopped at once, straightened up quickly. His dark face took on a swift mask of impassiveness, and he made a resigned gesture with one hand. "I come," he said, and suited the action to the word.

When he was standing in front of us he seemed more hang-dog than at a distance, and his black unreadable eyes darted from one of us to the other; there was an intense and virulent smell of onions about him. Onions or garlic, whichever was worse.

"Those people who were just here," MacMasters said. "Who were they?"

The man shrugged. *"Quién sabe?* People to buy."

"To buy what?"

"One to buy picture. Others to find out."

"What sort of a picture?" MacMasters asked.

The man shrugged again, and didn't speak.

"There was a girl here several days ago," MacMasters said. "A girl who plays the tennis."

The man, who had been looking at the Sergeant, glanced sidewise at MacMasters; his eyebrows went up slightly and he seemed to shrink into himself a little, to tighten up. "Dead, eh?" he asked. "I see in the paper."

"She's not dead," MacMasters said. "The girl she played against is the dead one. What did the girl buy from you?"

"Buy? Buy nothing. You lock me up because she buy nothing? I don't know."

"You know," MacMasters said. "What did you go to her hotel for?"

"She write letter. I go."

"She was here, wasn't she?" MacMasters asked.

"Si, si."

"And when one of my men came in after her she was gone. The woman said she hadn't been here, that nobody had been here."

"Old woman make mistake," the man said, shrugging again. "She not know. Me in shop, girl come in, I go out back door with girl. I tell woman I go out. Woman not see girl."

"What did you go out the back door for?" MacMasters asked, and added in an aside to me: "I knew it was a mistake for that fool to come in. They've had time to cook up an alibi."

The Spaniard listened to this, his head forward and the garlic coming in waves. "Cook?" he asked. "Cook nothing. Go out back door to buy."

"Damn it!" MacMasters said. "What did you buy? What did the girl want to buy?"

The Spaniard stared at him with narrowed black eyes, and shrugged. It was a very final shrug.

"Ah, me," MacMasters said. "If I had this gent in the States I'd beat him half to death with a rubber hose. What did the man and the woman want tonight?"

"They would know what the girl of the tennis bought. I not tell them. I not tell you. I am lawful man."

MacMasters swallowed this, and asked: "What sort of a picture did the other man want?"

"I never hear of him, this picture. Picture of man like Jesus, very bad all the same. Italiano, most old."

"What did he come to you for, then?" MacMasters asked. "Who sent him? Why didn't he go to the big dealers?"

"Quién sabe?" the Spaniard asked.

"Oh, rats!" MacMasters said. "Enough is enough. Sergeant, get this man fingerprinted tomorrow and look him up. Let's get out of this, and shake him down later." He turned away, saying as he did so: "Good night, my friend."

The Spaniard stood motionless, and when we had reached the door said in a tone which sounded sardonic in the extreme: "Good night. *Vaya ustedes con Dios.*"

"A sense of humor," MacMasters said, as we got into the cab and started off, "is a grievous thing, at least for us. It piles the work up. That dago knows exactly how far I can go with him. He's heard about the cute little thing they have in this benighted country called 'Judges' Rules.' No third degree, so I'll have to work three men to death to find out about him." He took out a package of American cigarettes, lit one, and spat a crumb of tobacco out. "He told the truth, I think, as far as it went. Miss Dwight assuredly bought something, and it's up to us to prove what it was; maybe Andrews even wanted a picture. What do you think Miss Dwight bought?"

That seemed to be rubbing it in a bit too much. "Christmas presents," I said with some asperity, "for the girls back home."

"Now that's an idea," he said. "Mandrake roots or the like, eh? He must have had them in that litter. Did he remind you of the man you tangled with at Azarin's?"

"He was short," I said, "and so was the other one. They both eat the same thing, apparently. I don't see how they survive the garlic diet very long. What interests me is how everybody finds this one man. Betty Dwight found him, Andrews found him, Gasden and Mrs. Cosgrove found him. They could have found him through Betty, of course, but how about Andrews? What did the Spaniard at Wimbledon look like?"

"Sergeant, find out tomorrow from Hajos' man," Mac-Masters said. "You know where to flush him. Take him along when you get the fingerprints if it's necessary."

"Tomorrow's Sunday, sir," the Sergeant said.

"He's always in the bosom of his family on Sunday," MacMasters said. "He's a pillar of the church. That will make it easier."

"You know a lot about him," I said.

"I know a lot about a lot of people," MacMasters said. "My brain's the handiest little indexed file you ever saw."

I was becoming aware of that.

"Take Lady Irene now," he went on calmly, and threw the stub of the cigarette out the window. "She has a house off Hyde Park, with a lot of damned expensive pictures in it. Most of them came down to her, but she's bought two or three in her time."

"Did she buy any of them from that Spaniard?" I asked.

"Ha!" he said. "You're beginning to deduce things. It was a wise move when I made you a deputy. Unfortunately, she bought them all from big dealers. They were all well publicized sales. A smack in the eye for the dirty Yanks, as she implied herself. It's amazing how the British poor cheer up when some patriotic soul—who's been taking the extra slice of bread out of their mouths for years—pays that bread money to keep a masterpiece in the Empire. Isn't that the hang of it, Sergeant?"

"They were fine paintings, sir," the Sergeant

"The Sergeant won't discuss Socialism," MacMasters said. "Confusion to him, and let him take what he gets. Lady Irene, therefore, has a fair name among the masses. She's rich and patriotic and handsome, and she has a way of not getting publicized when she's on the Riviera. She's been discreet about her lovers and her gambling losses, more discreet the last several years than formerly. She was very glad to see Azarin. What construction would you put on it?"

"That she's been pining for him ever since he went to California," I said sulkily. I was beginning to see where all his talk was leading; he was giving me a lot of information about Lady Irene and Andrews and was going to shove me off on them whether I felt like being shoved or not. "She certainly seemed overjoyed at the sight of him."

"And he?"

"Not so overjoyed. He controlled himself very well. Even better than Marie."

"Doesn't that interest you?" he asked, and yawned. "It's a nice little set-up. Azarin comes to England and accidentally runs into a lady who longs for him; he has with him a girl who by Hajos' account isn't his niece; the girl and the lady, both with tender passions, meet and exchange words; the lady begins to go to his house, as discovered by you; and, with great éclat, the other suddenly dies on the tennis court." He yawned again, luxuriously and mightily, and stretched his arms. "If you weren't so damned intent on one side of this affair you'd soon see that I was giving you the chance of a lifetime to clear your own girl. Do you do it? No; you think I'm putting you off to get you out of the way. You sit there and sulk."

The irritation which had been growing on me since the start of this harangue flared up. "I'm not sulking," I said in a passion. "And if I was what good would it do me? You're going to keep me away from Betty Dwight; why don't you say so and be done with it? I don't want to sound like an ass," I went on, "but you should be able to see how I feel about it. Instead you go along as if I had no interest in the girl at all. You've got enough material for a lot of tough questions for her, and you can't expect me to sit by and be comfortable about it. If this Andrews angle's so important why don't you work on it yourself? You know damned well you want to get me out of the way."

He sighed, a little theatrically. "Oh, no," he said. "Not at all. You can be there and lend aid, even if she has managed to get on without you all her life. She's made out fairly well, at that, it seems to me. Of course I've got some tough questions for her. I thought, at this stage, it would make you more comfortable not to hear them. But sweet reason gets me nowhere. You can come along when we see Miss Dwight; but whether you like it or not you're going to play with

Andrews. Why don't you make something of that? Why don't you occupy your mind with toil? If I were you I'd start out with a logical action, such as checking with Bellevue to see what's really wrong with Andrews."

There was no getting around him. He talked on so persuasively and so logically that it was impossible to estimate where I stood with him or what he thought. "It all sounds good," I said. "It sounds so good that I'm sure there's something wrong with it. I always feel that way when an Irishman gets working on me."

"I'm not sure I'm Irish," he remarked. "I think I'm a glens-of-Antrim Scot. However, that's beside the point. What concerns me is that I've found something of value in Gilbert and Sullivan. I loathe Gilbert and Sullivan; but they were right when they said a policeman's lot is not a happy one. Do you like Gilbert and Sullivan, Sergeant?"

"Very much, sir," the Sergeant said.

It was hopeless. And then, as I sat staring at MacMasters in exasperation, a thought struck me. "Listen," I said. "Are you putting on this act to spare my feelings? Do things look worse than I think they do? I know so damned little of this—"

He raised his hand. "We're in front of your hotel," he said, and I looked out to see that we were indeed in front of it, with the doorman looking through the cab window in some distress. "I'm damned," he went on, "if you don't go a long way for punishment. I told you you thought about that girl too much, so I'll tell you one thing more that may divert your mind. As sure as the devil, Azarin's going to make a perfect bloody nuisance of himself accusing you. You were pretty thick with Miss Dwight on the boat; you went to his house and acted very strangely for a guest, and now he's got you in a corner because you did. It was a fool

thing to do, and you can spend the rest of the night thinking about it."

He opened the door of the cab and I got out without another word. I'd never thought of that angle of it before, but
I thought of it plenty as I walked down the hall from the
elevator. I had surely been incredibly naive; but then, I'd
been in such a lather about Betty that I'd been naive about
everything. MacMasters might be up to a game too subtle
for me, but I had to admit that some of the things he'd said
were reasonable. Like occupying my mind, for instance. If
my mind had been occupied I wouldn't have said so many
fool things to him. It suddenly occurred to me—for the
first time, apparently—that I was as suspect as the rest of
them. Because MacMasters had checked me with Captain
Brererton I'd somehow got the idea that I was, in his eyes,
perfectly guiltless. Probably the way he talked—telling me
things, sketching in characters—had strengthened the idea.
Policemen seldom took suspects around with them while
working on the suspect's case. However, I was so confused
at the moment that I didn't know where I was or what to
think. I didn't know what anything meant, what MacMasters really knew, whether he was taking me around to keep
an eye on me, or whether he really intended to make use of
me with Andrews.

As I considered my new and extremely anomalous position I felt very much ashamed of the way I'd gone on to him
about Betty. I had been childish, and it had taken MacMasters' speech about my position to wake me up to the fact. I'd
stop tagging along, saying people were putting things over on
me. Maybe they were, but I intended to follow his lead and
see where it took me. If it took me to a place I didn't like,
then would be sufficient time to do something about it.

It was at this juncture that I discovered I was standing still in the middle of the corridor, making gestures to the walls. I looked around quickly, saw no one, and started again for my room. I was still thinking about Inspector MacMasters when I got to the door, and absently turned the knob before I got my key out. The door opened and I almost fell into the room. The light was on, and Gasden was sitting on the bed. He started to his feet, saw me, and sat down again, limply staring.

"What the hell," I demanded, "are you doing in here? How did you get in? It's about midnight. You ought to be in bed."

"They let me in," he said, still staring. "I told them I was a relation and had to see you." He looked frightened and relieved at the same time. He was rather pale and apparently sober. I had walked over to him by then and saw that he had the shakes, although he tried to control them by holding one hand with the other. He stayed on the bed looking up at me, his eyes a little bloodshot and wide but calmer. There was some sort of fear on him, but my entrance had removed it a little. "You're a good guy," he said. "Sit down, can't you? Sit down, you make me nervous standing up. I wanted to talk to somebody, and I couldn't think of anybody but you."

"Any bartender would have done," I said, still angry at his intrusion.

"Bars are all shut," he said, accepting the sarcasm without noticing it. "You're not in the U. S. A."

I sat down, feeling a little ashamed of my remark. "What is it?" I asked in a more civilized tone. "What sort of a jam have you got yourself into?"

He leaned forward. "I don't know," he said. "Mrs. Cosgrove and I were only having fun. We found out about a

place in Limehouse and went there, and then a guy named
Andrews came in. He's a son of a bitch, that guy. He's a
first-class, self-made son of a bitch if I ever saw one. I never
did anything to him. I never saw him before. He wanted
to know what I was doing there, and I was a little bit lit so
I told him to go air himself. Then he said he'd been there
first, and if it was money I wanted he'd give it to me. I said
what the hell good would money do me because I'd only
give it to some bartender, and with that he got the nastiest
look on him I ever saw. By God, he did, and before that
he was a nice-looking guy. And with this look he says I'd
join Marie Azarin on a slab damn quick if I ever showed up
there again. So then Aunt Bea steps up to quiet things down
and it seems like she knows him. And what did he do but
tell her that he wouldn't stand interference, and for her to
get me out of there and go back to things she knew about.
Then he turned to the Spaniard and says: 'Don't make any
mistakes. There's one dead now, and there'll be more maybe. Keep your mouth shut.' The Spaniard shrugged and Andrews turned to me and said if I didn't get out he'd throw
me out. Oh, hell, we finally all went out together and he
went away, but after I left Aunt Bea at the Dorchester I saw
there was a man following me." He stopped and stared at
me. Only then did his face take on expression; all through
his long speech it had held none at all, he had rambled
on as though talking in his sleep. The sudden widening of
the eyes, the forward thrust of his head, was startling. "By
God!" he exclaimed. "Maybe he meant what he said! What
do you think, Cameron? What do you think?" He suddenly
became very agitated. "Look, he talked about Marie Azarin
being on a slab, and then the guy followed me. Sneaking
along with his hands in his pocket. A big guy, tall as hell.

He was lame in one foot. He got close to me once, under a light, and his face had a long scar on it." His eyes grew wider; he jumped up and looked wildly about. "Do you hear anything?" he shouted, and began to run around the room.

In that instant I saw, as clearly as though he had been standing in front of me again, the tall man with whom Betty had talked for a moment in Hyde Park the day of the match; then Gasden's row drowned everything out.

"Sit down!" I shouted back at him.

As suddenly as he had got up he collapsed on the bed again, shaking badly and staring. "Ah!" he said, and took his head in his hands. "A great girl," he said in a muffled voice. "Fun. What in the name of God she's got into . . ."

"What did you go to Limehouse for?" I asked.

"Aunt Bea," he said, without moving. "Aunt Bea found out where Betty went. Ah!" he exclaimed. "People are talking to me. I know it's a lie, because you're the only one here."

"Nobody's talking to you," I said, and going to the bureau dug out a bottle of Scotch I'd bought and got a drink into him. It probably wasn't the thing to do, but it brought him around a little.

"I can't go out," he said. "I've got to stay here. I can't go down where that man is. Andrews' man, isn't it? He'll kill me. He's waiting to kill me."

"Nonsense," I said. "Listen, what's Betty been doing?"

"Betty? She hasn't been doing anything. She is in the hotel. I don't know anyhow, we haven't been there."

"Do you know what she went to that shop for?"

"Aunt Bea asked her. She hasn't done anything else but ask her. Aunt Bea says she went there before, she says she's sure she went there before. Aunt Bea's worried as hell about her. She won't eat or anything. She . . . Oh, God, there it is again!" He raised his head swiftly, and shouted: "I won't! If I can't drink what the hell else can I do? What the hell else do I care about?"

There was a knock at the door. He jumped a foot and I went to the door and found a bellhop there; before he could say anything I told him to get the house physician as quickly as he could, and if the room next to mine was empty we'd put Gasden into it. He went running down the corridor, and I turned to Gasden. He had got himself into the far corner of the room and was standing there, terrified. "Easy," I said. "Easy does it. Come sit down."

He watched me narrowly for a moment, then sidled over and sat down on the bed. "They think I'm only a tennis bum," he said, in a low, confidential tone. "Only one more tennis bum. Let them try it." He made a choking noise. "Poor Betty wants to be champion forever!" he said, leaning forward and pointing a finger at me. "She wants to win, always. She almost didn't stay in it with that Australian girl—"

"For God's sake," I said, "don't go around talking like that. Do you want to get her into more trouble? Use your head, man, use your head."

"She can't last forever!" he said. "She was scared to death of that Azarin girl. What did she want with that Spaniard? What's she always sitting by the telephone for? I'll tell you why. She's afraid that Cynthia Blythe will call up and spill the—"

"What's Cynthia Blythe got to do with it?" I broke in.

"How should I know?" he said.

A knock at the door put an end to this. He leaped up again and made for the corner, and I went to the door. It was the doctor, a sharp-eyed, birdlike little man with a goatee. He stepped into the room; Gasden uttered a wild whoop and tried to climb the wall. The doctor halted, put his bag on the bed, got out a hypodermic syringe, and went into the bathroom. Gasden continued to scramble about, making the most shocking clamor; the doctor came out of the bathroom again, glanced at me, and we both went for Gasden. He was a handful, but we finally got the injection into him. He became quiet at once, and listened as the doctor talked to him in a low voice; after a little of this he allowed himself to be led out of the room. The doctor was gone about fifteen minutes, then came back for his bag.

"He's quieting down," he said. "He will be all right the rest of the night, I fancy."

"I'm very sorry for all the row," I said. "He got into my room somehow. He'd better be sent to a nursing home or some similar place in the morning. He's been drunk for a long time."

The doctor nodded. "Has he any relatives? Anyone to be responsible for him?"

"I don't know," I said. "I will be responsible for him until I can find out. I know him slightly. He's been hearing voices," I went on, in case he talked some more. "He's apparently got some delusion of persecution. He may talk about Miss Dwight, the tennis player, but there's very little actual connection. He used to be a great match player himself, before arthritis finished him. He's never been quite the same since."

"I see," the doctor said. "He's apparently jealous of Miss Dwight. An acute alcoholic hallucinosis, I daresay."

"He thinks a man with a gun's waiting out in the street for him, too."

He smiled slightly. "It should clear up shortly," he said. "I shall make arrangements and have him moved at once."

"Good," I said. "He'd better stay in the nursing home until he's quite rational. Keep in touch with me about him."

He went out. I was very tired, but not too tired to be thankful that Gasden had happened on me for his ravings. They were disturbing enough among friends, particularly the parts about Betty.

That brought me back to the place I'd been before Gasden interrupted me. I didn't want to let Betty in for anything; but as I examined my feelings in the light of what MacMasters had said and done during the evening I found that I had at last settled in my own mind what I was going to do. I was going to tell him all of it. He'd find it out anyway, I was sure of that. He had all the sources of information, and an unknown number of men working all over England. It was an unheroic decision, but the only sensible one I could come to. And, having made it, I finished undressing, went to bed, and fell into the best sleep I'd had since the affair started.

CHAPTER EIGHT

I had just finished shaving the next morning when there was a tap at the door, and opening it I found MacMasters standing in the hall. He was looking very fit, and there was a flower in his buttonhole; I asked him to come in. "I want to see how it looks on you," I said, "in a stronger light."

He came in and sat down in a chair near the window. "It's a concession," he said. "My mother used to like it. I always wear one on Sundays when I can shake the Sergeant. How did you sleep?"

"Very well," I said. I had been putting on my tie, and glancing at him in the mirror I met his blue eyes on mine; the expression in them didn't match the flower. It was speculative. "Very well," I repeated, "after I got started. Gasden was here when I came in."

"So?" he asked.

"He settled my doubts," I said, and told him the whole story. "There it is," I ended up. "You'd better rejoice at it. It was a struggle to get that far."

"It would have been more of a struggle if you hadn't," he said. "I've got a transcript of it all in my pocket."

I stared at him. "What?" I asked.

"Dictaphone," he said. "Very unBritish, but I wanted to make sure. The case can't get anywhere until we find the body, and I'm a little weary of wondering who everybody's for. Besides that, the event I spoke of has come to pass. Azarin's accusing you. There might be some connection between his choosing late last night to do it and Gasden's visit here, although I don't know what it is. He could have done it before."

"I thought he had," I said, "when you began to prophesy."

"No, not until after Gasden came in. There was a man following Gasden. In fact, there were two men following Andrews when he went to Limehouse. One of them stayed on Andrews and the other took Gasden."

"I'm beginning to think I did the smart thing," I said. "Are you shadowing everybody in this business?"

"Just about," he said. "Lady Irene went out to Azarin's last night after she got rid of Andrews. I've got to find that body. It hasn't showed up anywhere. Not in any cemetery or any place else. It's unreported, so it wasn't merely lost around Putney. It was took. I've got a canvass of all estate agents and things going on now. We might find that someone rented a house to keep the body in."

"It seems to me," I said, "that you're talking a great deal more than would suit the Sergeant."

"So I am. But if you'd admit to those statements Gasden made about Miss Dwight I'm not afraid of *you* for the moment."

"Tell me," I said, "where that dictaphone was. I'm beginning to feel entirely hedged in. In my mind I can see thousands of constables all over England running about, looking at corpses, talking to rental offices, searching vacant lots, stringing wires."

"It was in the next room," he said. "Oh, 'thousands at my bidding speed'. I'm a little Miltonic at times like this."

I was inclined to agree with him. "What did Azarin do?" I asked.

"He stayed home."

"And Betty Dwight?" I asked. I didn't like to ask that.

"She stayed home too. She's quite a home body. If she went about more it would be better."

"Tell me," I said, "what you think of it."

He looked at me for a moment, then grinned. "I'll tell you as much as might help you out," he said. "You can add this to the information I've given you on Lady Irene: Lady Irene and Azarin were very friendly while he was living at Cannes. Very friendly indeed, and you may make what you can of that. I think such understandings occasionally occur in the States. I've heard popular songs about them. According to the gossip, they seldom went to Azarin's villa; the secretary, Helga Lindstrom, didn't seem to approve of it. Lady Irene had quite a place of her own. When Azarin ducked out I think it was a somewhat quiet departure, a surprise even to Lady Irene. She missed him, and even began to indulge in a little morphia now and then. She probably still uses it. She's calculating, chancy and plausible. A nice girl." He took out his cigarettes, lit one and crossed his long legs. "Azarin," he remarked, and bent his head to sniff at the flower in his buttonhole, "was the love of her life, her *beau sabreur,* and then pulled stakes without so much as a goodbye. A nasty fellow." This seemed to amuse him; he grinned and sniffed the flower again. It was a ridiculous performance.

"Why didn't you bring me one?" I asked.

"You wouldn't have appreciated it," he said. "Americans are rather . . . ah . . . material, aren't they? Azarin, now,

always interested the Sûreté, but they could never get anything definite on him. Things happened to horses, to athletic contests, and on the Bourse. Some tuppenny crook
went to jail for them, and his family was never in want
while he languished. Azarin never made the mistake that
American gangsters do—he never grew arrogant with power
or played politics. When he went to the States he behaved
himself. How he found Marie nobody knows and nobody
seems to be able to find out. There was an uncle with whom
the adoption business went on, but he's completely out of
sight. If either Helga Lindstrom or Lady Irene—both of
whom seem a little jealous according to you—could be loos-
ened up it might be worth the effort."

It sounded like somewhat of an order. "And how," I
asked, "would one go about that little chore?"

"Woo them away," he remarked airily. "Woo them away
from this monster. Nothing of a job for an ardent young
man of your enticing construction. Of course, Azarin might
object, but that's just one of the hazards. Makes the blood
run faster." He was surely enjoying himself. "Ah, me," he
said, standing up, "I wish I were your age again."

"I wish you were a little older," I said. "I wish the Commissioner could hear you. I wish to God that you wouldn't
pick me out for your spells of levity. It gives me an empty
feeling."

"Somebody has to listen to it, and the Sergeant's busy. I
like levity. It is more fun than whistling in the dark as we
are doing now. Listen: a girl falls dead on the Center Court
and her body vanishes. No one was with her in the locker
room before the match that we can find except her own
masseuse. No common poison gives the symptoms she had;
hardly any common poison could be timed so confounded
fortuitously. Her opponent, Betty Dwight, apparently talked

to the masseuse on the boat when in an apprehensive state of mind. Betty Dwight has been to a questionable address, from which she vanished, and dealt with a Spaniard. A Spaniard was seen near the victim's dressing room, and also at her house. After the death of the victim her opponent disappears from the court and sits tight in the Dorchester. The masseuse doesn't move from Azarin's. Lady Irene moves about—to dine with Andrews and go to Azarin's house. Andrews—a crackpot—also goes to see the Spaniard, asking for pictures. See if Lady Irene sent him, and why. See what he's up to with Azarin. Did you get off a cable to Bellevue?"

"No," I said. "If he's as cracked as you say, what's the use of it? He's not important, according to you. He's just a confusion, and a minor one at that. Azarin, now. . . . What about Marie's injury?" I asked, suddenly remembering it. "Have you found out about that?"

"She got it in an automobile accident," he said, "according to Azarin. The night before the game. She sneaked out and went for a short ride with that Prussian you saw at Azarin's. It was, apparently, a bona-fide accident. They swerved to avoid hitting a dog, and hit a tree. The Prussian laid his scalp open, and Miss Azarin cut her arm. It's been checked very thoroughly, even to interviewing the man who owned the dog."

"Was a Spaniard at Azarin's house after it happened?" I asked.

"No. She and the Prussian got home fairly late, in a cab, and no one was there afterward.

"I've been thinking about the poison angle," he said. "If she wasn't poisoned, why would anybody want to conceal the body? Just to save it from being mutilated in a post-mortem? Did she belong to one of those sects who think you have to be entire to appear in Heaven? And if so, did she rise up and get out of the undertaker's car herself as a protest? You have a fine field of speculation there, if you could get a few werewolves into it. A few werewolves and a man named Dracula."

"A Spaniard," I said, a little viciously. I was growing irritated again by his levity, his werewolves and so on.

"Quite possibly a Spaniard," he said, surprisingly enough. "Wasn't it a Spaniard that you heard talking to Helga at the back door in the fog? Wasn't it a Spaniard that you bit? Did you see any marks of a bitten hand on the Spaniard in Limehouse?"

"I did not," I said in desperation.

"I think it pretty safe to say that the Sergeant will find the man Hajos' man saw at Wimbledon wasn't the man in Limehouse. There may be a connection between them and there may not. That's why I want you to find out all you can about Marie Azarin. There may be a connection between the bitten Spaniard and Marie. Andrews is still a house guest at Lady Irene's. Telephone Andrews that you're coming around this afternoon, then we'll go see Miss Dwight."

I had started for the phone, and when he mentioned Betty I had a sudden hollow feeling inside; but his eye was on me and I didn't hesitate. I found Lady Irene's number and called it, asked for Andrews, and sat staring at the floor until he answered.

"Hello!" he said. "Who is it?"

"David Cameron," I said. "I came over with you on the boat."

"Oh, yes. Yes, indeed. I've been wondering about you, you know. I'd like to see you. I . . . ah . . . hardly like to call Miss Dwight. How is she? How's she taking it?"

"I don't know," I said. "I haven't been in touch with her."

"Really?" he asked, in an indeterminate tone. "I didn't know where you were, of course. Could you stop here for luncheon? We'll have a talk."

"I'd like to," I said. "One or thereabouts?"

"Yes, yes, that would be all right."

"Good," I said. "I'll be there." I hung up, and turned to MacMasters. "That was painless," I said. "He wants to see me as badly as I want to see him."

"I thought so," he said. "You can have luncheon with him, establish a friendly footing so you can keep on going there, then meet me at my place on Half Moon Street in time for the Sergeant's report." He handed over a visiting card with his address on it and put on his hat. "Come along," he said.

There was nothing else to do; I got my hat and we went to the Dorchester. MacMasters didn't phone up. We went to the elevator, and instead of going to Betty's floor got off at the floor where the house detective had his room. He was still sitting behind his desk. In the daylight his fair hair was thin and a little streaked.

MacMasters nodded, and said: "Anything doing, George?"

George took a list out of his desk and handed it over. "It was too difficult to get a complete list of Miss Dwight's visitors," he said. "Several of our people recalled a rum-looking chap, very well got up. Spanish, or possibly Mexican. He was there once or twice. The drunken American, of course. A young lady yesterday. American by her accent, according to the lift boy."

"Describe her."

"About five foot six," George said. "Fair, brown eyes, well-dressed, walking with one shoulder a bit lower than the other. The right, that was. Hard to see. You don't usually notice it, I fancy, because she has a smooth way of going. Very neat figure. Rather pretty, but . . . um . . . dissatisfied-looking, you know. Sour, what? She stayed about half an hour."

"What time was she here?"

"In the evening. At 8:46. When she left she used the Park Lane entrance and walked off. Miss Dwight was alone then."

"So," MacMasters said, and studied the list. "Miss Dwight made none of these calls?" he asked finally.

"No, Mrs. Cosgrove made them all. Shops and that sort of thing, Nothing personal. Miss Dwight does very little. She even has her meals sent up, but she's been on the roof once or twice about sundown. She gave orders to be let alone, you know."

"And there were no incoming calls for Miss Dwight?"

"Oh, a great number, but she answered none of them. People calling about the . . . ah . . . match, you know. Other people. Photographers, and all that. Mrs. Cosgrove talked to them when she was about, and when she wasn't we had instructions to say Miss Dwight would ring them up at a later date."

"Their numbers are all here?"

"Oh, yes, we rang central back to get them, and mentioned you. I have another list of them about, all names and addresses, but we recognized them all. Miss Dwight has many highly placed friends here, you know. Last year and the year before she went about a great deal. Very posh. Of course, there were hundreds of telegrams. A lot of them weren't opened. I've saved her rubbish for you, but there's nothing in it. She's lying extraordinarily quiet, what?"

"Quite," MacMasters said. "I'll send a man to look over the rubbish. Keep collecting it, keep close watch on visitors and phone calls, everything. If the American girl comes here again could you spare a man to send after her?" George nodded. "Good. I doubt if she comes."

We went out, got the elevator again, and went up to Betty's floor. A feeling of revulsion had taken hold of me as the interview with George progressed, and it grew steadily stronger. There was a sort of shame in it for the way her life had to be gone into—the search of her waste baskets, the scrutiny of her phone calls and visitors, things like that. It was a miserable business, and there was no telling how much further it would go—or had gone, for that matter. It might be that they had found out other things—before the death of Marie—things MacMasters hadn't told me. As we stopped before her door I discovered in myself a strong inclination to bolt. Inspector MacMasters, possibly, had the right to invade her privacy; I wasn't so sure about myself. MacMasters had taken a stand beside the wall, out of sight of anyone opening the door.

"Knock," he said.

"Come out," I said, "where you can be seen. Don't hide there and jump at her."

He didn't move, but merely shook his head. I knocked, and after a short space the door was opened. It was Betty. The light was behind her, but even at that she looked a little tired; her face was composed, with a sort of closed, enforced composure, and her eyes held a strangely defensive expression. She stayed that way for an instant, then her eyes widened and her face lighted up. "David!" she said. "I've wondered. . . . Won't you come in?"

It seemed to me that I hadn't seen her for years, and that the interim had been a dolorous one. Then I remembered MacMasters. "Betty," I said, "I've a Scotland Yard man with me. He wants to talk to you." It was a stupid way to go

about it, but I wasn't functioning very well. I thought better
of the speech before I'd finished it, but it was too late by
that time. Her face composed again and the flicker of vitality vanished from it.

"Scotland Yard?" she asked, in a low tone. In the very
short space of time before MacMasters stepped out behind
me it all rushed through my head—the scene on the boat
deck, her look into the stands at Wimbledon, the tale of
her visiting the Spaniard in Limehouse, the many telegrams
which—according to George—she hadn't opened. "Chief
Inspector MacMasters," I said. "Miss Dwight."

MacMasters bowed, looking at her from under the hedge
of his eyebrows; Betty's glance, on me with a sort of protest-
ing unbelief, shifted to him. She made me feel guilty, as if
I had deserted to the enemy camp. She did not know Mac-
Masters had forced me to come along. She smiled slightly,
a smile which went no further than her lips. "How do you
do?" she said. "Won't you come in?" It was the second time
she'd said that.

She turned and we went in. The sitting room had no
flowers in it, where before there had been a great number
of them; with the dark paneling unrelieved by their color
the room seemed somber and cold. I caught a flash of the
green of Hyde Park through a window, trees with the sun on
them; then we were all sitting down.

"This is completely unofficial," MacMasters said. "Maybe even a little unorthodox." It was that gambit again; I
looked at Betty, but she was watching him. "You knew, of
course, that Miss Azarin's body has vanished?" he went on.

She came forward a little in her chair. "No," she said. "I
haven't read the papers. I . . ."

He waited for her voice to die out and went on. "This
has naturally put the police power into action. Bodies don't

vanish without reason, and it appears that the body was taken because the girl was murdered."

"I understand," she said. She was very still.

"You were close to all this; possibly you noticed something that would aid us to find the killer. There have been indications that Azarin, who is known as a gambler, made large, unconditional bets that Marie would win. She died; and because his bets were unconditional, he lost his money." There was a purring, soothing quality in his tone; it made the hair on the back of my neck stir as if a cold draft was blowing on me. I wanted to say: "Watch out! Watch out!" I tried to catch her eye, but MacMasters held it. "Perhaps you noticed something on the boat," he went on. "A glance, an equivocal action. You knew Azarin's masseuse, Helga Lindstrom, I believe?"

Her eyes flicked toward me and back to him again. "No," she said quickly. "I didn't know any of them. I am a little afraid of Mr. Azarin. I think he is a sinister man."

"Doubtless," MacMasters said. "Did you have any idea of how the betting went?"

"No," she said.

"Would it have been possible for Azarin to know that you had called in the ship's doctor?"

She looked startled at that, quite startled, then sat perfectly still. Only her eyes moved; they turned to me with an expression that was at once appealing and reproachful.

"Would it have been possible?" MacMasters repeated smoothly.

"I don't know," she said at length. "I . . . I had hurt myself in the storm the night before. The ship rolled violently. There was a vase of roses on my bureau, and when I saw it begin to tip over I jumped to catch it. I nearly fell, and wrenched my knee."

"You were much worried about that, I daresay. You estimated Miss Azarin as a capable opponent?"

"Yes," she said. "Yes, she was very capable."

"As capable as anyone you have ever met?"

"Yes," she said, in a low tone.

"And you told no one of this injury? Please consider. It would have been very valuable information to anyone intending to bet on such a prospectively close and important match."

She was looking at the floor now. "No one," she said.

"Do you think anyone might have noticed a slight limp?"

"I don't think so," she said. There was a short silence. She didn't raise her head, and I wondered if MacMasters was going to ask her next about her walk down to C deck, to Cynthia Blythe's stateroom. I sat waiting for it, tight inside; Betty was completely withdrawn, and her bowed head, with its cameo-like profile, was still and clear against the paneling of the room. "I was worried about my knee," she murmured, "and besides I didn't feel very well."

MacMasters' voice started again, with the purring note still in it. "You didn't see Miss Azarin before the match? You saw nothing at Wimbledon that would assist us?"

"I met Miss Azarin in the lower hall after the assistant referee came for me. Then we went through the door and around the backstop and on to the court. I didn't see anything. My concentration . . ."

"Of course," MacMasters said. "And since then, Miss Dwight: has anyone been here to talk to you? Anyone you met on the boat? Anyone living in London? Strangers, or people you knew before?"

It was all there. He was giving her a chance to talk about Cynthia or anyone else, to make a clean breast of it. I tried desperately then to catch her eye; and besides that, she should have known, by the question about the doctor, that they'd checked her up. Instead of telling anything she looked straight at him and said: "I requested them not to . . . let anyone come up. It was a terrible shock to me, Mr. MacMasters. I've never played such a match. I was nearly exhausted and my knee was paining dreadfully. And to have her fall . . . fall . . . I was very nervous before the match. There wasn't enough time to practice here. We sailed late because Mr. Azarin seemed determined to be on the same ship and I didn't want that. Then he got on it anyhow. And Marie Azarin made a scene in the dining saloon. Then there was my injury. I wanted the match so badly, and now it doesn't mean anything. Nothing. Would gamblers have killed her? That seems fantastic. I have always heard crime is too difficult in England."

A little animation had come into her voice, bringing the light, appealing timbre of it back again; but there was more than a touch of melancholy in the animation. She was like a little girl, sad and confused, wanting people to help her. MacMasters grinned slightly, and I felt immensely depressed; for she had denied, by inference, many things he knew to be facts. He sat quietly for a moment, his lips moving as though he were whistling to himself; then he said suddenly: "Miss Dwight, didn't you lose a fur jacket on shipboard?"

"Yes," she said, and went on quickly: "I'd hung it on a chair near the window in the cabin. That cabin had windows onto a deck. Then I went into the bathroom, and when I came out it was gone. I didn't notice it was gone right away, not until I decided to go out. I couldn't bear to stay in any longer. But the jacket was gone, so I tried to phone Captain Brererton, but his line was busy. I tried to phone him for a long time before I got him."

There was a sort of incoherence in all this—a sub-surface incoherence, hurried and a little desperate. She didn't usually talk in such a scrambled fashion.

MacMasters hadn't been looking at her; he had been staring somewhat abstractedly at the carpet, listening intently. Without looking up he asked: "How tall are you, Miss Dwight?"

"Five feet six, nearly," she said, and then a phone rang somewhere. She stood up and went out, returning in a moment to say that the Inspector was wanted. We had both stood up; he followed her and she came back alone. I was still standing; she stopped about eight feet away and we stood looking at each other. The room was very quiet, and we couldn't hear MacMasters; her brown eyes were on me with an unreadable intentness, and her brows were drawn down a little. She seemed to be trying to ask me something. I don't know how long we stood there with the silence between us. I didn't think. I didn't want to; and then, suddenly, there came to me a faint breath of her scent, like a field flower in the sun. It was a strange thing, bringing into the emptiness of my mind the most confusing visions—a meadow, bright with color, and a little brown-eyed girl in it; a complex kaleidoscopic thing with policemen and all the modern weapons of policemen in it, the whole grim, complicated and practically inescapable equipment of a manhunt.

"Betty," I said. "Be very careful what you say." Her head went back a little, and her eyes darkened. "Can't you speak?" I asked, after a moment. Her face didn't change at all, but she shook her head slowly once or twice. Then MacMasters came in. He was moving rather quickly; he glanced at her, and said: "We'll have to get on. Miss Dwight will excuse us, I'm sure. Maybe there won't be a hurry call next time."

He picked up his hat and handed me mine, and started for the door. He paused there, and said: "So sorry we have to run off, and many thanks. If you think of anything that might help us along the ground I've tried to cover, will you call Whitehall 1212? Goodbye."

She hadn't moved. She was standing in the middle of the floor, controlled and still, and nodded as the door swung to.

"Come along," MacMasters said, impatiently. "We'll be back again, and maybe sooner than you think."

CHAPTER NINE

I didn't want to say anything to MacMasters about Betty; MacMasters hadn't spoken; he was whistling his eternal John Peel softly between his teeth; and in order to change the current of my own thoughts I asked: "What's the rush? What's happened now?"

"We'll watch her," he said, apparently voicing his meditations aloud, "until something turns up. It will, sooner or later. I always thought that such a crime was impossible in England." He looked up and grinned slightly. "The lady has been well informed, but she should be a better actress. Her voice changed too much."

"So would yours," I said, "if you suddenly realized, in the middle of a conversation, that the cops were after you."

"Not at all," he said. The elevator stopped and we got out and stood a moment in the narrow second lobby among the little tea tables. "I wouldn't have started off so innocently. It was pretty clever, picking out the ship's telephone operator. The exchange is always busy at that time of night, and the operator would hardly remember one party making several calls."

"If the party raised hell because of the delay," I began.

"She's not the sort to raise hell," he said. "One of those quiet gals. Come into the front lobby and wait. I have to make a phone call before we go."

We went into the front lobby and I waited in the middle of it. The Maharajah of something and his entourage streamed by, but I wasn't amused by them. It would have taken a lot to amuse me at that moment, for it struck me that MacMasters was phoning to start the search for Cynthia Blythe. Betty had been too reticent about her, had evaded his leading questions too obviously. Betty and this Cynthia were much the same height and general build. They might easily be mistaken for each other in certain circumstances; and it was to Cynthia's cabin that Betty had gone shortly after meeting Helga Lindstrom on the boat deck. I couldn't have sworn for sure who it was I saw on deck in that marten cape. Who it was depended really upon the hour that the cape had been taken—whether immediately before Betty reported the loss, or a longer time before. I wasn't going to give this lead to MacMasters. There was too much danger in it. MacMasters' remark about Betty being too quiet was not encouraging. We would go next, I judged, to see Gasden; for Gasden knew about Cynthia.

"Gasden next?" I asked, as he came back.

He looked at me, I thought, a little ruefully. "Good old Gasden," he said. "Always letting people down. Come along." We took a cab, and I soon lost my direction; the shabbiness of London rolled by.

"What was the hurry?" I asked again. "You hadn't asked her all the questions you wanted to."

"Hadn't I? I couldn't think of any more that wouldn't have been impertinent. You didn't see Mrs. Cosgrove about, did you?"

"No," I said, and added: "Maybe she's in Limehouse."

"Don't be bitter, my boy. Everything will turn out all right, one way or the other."

"It's a brand of philosophy," I said, "too high flown for me. I still want to know why we got out of the Dorchester so quickly."

"You'll soon see," he said, and that was all I could get out of him. The cab went around corners and up side streets; in a few minutes we pulled up before a large brick house in a quiet residential neighborhood. There was a bobby in front of it who saluted MacMasters, and we went up and rang the bell. A uniformed nurse let us in and led the way up the stairs to a back room on the second floor. I didn't know what to expect by that time, but I wasn't kept waiting very long. The door opened to MacMasters' knock and it was all there: the two men who nodded to MacMasters, the other man with his little black physician's bag, and the sheet-covered figure on the bed. I stared at it and MacMasters' words came back to me again: "Good old Gasden. Always letting people down." He'd done it for the last time.

"Sorry," MacMasters said, "I had to let you in for this. Meet Inspector Trevelyan, Constable Ganderson and Doctor Hunt."

I nodded to them in turn and leaned back against the wall.

"You didn't find him there?" MacMasters asked, nodding toward the bed.

"In the closet," Trevelyan said. He was a big man with a moustache and a serious, square face. "The photographer's been here and gone, and we'll fingerprint later this morning. Ganderson has the gun. He was shot behind the ear, close to. Suicide, apparently—except that there was a man here early this morning using your name. They let him up alone. The deceased had had his breakfast, and had been quiet. Rational, in fact. The man using your name answers the description of the one who left Andrews to follow the deceased."

"What?" MacMasters asked, rather sharply. "A tall man with a limp and a saber cut?" He stood very quietly for a moment, and his left eye screwed up a little. "Go on, go on."

"You've seen him?" Trevelyan asked politely. "The man using your name said he was from the Yard, of course, and wished to speak privately to the deceased for a moment. He was here fifteen minutes in all. No one came in to see the deceased after that until about ten, to bring bouillon. He wasn't in the room, and the bars on the window were untouched. They looked into the closet and rang us up at once. It hasn't been established that the deceased was dead when the man left, but he died near that time."

The doctor nodded. "It is impossible," he remarked, "to time it more closely than that. There were no marks of violence."

"The deceased," Trevelyan went on, still in his polite tone, "had no gun with him. There was a large bandage secured with adhesive tape on his right side; the bandage was not removed when he was admitted here. Doctor Hunt removed it and found no surface indication of injury. However, the bandage was pressed in such a way that it appeared a gun was carried under the bandage. The skin also showed indications of this. The adhesive tape had been taken up and replaced."

"What you're getting at," MacMasters said, "is that Gasden wore a bandage to carry a gun around under it? Curiouser and curiouser. Wasn't there medicine of any sort on the bandage?"

"None," the Doctor said. "It smelt faintly of oil."

"They didn't hear any noise?"

"No," Trevelyan said, "they didn't. The gun's a .32. There were several blankets over his head, which were removed by the nurse."

MacMasters turned to the Doctor. "How well do you know this place, Hunt?" he asked. "Do you think they'd cook up a story about a man coming here, as well as the story of the bandage, to cover any possible negligence of their own? How fresh was that bandage? Do you have it?"

"Ganderson has it," the Doctor said. "I—"

"But they described the man," Trevelyan began, interrupting him.

"Gasden might have talked about him," MacMasters said. "He knew the man was following him. That's why he went in the Mayfair. Go on, Hunt."

The Doctor looked judicious. "Blake, at the Dorchester," he said finally, "is a sound man. He wouldn't knowingly patronize a dubious nursing home. However, they are difficult to check, and some of them would go a long way to avoid criticism. It might be well to take along samples of their bandage and tape for comparison. The bandage on the deceased is a rather fresh one."

"Take the samples," MacMasters said. "Put a full report on my desk as soon as you can. Trevelyan, I'll leave this all with you. Maybe this little stranger talked Gasden into shooting himself and maybe he didn't. You can find out. Good morning, gentlemen."

I followed him out to the sidewalk, where the cab was still waiting. "You take this cab," he said. "I'll go in and phone for another one. I want to talk to the nurses a little anyhow. I always liked fairy stories, but there was a limit to what I'd swallow. I—"

"You think this intruder shot him and put the bandage on?" I asked. "And that the nursing home said it had always been there, to save themselves the appearance of negligence? Or that they put it on themselves? Where did Andrews go after he left Limehouse last night?"

"He went home," he said. "Or rather, to Lady Irene's. She wasn't there, so he went out to Azarin's."

"And where did the man who was following Andrews go?"

"You've got me there. We lost him. We weren't set for him. Good Lord, I can't shadow everybody in the bloody British Isles. I'm shadowing threequarters of them now."

"And what's Azarin been doing?" I asked. "And Helga? Why don't you spend a little time on them?"

"Little man," he said, "it's time you hopped off for Lady Irene's. You've got to work like hell. Cynthia Blythe went to see Miss Dwight last night; Miss Dwight won't volunteer that information; Gasden died this morning, withholding from me any information on Cynthia Blythe; Cynthia Blythe and Miss Dwight talked together before the murder. One of them talked with Helga, and I'm a damned fool that I didn't pay more attention to Captain Brererton's report, particularly the part about Cynthia Blythe. I'd have had a man posted; I'd have had her by now. Bear down on Andrews. Scare him to death, alienate him from Azarin and see what he says. Get into the cab and out of my sight. I'll see you at my place later."

He shoved me into the cab and went back into the house. I gave the driver Lady Irene's address and settled back. It came into my mind that what MacMasters had just said would have put me into a cold sweat a day or two ago. Maybe I was in a cold sweat now, but it was somewhere inside myself; it didn't appear on the surface any more. I'd got that far. I fell to considering the affair. The things definitely known were few: Betty and Cynthia Blythe had been in communication; Andrews was being followed; Lady Irene was getting rid of Andrews and going to Azarin's house at every opportunity. MacMasters was going to find out about Cynthia Blythe. I was to find out about Andrews, and the more I found out, as well as the quicker I found it, the better. Why was he being followed, who was having it done, and why had one of his shadowers gone to see Gasden? He was, by what we had heard so far, after a picture; was it possible that his shadowers were guards hired by him for protection? Why had one of them gone after Gasden (who had quarreled with him) if they weren't?

So long as nobody knew what all this pother was about Betty would be connected with it—more than ever since the advent of Cynthia and the death of Gasden. Gasden had vaguely connected Betty and Andrews; and perhaps he had said too much where Andrews could hear him, just as he had said too much to me. The word "picture" might be code for something else. Perhaps Gasden had been a go-between just as Cynthia appeared to be. If this complicated method of not appearing in anything was in progress it pointed to Azarin, who had been mixed up in things for years without appearing in any of them. That Betty was following a plan of campaign laid down by Azarin (who had had long experience in such matters) seemed far-fetched. She couldn't have wanted to win the match badly enough to talk Mrs. Cosgrove into buying it from Azarin.

I tried to put this out of my mind as absurd, but it wouldn't be put out. Too many things contributed to it. We were passing the Victoria and Albert Museum by that time; soon we came out beside Hyde Park, ran along it for a way, passed the Dorchester and continued up Park Lane for a few blocks before turning off and stopping at Lady Irene's door.

I paid the cabman, got out, and was admitted by the butler and shown into the front room. It was a beautiful,

paneled room, silvery in tone, with a portrait over the fireplace. Andrews came in almost at once, in a morning coat
which set him off very well; but he seemed to have lost a
little weight, and I noticed again the sharpness of his face
which had appeared to me for the first time at Azarin's. His
eyes seemed cold and avid.

"I'm glad you rang me up," he said, shaking hands. "I've
been disturbed about Miss Dwight. How's she taking it?
There's been quite a lot of unfavorable publicity about her
since the match."

"I haven't seen much of her," I said. "She's not seeing
anyone."

"Really?" he asked. "She shouldn't do that. Do you really
think there's . . . ah . . . anything suspicious there?" He
stared at me. "Of course, I realize that my question may
sound impertinent to you, but it shouldn't. You know my
feelings about her."

"I seem to recall that you liked her," I said. "As for myself, I don't know what to think." We walked slowly over
to the fireplace, and turning, stood with our backs toward
it. "A C. I. D. man has been to see me," I said. "I wouldn't
be surprised if he came to see you. He's looking Azarin up.
Maybe he's looking us all up."

"Naturally," he said. "Naturally. I suppose you've often
wondered how I became intimate with Azarin after talking
to you the way I did about him." He looked at me, and I
looked back at him; there was a cold, intent and speculative
look in his eyes; but no fear. Evidently he wasn't afraid of
Scotland Yard.

"You had a good reason," I said, "and that's enough for
me." That seemed to please him; he smiled faintly, and
glanced sidewise at the door. As for me, I took a moment
to rearrange my thoughts. Inasmuch as he apparently hadn't

killed Gasden, it was probable that he hadn't had a hand in killing Marie either. I was a little nonplussed by this, for it narrowed things down closer to Betty. A great number of my speculations had very quickly been brought to nothing, and that didn't comfort me much; but I hadn't time to mess about at the moment. Lady Irene would be coming in soon. "Did you know," I said, turning to him, "that Gasden was dead?"

"Gasden!" he exclaimed. His mouth dropped open and remained that way for a moment; the pupils of his eyes contracted. Being a reflex and uncontrollable, this convinced me that the news was a surprise to him—and an unpleasant surprise at that. "When?" he demanded. "How?"

His eyes took on a withdrawn intentness; I could almost hear his brain working. Whatever deal he and Azarin had between them hadn't, apparently, included killing Gasden; I doubted now if it had included Gasden at all. He was frightened by this unforeseen turn of events; and while he was frightened it was my opportunity to frighten him still more and alienate him from Azarin as much as possible. "He was shot in the head," I told him, "in a nursing home. He came to see me last night. He'd just come from Limehouse, where he said he'd seen you and quarreled with you. He said a man followed him. He said it was your man."

He stared at me with a sort of fascination, and I bore down on him a bit more. "He was scared half to death," I went on. "I had to get a doctor to give him a sedative and send him to a nursing home. But even that wouldn't shut him up. He talked all the time. He said you'd threatened to kill him and put him on a slab beside Marie Azarin."

"Good God!" he exclaimed, and began to walk up and down.

"A Scotland Yard man saw him this morning before he was shot," I said. "That was why they let the second man in.

The second man said he was from Scotland Yard too. But he wasn't; he was the same man who followed Gasden from Limehouse last night." I stopped at that, aware that I'd said a little too much, shown too much knowledge of events. But he didn't realize that; he was too upset to co-ordinate what I'd said. He'd stopped walking and stood a few feet from me, biting his lower lip. He had a strange, collapsed look.

"What is your stake in this?" he asked suddenly, glancing sideways at me. "What are you in it for? Don't lie to me."

"Money," I said. "I had money on it. I think Azarin's done a job on me. I always thought he was going to. He started on the ship."

He considered this for a moment, his eyes restless, trying to weigh what I'd said against what he'd seen of me. He was getting some self-control again, and as he did it a sort of secretiveness became evident on his face—a foxy, calculating secretiveness that had something mad in it.

"We can be of value to each other," I said quietly, and he glanced swiftly at me again. "What I've told you will help you prepare for the Scotland Yard man who'll be around. I don't care what you're up to. Remember that. But I'd like to know if you've seen, at Azarin's, any evidence that he sold the match and then had to kill Marie because he couldn't control her. She was very ambitious, you know." He half turned to me at this, changed his mind, and stood staring for a long time at the carpet. His fingers moved slightly and incessantly at the seams of his trousers. "Do you know a girl named Cynthia Blythe?" I asked. He didn't seem to hear that. "You were surely right," I went on, to push him a bit more, "when you warned me to steer clear of Azarin."

He looked up at that. "Yes," he said. "He's got us both in a frightful mess." He raised one hand and rubbed his cheek, then fixed his eyes on me. "He bet heavily on Marie," he went on. "Why would he kill her?" The sly look came back to him again. "Maybe he had an arrangement with the book-maker," he said, "as an alibi. That man you fought with the night you were at Azarin's had some sort of a message which upset Azarin and Miss Lindstrom. There was something about money in it. They tried to keep it very secret. They tried to keep him away from Marie. After the fight they almost pushed her upstairs to keep her out of his way, because he was hurt and made a great outcry." Strangely enough, he began to sweat; I could see the minute drops of perspiration on his forehead. He wiped them quickly away, glanced at the door again, and said in a lower, secretive voice: "None of this must get out as coming from me, but it would be like Azarin to bring Marie over here as a sort of blackmail. And Mrs. Cosgrove could pay it." He looked around quickly, licked his lips, and suddenly walked to the bell-pull and gave it a yank. "I want a drink," he said. "I feel very queer."

We stood silently looking at each other for a moment; then we heard a muffled exclamation in the hall outside the door, an indeterminate, stifled noise as the butler, looking a little perturbed, came in. Andrews was staring at him.

"What was that noise?" he asked. "That noise in the hall?"

"Cook's little girl, sir," the butler said. "Brought for the day, sir. She'd broke away and got abovestairs, sir."

"See that she doesn't do it again," Andrews said. "I want a whiskey and soda. Cameron? Two whiskey and sodas. And please tell Lady Irene Mr. Cameron is here."

"I don't think Lady Irene has come in yet, sir," the butler said.

Andrews stared at him. "Not come in?" he asked. "When did she go out?"

"About an hour and a half ago, sir."

For an instant Andrews' face got out of control. Complete surprise, denial, then consternation crossed it swiftly and as swiftly faded into what seemed to me an enforced and uncertain composure. "Very well," he said in a tight voice.

The butler went out, and for a short space of time Andrews didn't move. He was completely motionless; but in his tense pose he managed to convey the impression of a man in swift and terrified flight. Then the sweat broke out on his forehead again. His eyes darted about the room, and when they came to me he gave a start.

"You'll have to go," he said. His voice sounded like a croak. "You'll have to go at once. I'll get in touch with you as soon as I can."

He began to push me toward the door. When we got into the hall the butler appeared from somewhere and handed me my hat; Andrews kept pushing me from behind until we came to the front door. He squirmed around and got it open; we almost fell down the steps, and as we reached the sidewalk he jumped from behind me and ran out into the street in front of a cruising cab. The cab pulled up with a screech; he jumped into it, leaned forward and spoke rapidly to the driver, and the cab whirled away. It turned the first corner, and was gone.

CHAPTER TEN

I could hardly have been blamed for standing by with my mouth open at the finish of this scene; for it had happened so quickly that by the time I realized what Andrews was up to he had vanished. At one moment he had been all around me, pushing and pulling; the next moment he had been scrambling wildly into the cab; the moment after that even the cab was out of sight. I straightened my hat, which had been knocked over one eye, recovered my breath, and after a short but scattered interval of thought I came to the conclusion that Andrews was on his way to Wimbledon Common. He had shown a great unwillingness to leave Lady Irene and Azarin together; and hearing that she had stolen a march on him and got out of the house the only thing he could think of was to join them as quickly as possible. My luncheon with the pair of them, to which I had looked forward with great interest, would probably never occur now. That was regrettable; and as I stood there wondering what to do with myself it struck me that I wanted to go and see Betty.

It wasn't very far to the Dorchester; I walked back to Park Lane and along to the side entrance of the hotel. The side entrance was never used much, and I didn't want to attract any more attention than necessary. I wasn't at all sure that

I should be there; my presence had an air of running with the wolves and hunting with the hounds; but MacMasters hadn't warned me not to see Betty, so I decided to chance it. I couldn't help a feeling of nervousness, and once I was in the rear lobby the feeling increased; for there were a lot of people moving about, guests and formally dressed functionaries and attendants, and they all seemed to be covertly watching me. That, I told myself, was because I was aware of the scope of MacMasters' surveillance. An atmosphere had suddenly surrounded me, as though I had entered a different world; and for the first time I appreciated with my nerves instead of my mind what Betty must be feeling, what they all must be feeling; and as I finally reached the elevators I thanked the Lord that Scotland Yard wasn't after me. But, curiously enough, that thought didn't seem very convincing.

The elevator started up, and I didn't give the number of my floor until everyone else was out of it. When I did give it the elevator boy glanced at me and away; I got out and walked down the corridor feeling that doors opened slightly behind my back, with eyes peering out of them. After knocking at Betty's door I looked around quickly. The corridor was calm and deserted, and all the doors were shut. Then Betty's latch clicked, and she was standing there with the same defensive look that had been on her face earlier that morning. It changed as quickly as before; but this time, instead of the spontaneous lighting-up of her features, there was a reserved smile. She didn't speak, and there was an awkward moment of silence; I stood looking at her like a cigar-store Indian.

"Please come in," she said, and opened the door wider.

I went in. There still weren't any flowers, and the room seemed colder than before despite the sunshine flooding it.

I stopped in the middle of the floor, and we stood looking at each other again.

"Betty," I said, "we can't stand staring at each other like this. It's ridiculous."

"Is it?" she asked. There was something wooden about her, wooden and expressionless; it was really amazing that her vitality could be so completely subdued.

"You were glad to see me before," I said. "You can't deny it." She didn't try. "I couldn't help it if Inspector MacMasters was there," I went on, apologetically, "and I asked him not to hide against the wall." She didn't say anything to that either; and even allowing that her nerves were in bad shape I began to be a little irritated by her silence. After all, my own nerves weren't so good either. I'd heard a lot of strange things. What I wanted at the moment was her explanation of them. I granted that she couldn't explain them unless she knew what they were; but at the same time I couldn't very well ask her in so many words if she'd made a deal with Helga Lindstrom, or with Cynthia Blythe. I'd come, unthinkingly enough, with a subconscious conviction that she'd tell me. I began to see that I'd put myself in a nice hole by a prize example of wishful thinking. "Let's sit down," I said, in desperation.

We sat down, on opposite sides of the room. Looking at her, at the still, clear-cut face and the brown eyes, I couldn't think of anything else except how differently she had looked that moonlight night on the boat deck; and then I recalled the mental picture of the little girl in the sunny meadow bright with flowers that had come to me earlier in the day. "Betty," I said. "You must answer my questions."

"Why should I, David?" she said in a low tone. "You never came. I wanted to see you very badly. It was horrible, having her fall like that and then finding out that she was dead. I couldn't stay at Wimbledon. I . . ."

"But you wouldn't see me here," I said. "I tried to get to you. I phoned, and they wouldn't connect me."

"I told them to put you through," she said. "I told them not to put anyone through except you."

There was something queer about that. "You told them?" I asked. "If you'd told them they'd have done it. I gave them my name, and argued about it."

"I told them to put you through," she said again.

"I should have come up without phoning," I said, and then rashly added: "Other people did it, didn't they?"

If I'd suddenly stood up and pointed a gun at her it wouldn't have brought about a more startling reaction. She straightened in her chair as though a piece of ice had been put down her back; her eyes widened; and then, as quickly, she was looking at the floor, still and relaxed again. The movements had been so swift and had flowed into each other so smoothly that I was left in doubt for a moment whether they had actually taken place. She didn't answer. "Why don't you admit it?" I demanded. As I stood at the window looking at the trees, her voice, light and with that appealing timbre, said: "David."

The sound seemed to hang in the air, with a strange power of endurance; and there was something insinuating about it. It got past my defenses and my confusion. I turned. She had stood up, and was moving into the middle of the room with that beautiful co-ordination—the same co-ordination that had made me think my eyes had deceived me a few minutes before.

She stopped. "You have to believe me, David," she said. The appealing note was still in her voice, it was stronger than ever, and then a sort of uncertainty came into it. "No one . . ." she began, and her voice died away.

I had leaned forward, waiting for her to speak again, but she didn't. She merely watched my face, then shook her head slightly and bowed it. "Blast it!" I said. "Aren't you aware by this time that they know everything you do, every phone call you get, everybody who comes here? Why did you jump when I said other people had come up? And after you jumped why did you try to hide it? Even Mac-Masters said you should have been a better actress. Betty," I said, "Betty. They know everything. You can't stay quiet and think they won't find out. If you don't tell them they'll find the others and make them tell."

She stood up very straight; she was furious. "How dare you try to implicate me in this terrible Wimbledon crime— in any way at all! I have no connection with the death of Marie Azarin, through Cynthia Blythe, Azarin, or anyone else," she said. Her eyes were wide and flashing and she was trembling all over. "You are working with Inspector Mac-Masters and have come here to try to spy on me. I never want to see you again!" She ran to her room and slammed the door.

The door into the hall was very hard to open; it seemed to be possessed with an animate desire to keep me inside, and then suddenly it was free. It swung with a jerk, almost knocking me down, and Mrs. Cosgrove was standing on the other side of it with one hand out.

"David!" she exclaimed. "Well, of all people!" She dropped her hand and leaned forward, looking at me closely. "Why, my dear boy, you look as though you'd seen a ghost! An *actual* ghost! I'm sure that Betty hasn't treated you nice-ly. She's been so difficult. Where *have* you been, David? I've wanted to see you so much. I haven't been able to find poor Charley, and I've been every place that one could possibly imagine. There was the nicest man in the Claridge bar—I think he must have sold drinks, because he wore a white apron—and he told me that poor Charley often used to come in and talk about his *dear* mother."

"Charley?" I asked stupidly. Her flood of talk had rolled over me, and I'd only heard half of it consciously. "Charley?"

"Charley Gasden," she said. "Now, you know perfectly well whom I mean. You remember how *amusing* he is."

That was like a spray of cold water. "Have you looked for him in Limehouse?" I asked.

A remarkable change went over her face. She glanced around quickly, and her glance came back to me; it was almost furtive. There was a beady quality about her eyes, like the eyes of an old monkey, and she edged around me and got her back to the open door. "Limehouse?" she asked. "Limehouse? Don't you mention that. Don't you *dare* mention it. You must be *very* nasty today if all you can think of is things like that. You had better go home at once. *Good*bye."

Her hands were trembling, and there was a frightened look on her; she stood up in the doorway, diminutive but solid. I backed away, bowed slightly, and started down the hall; she stood in the doorway, watching me until the elevator came and took me away.

I was glad to get into the street again. My knees felt shaky and there was a strange, gone feeling in the bottom of my stomach. It had all been too much for me; I'd gone through too many emotions and found out too much—or, at least, had too many things pointed out to me. I walked along Park Lane until I came to South Street, turned up and followed that to Farm Street, and came out on Berkeley Square. I'd often been curious to see Berkeley Square because of a metaphysical play connected with it that I'd seen some years before, but that day it had no charms for me.

My first double Scotch in the bar of my hotel showed a tendency to bring on tears, rather than to cheer me. I got out of the bar feeling ashamed of myself. It was surprisingly late; I had some lunch and went up to my room. I couldn't stay in it. I went out again and walked to Green Park and roamed aimlessly an hour or so before I caught a cab for MacMaster's flat on Half Moon Street.

The man who let me in was built like a stone column; there was a lot of bone and lithe muscle packed into him and there was a network of wrinkles at the corner of each eye as though he'd spent most of his life squinting into the sun.

"Is Inspector MacMasters in?" I asked.

"*And* the Sergeant," he said, as though he meant: "*And* the cat." He took my hat, and added: "This way, sir."

I followed him down the corridor, which had built-in bookshelves and a long glass case full of dully gleaming guns, into the large room in the rear. MacMasters and the Sergeant were sitting together on a divan before the fire-place. MacMasters waved and the Sergeant stood up. It was a very cheerful room, with furniture that contrived to be delicate and masculine at the same time; there was a baby grand piano in one corner and bits of old carvings—Cambodian, Chinese and Aztec—scattered sparingly about, several handsome etchings of wild ducks and geese.

"Come over and sit down," MacMasters said. "Nick, bring him a Scotch and soda."

I walked across the room and sat down on the divan. "Well?" MacMasters said. "You don't seem to be full of cheer."

"I went to see Betty Dwight," I said, and avoided the Sergeant's eye.

"A sound idea," MacMasters said, and stretched his legs out. "A man can't live by second-hand suspicions alone."

"Don't be amused this time," I said. "I didn't like it. I . . . I had a bad half hour, if you want to know."

The man came in and left my drink on the table; Mac-Masters looked at the Sergeant and nodded slightly. "They'll do it every time," he said. "Get your book out, and we'll hear the worst."

A sort of professional detachment descended on the pair of them, and that made it less difficult; but even at that it was bad enough. I gave a somewhat amended version of what had happened. As I proceeded the Sergeant became more British oak all the time; MacMasters stared at the ceiling. His face was unreadable, but there was an atmosphere of irony about him. "There it is," I said, when I'd finished, "and be damned to it."

"You're a menace to womanhood," MacMasters said finally. "An emotional soul like you. Even Mrs. Cosgrove, eh? You didn't mention good old Gasden?"

"I didn't have the chance," I said wearily.

"That's too bloody bad. You're tired, I take it?"

"I am," I said. "I'm tired to death."

"Ah, me," he said. "And naught but the stump of Dagon remained. Well, we did our best. What about Andrews?"

"Oh!" I said. I sat for a few minutes pulling myself together, for it was all very confused in my head. Then I told them about that. The only time MacMasters interrupted me was when I got to the cook's little girl being in the hall, at which he said in a low voice to the Sergeant: "See if the cook has a little girl." After that nothing broke in but the soft sound of the Sergeant's pencil.

There was a longish silence, then MacMasters said: "It's a good thing you saw him first, while you were in your right mind. You did a handy little job on Andrews. You agree, Sergeant?"

"Quite, sir," the Sergeant said.

"And he seemed ready to swap details, eh? He wasn't afraid of the Yard?"

"No," I said. "I don't think he was."

"And his pupils contracted when you mentioned Gasden's death, eh? You're coming on at a ferocious rate. What inspired you to get so efficient?"

I said, "I got to thinking on the way there that perhaps Azarin had sold the match to Mrs. Cosgrove. That would make Betty Dwight merely an accessory. He fell in with that idea."

"After you mentioned it."

"Of course," I said. "I started the ball rolling. He was almost afraid to talk with me. He's afraid of Azarin too. He's afraid like all the rest of them. He didn't want Lady Irene to hear him letting Azarin down."

He grinned. "And where do you think he went after he so impolitely walked out on you?"

"To Azarin's," I said.

He shook his head. "No," he said, "he didn't. He just bolted into the blue. He got off so quickly that our man wasn't ready for him. He's vanished."

"Vanished!" I said. They were all vanishing. I sat staring at MacMasters in a somewhat stupid fashion.

"Vanished," he repeated. "Evaporated. I have a notion that he didn't trust the cook's little girl. If Andrews didn't catch you up on your knowledge of Gasden's death, maybe the cook's little girl did. It was a happy day when I decided to enlist you in the ranks of righteousness, my young Romeo. It happens that Lady Irene wasn't at Azarin's today, either. At least, she wasn't there up until three o'clock."

"Then she was in the hall!" I said. "She heard him, and he knew she heard him! She hadn't been out at all."

"Not so fast," he said. "Wait until the Sergeant talks to the cop on the beat. The little girl concerns us until we find out about her. It may be that Andrews went through that act to establish a lack of knowledge of what Azarin was up to—or it may be that he was really frightened. Time will tell—Time, the old gypsy man, according to the poets. Did you ever see Time in the semblance of an old gypsy man, Sergeant?"

The Sergeant tried hard, but he couldn't manage it. "I can't say that I have, sir," he said.

"Exactly," MacMasters said, and turned to me. "Enough for you, however. You've held the stage long enough. I went to Wimbledon, and the most impressive thing I saw there was a sign of varnished wood over the swinging doors into the Center Court, with Kipling's immortal words on it—'If you meet with triumph or disaster . . .' Very impressive sentiments, eh? Especially for the vanquished. Lets 'em console their souls with rhetoric. It shows what a civilized race the British are. Right, Sergeant?"

"He was a good poet, sir," the Sergeant said patiently. "If you'd hear Blaycock at the Yard do 'Boots,' sir . . ."

MacMasters took a drink. "Someday I hope to," he said, and got down to business again. "There's been a great stir going on about the courts since Saturday. Fingerprinting, interviews with everybody, searches, God knows whatnot. Regular Scotland Yard procedure: footwork, hundreds of interviews, sifting and correlation of evidence. None of the flashy stuff—dust analyses and the like—after the fashion of the upstart Americans. And very little's come of it. Several people remembered a Spaniard—or a Mexican. And they remembered the gambler Hajos' man watching him. There was only one man—and he admitted to being a little drunk at the time—who said that this Mexican anomaly was standing about when Miss Dwight's car came in. He said the anomaly made a sort of gesture when Miss Dwight looked at him. Raised his right hand a little, and looked as though he wanted to say something. She went on by him."

I didn't say anything. "So far as I can find out, on the day of the match Miss Dwight left the Dorchester with Mrs. Cosgrove by the side door, drove to Wimbledon, and went right into the members' dressing room. It has cubicles in it. She dressed and went to the outside court with the Wimbledon pro and warmed up for about eight minutes. He says she was nervous, he noticed it especially, he's helped her warm up before, and there was never any sign of nerves. Then she went back to the dressing room and waited for her call. I can't find that she talked to anyone except the pro. The Assistant Umpire hadn't anything unusual to report; he accompanied her from the dressing room into the hall upstairs, unlocking the door into the hall. They went down the stairs into the lower hall which leads to the door into the Center Court. The upstairs door is kept locked because the members' tea room's up there and royalty uses it. She met Marie Azarin in the lower hall; they said, 'How do you do?' The three of them went through the door, under the Royal Box, and around the backstop. The Assistant Referee was with them until they were around the backstop. They didn't get near each other, and didn't speak."

"What about Marie Azarin?" I asked.

"Nobody knew more about her than the dressing room attendant told us. She apparently drove to the court with Helga Lindstrom, and the two of them were swallowed up in Marie's cubicle. Nobody saw anyone else come in or go out. All fingerprints in the cubicle are accounted for, including Marie's. None of the trash cans yielded up a thing.

Helga Lindstrom stayed in the dressing room and Azarin was in the stands. So were Andrews and Lady Irene."

"Helga Lindstrom didn't come out to see the match?" I asked.

"No, I stopped in at the house and had a friendly little talk with Helga and Azarin. Very friendly indeed. They haven't been out of the house, either of them. We're watching their mail, their telephone calls and their visitors—all of which are practically non-existent so far. They haven't moved since the match; they sit like a pair of Cheshire cats—the same thing Miss Dwight's doing, for the matter of that. And they're up to something. I can feel it in my bones, but all I can do is feel it."

He took another drink. "I didn't ask them any funny questions, any more than I asked Miss Dwight funny questions. There was a man there, a Spaniard. How could they deny that," he put in, parenthetically, "when you were there? In fact, they volunteered the information. They said he wanted contributions for the Loyalists. Azarin lived in Spain at one time. That's in his dossier. There was a little rumpus with the Spanish Government a few years ago. He admitted it, blushingly, and said the man had made himself unpleasant for that reason. A favor to be returned, don't you know. Oh, yes, and while I think of it: the Sergeant took Hajos' man to see the Spaniard in Limehouse. It wasn't the same Spaniard that had been at the courts. The one in Limehouse is named Soledad, Garcia Jesus something something and something Soledad. There is a faint suspicion that he might sell morphine and such oddments."

I remembered something he'd told me. "Lady Irene," I said. "Didn't you say she used dope?"

"Stout fella," he said. "He recalls that, and it makes a connection. Lady Irene might have dealt with him. But if he sells morphine he might sell less pleasant powders—to people who vanish out the back door."

Ignoring his hint at Betty, I said, "But listen: Lady Irene's always wanted to shake Andrews. Maybe she sent him there to get him out of the way. If he's not in on the murder he's in on something else. He's hunting for something, and he's enlisted Azarin to help him. It all bears out. Azarin's keeping an eye on him, and sent the men (one of whom may have killed Gasden) to follow him. Andrews—"

"You're moving along," he interrupted me. "I told you that Andrews was your high point. You've started something there. I couldn't have done it; he'd have been all set for a policeman; but you were a fellow conspirator, and he believed you. He didn't have the same resistance."

The man came in, and MacMasters turned to him. "Telephone, sir," the man said. "Scotland Yard calling."

"Take it, Sergeant," MacMasters said. The Sergeant got up, and we waited for him. Neither of us spoke; we sat looking at each other, a little tense.

In a moment the Sergeant was back, holding his notebook. He was tense too; there was an air of relief and manfully subdued excitement about him. "The Assistant Commissioner, sir. I told him you were in the bath at the moment. They've found the body, sir."

"Marie Azarin's body?" MacMasters asked. He stood up, with the tight, careful movement of the waiting hunter when the game emerges from cover.

"Yes, sir," the Sergeant said. "A house in Fulham, sir."

"Did they get anybody?"

"A Spaniard or Mexican, sir, as near as I can make out. They're holding him for you there, sir. Shall we go at once?"

"We shall," MacMasters said. "Maybe we're out of cover. Tallyho's the word, isn't it, Sergeant?"

For once the Sergeant was on firm ground. He'd been patient about Socialism, Art and Kipling, but there was nothing equivocal to him about fox hunting.

"Possibly even yoicks! sir," he said, in a tone which brooked no contradiction.

"Yoicks! it is," MacMasters said. "Let's get our hats."

CHAPTER ELEVEN

It was getting on for twilight when we reached the house—a wretched one, of dirty yellow brick, with a tiny plot of trampled grass and a mournful bush in front of it. Not even the declining sun, with its power of softening squalid things, could do much for the miserable neighborhood. There was a constable on the sidewalk and several cars at the curb, but not many people. They had apparently all gone into their houses to peep through the windows; a lone and famished-looking cat crossed the street some distance away as we got out of the cab. The constable saluted, and we went in. There was another constable just inside the door. He saluted too, and said: "They're upstairs, sir."

"Where's the body?" MacMasters asked.

"They've taken it, sir."

There was a heavy, damp, mildewy sort of smell inside the place; a few cheap and battered pieces of furniture stood about, and the walls were cracked. The whole thing had a weary and desolate air as though ready to fall down about our ears. MacMasters led the way up the shaky stairs; a tall, red-haired man came out of the back room and said: "Hullo, Mac. We've got your bird in here."

We went in. The room had a broken-down, frowsy bed, a sagging bureau, and a large, horribly colored picture of a Saint Bernard dog. A tall man, very broad in the shoulders, was standing near the bureau, and nodded; the prisoner, a medium-sized, chunky man, was seated on the bed. He was obviously a Mexican; he wore small, pointed, patent leather shoes, a good suit, and no necktie; his angular, dark face had the patient, wistful quality of a trapped animal's, and his right hand was mostly covered by a dirty bandage. His black eyes fixed on MacMasters.

"So," MacMasters said. "This is it. Did somebody bite you, my friend?"

"Yes," the man said. His tone was rather submissive, and he didn't have much of an accent. "Yes, I was bitten."

"What's your name?"

"Tomayo," the man said. "Felix Tomayo, Señor."

"You were bitten at Wimbledon, eh? At the house where the girl was?"

"Yes," Tomayo said.

"Maybe I won't need the rubber hose this time," Mac-Masters said. "Why did you go there?"

"The girl, she is mine, Senor. I am the *tio*, what you call . . . oncle, yes? I am the oncle of her."

"She was adopted," MacMasters said.

Tomayo gestured, throwing his hands up. "No!" he exclaimed. "No! This man, he pay me money. He see her play the tennis, and pay me money to take her."

"Not enough money, eh? You want more, is that it? You never signed papers?"

"No, no papers. I help her grow up, she sing in *cantinas,* dance, in California. She play the tennis in the public tennis place because of not much money. The man, he see her and come to me. He give me money, much money. He make her the good player, the best player. She play like she dance, very good. I want more money, I go ask for him." He shook his head. "Maybe later. What for later? I am the *tio*."

"So you are. Who was the girl's father? What was her name?"

"Her name Mariposa, Señor. Her father, who can tell? A gringo, I think. A gringo who looks for the oil."

"This man who paid you the money—he was her lover?"

Tomayo shrugged. *"Quién sabe?* She would get the priest, I think. It is better." His eyes gleamed. "Out of the *cantina*, out of the poorness. She did not like the poorness, that one. She make a face at it, so." He made a graphic face of disgust. "A girl of much . . . *orgullo* . . . *ambición*, yes? It eat her . . . here." He touched his heart.

"Maybe Azarin did promise her something," MacMasters said. "The other two wouldn't have liked that much." He turned to Tomayo again. "Do you think he'd kill her?" he asked.

Tomayo shrugged again, and didn't say anything.

"You came on the boat with them?"

"No," Tomayo said. "I come before, and live in this house. No one want me, I am the bad oncle. No one must know about me. She is a white girl."

"Then what the devil," MacMasters said, "did you want with her body? What good was she after she was dead?"

"They cut her up," Tomayo said. "They put her in the fire. *Hereticos!* Sometime I get the priest."

"That's about it," the red-haired man said. "He had her laid out in the cellar. A couple of lilies, two tall, cheap candles, a crucifix, all the rest of it. Some queer marks on the wall, too. He's Indian, mostly, what? All mixed up about the Church and the old gods too, I daresay. Maybe it's just as well we found her when we did."

"When you laid out your niece," MacMasters said, "did you take the bandage off her arm?" Tomayo nodded. "Was there anything under it? A capsule, for instance? The little holder that medicine comes in to be swallowed easily?"

Tomayo's eyes flicked toward the window and away. "No," he said, and his hand came up and rubbed his chin. "No, Señor."

MacMasters stood looking at Tomayo for a long moment, whistling quietly between his teeth. "Well," he said finally, "she flew a pretty long way at that. Did you know the other tennis player, Miss Dwight? Did you talk to her?" Tomayo shrugged. "You spoke to her at the courts, the place of the tennis. When she came in in the automobile."

"I put on her the sign, Senor. I wish Mariposa to win, yes? The sign," he said, in a tone which suddenly became downcast, "he is not a good one. Now, no more money for me."

"You were in the Center Court?" MacMasters said.

"No," Tomayo said. "All the time I am outside, I hear what the tennis does."

"I'm afraid so," MacMasters said, and gave it up. "You might as well take him in," he said to the red-haired man. "Have an interpreter talk to him, fingerprint him, give him a workout. I'll see what you've got in the morning. Be careful he doesn't fly away. If he could get that corpse in here by himself he's one of the minor marvels of the world. How did you find him?"

"Through Lord Twembly's house agent. Lord Twembly owns most of this section, you know. We questioned the pub-keepers first and got a lead on Tomayo. He'd been here about three weeks, paid in American money, and gave his real name. We rather concentrated on this section, because the A. C. thought it all had such an accidental air. The fog couldn't have been foreseen at this time of year, and the A. C. thought the body would be hereabouts for a few days until things calmed down. We were watching everything that moved. But even at that we were lucky, what?"

"Lucky enough," MacMasters said, "for such a cockeyed body-snatching as that. It doesn't belong with the rest of it. How about the cut on her arm?"

"No indication of anything," the red-haired man said, and turned away. They got Tomayo to his feet and took him out between them.

MacMasters stood listening to them go down the stairs. "Of all the damned irrelevant anticlimaxes," he said finally. The Sergeant looked somewhat downcast too. "It seems," MacMasters went on, "as though our Mexican friend was a pious lover of the truth. You don't think Azarin could have set him up, do you, Sergeant? Had him give his right name and all that, just to push him over when the time came?"

"Maybe a woman, sir," the Sergeant said, with a touch of glumness. "The matter has a certain female inconsistency throughout. It was a woman Mr. Cameron heard him talking to, sir. But begging your pardon, sir, I think it was purely an accident."

"Amen," MacMasters said. "Let's trickle back to the Yard and have another go at him. He's depressed me. If it's not too late I'll stop and sweat Hajos out a little, now that we have the corpse."

We went out, climbed into the cab, and rode somewhat silently back to the Mayfair; I got out there, MacMasters gave me an elaborate farewell salute, and they went off. I ate some dinner and went up to my room, feeling if anything a little more cheerful than I had in the afternoon. There was no reason for it, except that I had seen MacMasters a bit down in the mouth. Not that I felt like singing; I was a long way from that; but I began to have a vague feeling of hope. Maybe Betty had good and totally unguessed reasons for the way she'd acted. After all the pother about the body of Marie, nothing had come of it; and surely, I thought, if any sort of poison had been used they would find it. It might all turn into a tempest in a teacup after all.

I relaxed a little, decided to read awhile in bed, and the next thing I knew it was morning and the reading light was still on. I took a bath and had breakfast and a paper sent up; and while I drank my coffee I came on an item—hidden carefully, after the British newspaper fashion—about a celebrated picture dealer being knocked on the head in his home the night before. He hadn't been killed and nothing had been taken, but his private collection had been badly upset and rummaged. All of the servants except a maid had been out; she had been asleep and had heard nothing. The dealer had caught only a quick glance at his assailant before the blow.

At this moment the phone rang. It was Lady Irene's butler, who asked me to hold on a moment; Lady Irene wished to speak to me. I nearly fell off the chair, but managed to sound calm when her voice came through. There was a short colloquy, during which she reminded me that she had met me at Azarin's, and begged my pardon with the utmost graciousness for the disrupted luncheon.

"I am frightfully worried about Horace Andrews," she went on, after I'd made the appropriate noises. "He must have gone quite mad. No one knows where he is. Have you heard from him? Do you know where he is?"

"Have you tried asking Scotland Yard to find him?" I asked. The feeling descended upon me that there was a good deal more to her phone call than met the eye.

"Of course," she said. "Mr. Cameron, you were a friend of his. He spoke of you frequently. Did you notice . . . anything a little strange? I thought . . . but it is so difficult over the telephone, don't you think? The last few days I have wondered, I have been quite disturbed. And then to have him dash off like that—"

I wondered what she was getting at, then it struck me that her disjointed talk was a way of maneuvering me into some sort of an appointment. She wanted to see me. "He was very strange," I said. "The way he ran off was most peculiar."

"I feel as though I have a duty toward him," she said. "If, possibly, you could tell me what he has said to you we might piece together something significant. In his condition he must be found. I'm quite sure you would like to help me."

"Yes," I said. "Possibly you would have lunch with me. At the Ritz, perhaps?"

"That would be quite nice. At twelve-thirty? The time is rather tiresome, but I think we have a great deal to talk about. Thank you."

"Not at all," I said, and hung up. I started to walk across the room, considerably puzzled, and before I reached the window the phone rang again. It was MacMasters.

"Good boy," he said.

"What's good about me?" I asked.

"You've got them coming to you."

"Good Lord," I said. "Do you mean that you heard all that?"

"Most of it, my lad, most of it. No use overlooking any bets, particularly since the corpse let us down."

"Let you down?"

"No indication of anything. Superficial appearance of a peritonitis, but no peritonitis—as they discovered when they did the post-mortem. The superficial appearance was what fooled the doctors at Wimbledon. They thought she had a peritonitis because the poison acted that way. She just died, all full of health. That lets Tomayo out. There's no object in stealing a corpse to conceal poison if the poison is of the sort that leaves no souvenirs behind it."

"What could it be?" I asked.

"It could be histamine, but none of the bloody Home Office experts think it is. Histamine doesn't give peritonitis symptoms."

"But listen, what are you going to do now? I mean, it's all no place, isn't it?"

"Everywhere we've been is no place. We've wasted a lot of barks up a lot of wrong trees. I've been thinking about a man."

"Oh," I said.

"You've just thought about him too, eh? You've just re-membered that you saw him, eh?"

"How did you know I saw him?" I asked.

"Recall," he said, "that you asked the Sergeant to watch out for Miss Dwight. It was a lively little notion, maybe. However, it's up to you now. See what you can get from our noble peeress, and tell her nothing. Tootle—"

"Wait a minute," I interrupted. "What are you doing?"

"Looking for Cynthia, my boy. Who is Cynthia, where is she? The head waiter at the Ritz has a table for you."

"With a dictaphone under it?" I asked, and there was a click from the other end of the line. Being stalled by the dead-end created by Tomayo's interference, I gathered, he'd gone back over the early notes searching for a hint and found the report of the guard I'd requested for Betty. That didn't make me feel any better; and I had the idea that Mac-Masters was about to change his indirect methods, which were getting him nowhere, for more direct ones. He had a body now, even if it wasn't much actual good to him at the

moment—at least, so far as clues went. It was good enough
in a court. His hands had been more or less tied before it
had appeared, but they were untied now. He needed Cynthia Blythe; he needed her badly; and he needed the tall
man with the saber cut. Also, he didn't have to be so discreet
with his questions any longer. Betty, I feared was going to
regret the way she had talked to him on his first visit.

I didn't want to think about that, and began to read the
paper again. There was a fair amount of copy about the
death of Marie still in it, more or less repetitious, but nothing about the body being found. That had been held out,
and the omission made me more uncomfortable still. The
impulse came on me to see Betty again, to try to talk to her
calmly. After walking about the room for a while, I called
her up, and once more the desk refused to connect me. I put
up an argument; I told them she had said to connect me and
no one else; but, as before, I got nowhere. They refused to
do it, and insisted they had their instructions.

When I got through with that and calmed down, it was
time to dress; then I walked to the Ritz and waited in the
lobby. In about fifteen minutes Lady Irene came in, looked
about, saw me, and came over. She was extraordinarily
handsome, dressed in blue, and her make-up was practically perfection. There was a buoyancy about her that hadn't
been there that night at Azarin's; it was noticeable in her
gait as she crossed the lobby and more than noticeable in
her face. She looked five years younger; she was one of the
most desirable women I had ever seen. I hadn't thought of
her in this way before, and I wondered what had happened
to bring the change about.

"So good of you," she said.

"I couldn't do less," I said. "I was very fond of him." We
started for the dining room; she attracted a great deal of

attention, and I was keenly aware of her. It was like something out of Michael Arlen.

There was a little small talk which I don't remember, and we ordered something which I don't remember either; the hovering waiters departed, and we sat back.

"We must be systematic, must we not?" she asked. "If you will tell me about the boat first, I think that would be best."

"Nothing happened on the boat," I said, "that was in the least extraordinary. We talked quite a bit about tennis, of course. He wanted to see Miss Dwight win, I think."

"Yes," she said. "I did too."

"Really?" I asked. "I thought, naturally, that as you knew Mr. Azarin you would have wanted his niece to win."

"Mr. Azarin is an old friend," she said, "but I did not like his niece. She was an ambitious, headstrong girl, and had no scruples about using him to the fullest advantage. He is too generous with women. Even his secretary has bullied him for years."

I recalled her remark about Azarin living in the same house with a creature like Helga. "He doesn't look the sort to be bullied," I said, and racked my brains for some way to get away from this polite conversation.

"That woman," she said, "would wear down the resistance of anyone. She was a Scandinavian peasant, and has all the inhuman single-mindedness of the type. She has taken more and more of the details of his life under her own management. It would not surprise me if she has the mad idea of marrying him." She laughed suddenly, a scornful and contralto laugh. Then she smiled at me, a smile that was for me alone and made the two of us a sort of entity, a secret and friendly alliance against a preposterous condition. It was very flattering. "I have often wondered if Helga was quite

sane. She hated Marie, of course, because to her Marie was
an interloper—attractive and young. Young, before anything else. And Marie was not kind to her. Marie was really
extraordinary in thinking up aggravating ways of being
disagreeable." The waiters descended upon us and fussed
about, uncovered dishes, and finally departed once more.

"Marie, of course, made much of Mr. Azarin. She knew
on which side her bread was buttered. I have seen Helga
stand with the oddest expression when Marie staged a scene
of affection with him." She said, with another one of those
inclusive smiles that made me one of the clever ones with
a complete insight into the ways of designing women, "I
don't know what went on in Helga's mind, but it must have
been beyond civilized comprehension. Something dark and
violent, I've no doubt. I've frequently wondered . . ." She
stopped with a slight show of confusion, and said: "But this
is quite a way from Horace Andrews, isn't it?"

"I'm not sure," I said, and decided to skirt the edges a
bit. I was sure now that the Sergeant would find the cook
had no little girl; that it had been Lady Irene I'd heard
in the hall. "He was quite palpably frightened by Marie's
death. Scotland Yard men had been to see me, and I told
him they'd probably look him up. After the body vanished,
you know . . ."

"Oh, quite," she said. "Odd, wasn't it? They haven't
found it?"

"Not that I know of," I said. I looked straight at her. "I
was interested in the final match at Wimbledon and I knew
that Horace Andrews had some sort of an understanding
with Mr. Azarin. Not about the match, necessarily; perhaps
about something else. It struck me that maybe the match
had been arranged, and I went to Horace to see if I could
find out. I wanted to trade information with him."

"You think that Mr. Azarin arranged to lose?" she asked. "That's absurd. He lost a good deal of money himself. I happen to know. He has arranged matches in the past, possibly, but not this one. It is too difficult in England. Besides, he was quite confident. He knew that the Dwight girl wasn't in condition."

"Do you know whether Andrews' understanding with Mr. Azarin was about the match?" I asked.

"I'm quite sure it wasn't," she said.

I fell into an appearance of deep thought, carried it on for a space, and suddenly emerged from it with a start. "I'm sorry," I said. "I . . . ah . . . I think you must be right. If so, it would seem that Horace suspected Mr. Azarin of something, of a hand in Marie's death if you like, and saw his own efforts in danger through no fault of his own. Rats deserting the sinking ship, you know." I didn't think she'd object to Andrews in that comparison; she was working too hard for Azarin.

Her fork was halfway to her mouth. She stopped long enough to murmur, in a rather preoccupied fashion: "Yes." It was said quietly, but with an intonation that was unconscious and perfectly blood-chilling. It was the first time she'd forgotten herself. Or maybe she hadn't forgotten herself; maybe I'd convinced her of my pretensions. I wondered at what moment she'd begun to listen in the hall, whether it had been before we started to talk about Gasden or afterward. "Yes," she said again, in a normal tone. "I am sure now that he was mad. He was mad once before, you know."

"I know," I said, a little absently. The intonation of that first "Yes" still seemed to ring in my ears; and from the sound of it I knew things would go hard with Andrews if he didn't keep out of reach. Something would be "arranged" for him.

"He can't go about like this," she said. "He will get some-one into trouble, or get into it himself."

"If you knew what he was mad about," I said, "we might know where to look for him."

They took our plates away, and we both refused dessert. She looked at her watch; a small and secret smile crossed her face swiftly and was gone. "I wanted to ask you that," she said. "I thought he might have told you."

"No," I said, "I never asked." A sudden weariness descended on me. I was getting nowhere, it seemed to me, and there had been a subtle withdrawing of her interest. Nothing that was visible to the eye; apparently I was still the center of her attention; but there was something hollow in it. It was as if she had accomplished her purpose in seeing me and now had her mind on something else.

"Then there seems nothing we can do now," she said, "and I must go off in a moment. I am so sorry, for Horace's sake. You must get in touch with me at once if you hear anything. We must find him." She stood up, and I did too. "It was really very nice of you, and horrid of me to dash off like this. You will forgive me, surely?"

"Yes," I said. "Of course."

We crossed the dining room, and when we reached the door she paused and shook hands with me.

"I'm frightfully sorry," she said. "You have been very kind. Thank you so much."

"A pleasure," I said, "it was a great pleasure." She rewarded me with a brilliant and completely artificial smile, and walked off.

The buoyancy was back in her stride again, and I watched her back for a moment. And then, as my eyes left her and wandered about the lobby, I saw a man stand up. He was very tall, and there was something in his carriage that caught at my mind. He faced me for an instant and I stared at him. His features, full face, were like those of the man I had seen with Betty in the Park. When he turned the resemblance ceased, for his profile wasn't the same; the nose was different, smaller and straighter. But there was a similarity in his carriage, too; he was very like the man with the saber cut in the way he carried himself. But this man had no saber cut, his profile wasn't the same, and as he started out after Lady Irene he had no limp.

CHAPTER TWELVE

Someone tapped me on the shoulder. I turned; it was Mac-Masters.

"That man," I said, pointing after him. "The tall one. I think he's the same one that followed Gasden."

The man was almost to the door by that time. MacMasters walked swiftly over to the desk and spoke to the clerk; they talked for a moment and he came back. "His name's Batt," he said. "He lives here. He's been living here for some time. Let's move on. Meet me at my place in half an hour or so. The Sergeant's going to be there with some notes."

He went off at top speed. After returning to the dining room and paying my bill I went out and started to walk to the Mayfair. I felt sure that the tall man and the man with the limp were the same. I'd seen the man with the limp close to, and remembered his features perfectly; limps and saber cuts were easily simulated, and so noticeable that no shadower would go out equipped with them if he didn't intend to be noticed. If this easily-followed man talked to Betty in the Park, somebody put him up to it; if he took the disguise off when watching Lady Irene, whom could he be working for? According to Lady Irene, it was Helga.

I began to feel excited about this, I began to see a faint ray of hope in it. MacMasters, I thought, would laugh me to scorn, but I intended to follow it through. I quickened my steps, and just about as I'd reached the Mayfair I saw on a news poster: "ART DEALER ATTACKED BY MANIAC." Could it possibly be Andrews? I wondered. I bought a paper and took it to my room; I had a few minutes to wait, so I sat down and read about it. Sir Eric Manley, the noted dealer and critic, had been rushed to the hospital with severe head wounds, unconscious. According to the testimony of his first assistant, Sir Eric had had an appointment that morning with a man who gave his name as Gunther von Eppe; this von Eppe (who, it was discovered later, couldn't be found in the *Almanac de Gotha*) and Sir Eric had conferred in Sir Eric's private office for upward of an hour. Then von Eppe came out, closed the door behind him, and walked away. The first assistant, a few minutes later, had gone in to see Sir Eric and found him lying on the floor in a pool of his own blood, struck down with a Greek amphora. The first assistant, who had been curious, had noted von Eppe carefully when he came in, and his description tallied pretty well with the description given by Mr. Algernon Garrett, the dealer who had been attacked in his home on Sunday night.

The papers said the assistant had a hobby of knowing foreign nobility; it was a sort of snobbish pastime of his; and he had never heard of Gunther von Eppe. He had even spoken to Sir Eric about this, and so on and so on. The details passed smoothly into an attack on the police and ended up by asking a few questions about the Azarin-Dwight affair. There was too much, the article said, that was puzzling in Scotland Yard's method of handling the case. Allowing bodies to vanish, and so on. It was odd, remarked the writer,

that the arrival of Americans seemed to furnish the impetus
to start such strange goings on.

There was even more of it, but that was enough for me.
I was sure that something would be said about Betty, and I
didn't want to read it. I put the paper in my pocket, went
downstairs, and took a cab for MacMasters' place. The man
let me in, bowed, and took me back to the rear room. Mac-
Masters was standing before the fireplace, reading the paper
to the Sergeant; he broke off when I came in, and said:
"Here's one of them, Sergeant. One of those Americans. Do
you see what you started Andrews off on, you blackguard?
He'll polish off every art dealer in London if we don't catch
him."

"Is it really Andrews?" I asked.

"I'm sure of it," he said. "And so are you. But I'll have
him in a day or so. He's too consistent. Did I tell you I
checked with Captain Brererton on him? He didn't send any
cable that night."

"Did he kill Sir Eric?"

"Sir Eric will survive, by virtue of a quite Neanderthal
skull, but he won't be talking much for a few hours. Have
you seen Miss Dwight this morning, by any chance?"

He had something up his sleeve again; I could tell by his
tone. The Sergeant had an air of keeping carefully out of
it; his glance was modestly on the floor. "No," I said. "But
what of it?"

"Ah," he said. "I thought you might have dropped in to
ask her about the man in the Ritz."

"What's the man in the Ritz got to do with it? He was
watching Lady Irene. But he's the same man, I tell you."

"You're sure of it?"

"Positive," I said. "He almost walked over me that day he
asked Betty for the time in Hyde Park."

"You're quite sure of it?"

"What the devil is this?" I demanded. "I tell—"

"Now then," he cut in. "Now then, as the constables always say. I only wanted him identified. It seems that before he appeared in the Ritz in one incarnation he asked Miss Dwight the time in the Park in the other incarnation. Confusin', what? Confusin' as all get out."

"Go on," I said. I wanted to hear all of it before I said anything.

"One of my young hopefuls, taking his ease along near the side door of the Dorchester, happened to catch a passing glint from a mirror in the Park; and being a man of inquiring mind he walked over. There were no more glints—but lo and behold!—when my man got near him, he saw he had a saber cut and a limp. We're looking for this gent all over London and can't find him, so my young man watches. Presently Miss Dwight comes out of the side door, crosses over into the park, and sits on a chair for a while, then starts to return to the Dorchester. The man with the limp, hovering nearby, moves casually over to her, asks the time, and departs. The young man (who, I must tell you, was assigned to the side door of the Dorchester just in case Miss Dwight felt like taking the air) is in a quandary; but as Miss Dwight wends her way back toward the Dorchester, where there are other interested parties lying in ambush, the young man trails the man with the limp. But—alas!—the man with the limp somehow manages to evaporate from before his eyes. In the neighborhood of the Ritz, I may add. The old stunt of getting into one door of a taxi and out the other, I think. If the young man had read Sherlock Holmes, instead of serving on the Afghan border and learning about heliographs, he'd have known better. Comments are now in order."

"They hardly seem necessary," I said. "He puts on that saber cut and limp when he wants to be seen near Betty Dwight, and takes them off other times. He knew there was a man at the side door, and flashed the mirror into his eyes purposely. Don't you see," I asked, "that he's been deliberately planted to make things look bad for her?"

He rubbed his hands and managed to look Mephistophelian. "And why," he enquired, "did Miss Dwight choose to come down to the Park, for the first time in days, immediately after the signal was given with the mirror? That's confusin', too. Also, there was a lady named Cynthia Blythe who called her up this morning. At 11:45 a.m. Miss Blythe left a message at the desk to be delivered to Miss Dwight. It was 'I will call again.' More comments are now in order."

"Couldn't the man have left it? He knows Betty's line is watched. What about Helga Lindstrom?"

"Miss Lindstrom," he said, "was in Wimbledon. She didn't leave the house, although Azarin did. No phone calls were made from the house."

"What did Azarin do?" I asked.

"Azarin," he said, "went to Lady Irene's, and from Lady Irene's to the bank. It appears that Lady Irene gave Azarin a large cheque. The only phone call from Lady Irene's this morning was to you. After going to the bank Azarin bought a few articles of wearing apparel, visited a wine merchant, and returned to Wimbledon. Lady Irene, before meeting you, visited her hairdresser. Cynthia Blythe's call was made in the Berkeley Hotel, but it was all done so quickly that they couldn't call back and have someone intercept her. Azarin called Lady Irene before going to her house, but only requesting to see her at once. There are a few other incidentals I might tell you, such as this: my man, Nick, hearing me speak of the Spaniard in Limehouse being so close-mouthed, took himself there last night and smacked the Spaniard around. I want it clearly understood," he went on, with a sly sort of grin, "that I had nothing to do with this. It was purely unofficial, totally unconnected with me, and entirely reprehensible. It came from an excess of zeal on Nick's part, it was an embarrassing evidence of misguided loyalty. I have spoken to him with the utmost harshness about it; but he found out that Lady Irene, up until several weeks ago, bought morphine from the Spaniard. At that time he refused to handle it any more, he got frightened. And Miss Dwight was buying what the Spaniard called a 'present for someone.' Further than that, Nick couldn't get.

"I dropped in to see Hajos, the gambler," MacMasters went on, "after I left you last night, and pitched him such a tale of finding the corpse and a few other little incriminating incidentals that he'd have come clean to save his own hide if the bets had been crooked. The bets weren't crooked; Azarin, I am sure, actually lost the money, and felt the loss of it so badly that he had to get more from Lady Irene to stay afloat. What he gave in return we have yet to find out; but knowing the lady's passion for him we might hazard a guess that he promised to marry her. He got away from her once, remember, and she's not the type to have him do it again. We will talk at length with Lady Irene shortly, her remarks to you at luncheon were most interesting. She was, of course, protecting Azarin; she hates Helga, and small wonder. The cook, incidentally, has no little girl. Lady Irene must have been listening in the hall; for she was much more interested in quietly laying bombs under Helga than she was in hunting for Andrews. She hates Andrews for gumming things up. Did you notice her intonation when you made that crack about rats at lunch?"

"Yes, I suppose you had a microphone under the table as usual," I said without surprise. I was growing a little confused with all his rhetoric. "Yes," I repeated. "But what's all this got to do with the saber-scarred man? You talk too much."

"Oh," he said airily, "I admit it. If I listen long enough to my own verbosity I'm liable to get somewhere. But to go on with the man with the scar who was following Lady Irene, and conferring with Miss Dwight. Do you believe Azarin innocent of all this pother? Does he know what's going on? He didn't want to sell the match, he wanted to win it; he put up a lot of good hard money, and when he lost, it put him into a hole. I think he didn't want to go to Lady Irene, or he'd have done it before. You said that he wasn't glad to see her when he got off the boat. I don't think he killed Gasden, either. The bandage and tape checked—not with the hospital's—but with similar bandage and tape found in Gasden's rooms. No one, according to Gasden's landlady, has been in his rooms for weeks except himself. There aren't many kinds of bandage and tape, and we still aren't quite positive; but the dear old experts think that Gasden had been wearing that little private holster of his for some time."

He stopped and shouted for Nick. That worthy appeared in the doorway, received an order for three whiskey and sodas, and disappeared. "Dry work," MacMasters said. "Drier for you than for me." He was quiet for a moment; Nick brought the drinks, and MacMasters buried his nose in his and swallowed nearly half of it, then backed up to the fireplace again. "Look, now," he began again. "Let's go back a bit. Helga and Miss Dwight—or Helga and Miss Blythe—got together on the boat deck that night. Miss Dwight and Miss Blythe were, and are, in communication. Both Miss Dwight and Helga had cause to dislike Marie Azarin and want her out of the way. Azarin didn't want her out of the way; he bet his money on her. That he liked her, or was in her power, enough to bother Lady Irene is evident; and if Marie bothered Lady Irene she also bothered Helga. Lady Irene and Helga would probably work independently of each other. They're both what we might term Azarinites—a jolly little society. Marie rode rough shod over all of them; she is half a sa— half a savage, as Lady Irene was about to say at Azarin's house that night. Her origin is obscure; she was tremendously ambitious. Our unfortunate friend, Tomayo, said that Marie adored Azarin, and nothing but marriage with him would suit her. Miss Blythe might have known about this from Helga; Marie, to bring Azarin's and her own ambitions to their fulfillment, must win from Miss Dwight. Helga gets into communication with Miss Dwight through Miss Blythe or the scarred man in some way, and keeps her eye on Lady Irene; also on Andrews. For she doesn't know how much Andrews has found out. The scarred man is working for Helga, because if he was working for Azarin he wouldn't bother with Lady Irene."

"So," I said. "And why would Betty connive at all this merely to get Marie out of the way? It's foolish, it's too elaborate, it's unnecessary, it's rot."

"Maybe," he said, "she planned it all. She was the one who bought the 'present' in Limehouse; she is the one whose aunt has a lot of money. She—"

"Have you found that her aunt spent a lot of money?" I asked. "And if her aunt spent a lot of money, why doesn't Azarin have it? Why does he have to borrow from Lady Irene?"

"Maybe," he said, "Helga got it, or will get it. I have found out that on the day after she landed Mrs. Cosgrove cabled to her bankers to put $300,000 to the credit of Miss Dwight in a London bank. I found it out this morning."

"Further," MacMasters went on, "I have picked up another small item. The day after Miss Dwight visited Limehouse—the visit that we know of, of course—she went to the bank. This seemed a natural enough thing to do. Everybody visits banks. But, after finding out about Mrs. Cosgrove's generosity, I checked at the bank. It seems that Miss Dwight, instead of withdrawing a nominal sum, withdrew $8000—£1600—in cash. The down payment, eh? Maybe the Mexican in Limehouse knows something about it, and I've got a crew working on him."

"Why," I asked, "don't you ask Miss Dwight about all this? Or Mrs. Cosgrove?"

"It saddens me that I can't. It wouldn't be cricket. Also, I want to get my hands on Cynthia Blythe and segregate her first. Also the accomplished man with the limp. No use wasting my powder." He finished the rest of his drink, put the glass down, and said suddenly: "Sergeant, ring up Lady Irene and ask her if we may call."

The Sergeant went out; in about five minutes he was back again. "Lady Irene is not at home, sir," he said. "She's gone to Azarin's."

"Tantivy!" MacMasters said. "We'll whisk along to Azarin's, then, and pow-wow the lot. It might be fun. Nick!" Nick came in. "Get my car around, will you? And hold any messages that may come through here. I don't want the Yard calling up Azarin's house."

"You don't want me?" I asked, when Nick had gone out.

"But yes," MacMasters said. "Oh, but yes. You'll be fine backing to a few little questions I might want to ask."

We went out and got into the car, a Packard convertible with the top down. "I didn't buy British," MacMasters said, as we started off, "because I didn't buy British. This mechanical marvel reminded me of the fine time I had in the States hunting mountain goats. They're wonderful creatures, with just the right amount of conservatism."

He was a reckless driver; I sat with a sort of expectant tenseness stiffening me out. The Sergeant, who had the back seat to himself, sat with his eyes on his shoes and a fatalistic expression on his face. Nothing happened to us, however; we reached Putney Bridge and sailed over it, and MacMasters put on more speed. When we came to the golf course he slowed up, turned right, and drove along for a block or two before we saw a constable. We pulled up alongside the constable, who saluted.

"Anything doing?" MacMasters asked.

"A tall man stopped at Mr. Azarin's an hour or so gone, sir. He was inside about half an hour, and returned toward London. He was driving a Bentley. A clean-shaven, dark man, sir."

"Somebody went after him?"

"Yes, sir."

"Material there for a pious hope," MacMasters said. "Many thanks."

We went on again, winding about, and finally pulled up before Azarin's. Seen in the daylight, without the fog, it was a very nice place, half timbered, with quite a large lawn well planted with shrubbery. There was a two-car garage on one side, well in the rear, and a Rolls-Royce was standing before it. The garage doors were closed, so the Rolls was apparently Lady Irene's. We went up the walk, and a maid let us in. After we'd been standing in the hall for a moment Azarin came out, wearing striped flannels and a rather startling tweed coat. When he saw me he hesitated for an instant, and his face lost its sly, sleepy look as his eyes widened; but he caught himself at once and smiled.

"How do you do?" MacMasters asked. "You know Mr. Cameron? I brought him along to get everything straightened up. There's no use of you two being sore at each other. Waste of time."

"No," Azarin said. "Of course not." He shook hands with me with great aplomb; he smelt as though he'd had quite a few drinks. His skin still had that faint, oily shine on it. "Of course not," he said again. "I did Mr. Cameron an injustice, but it must be admitted that my nervous system had been very badly shocked."

"That's so," MacMasters said, agreeably.

Azarin nodded, without taking his eyes off MacMasters. They were slightly bloodshot, and the whites were a liverish color, but they didn't look apprehensive or frightened. They really had no expression except a waiting watchfulness, and that wasn't very pronounced. In the short silence before anyone spoke I stared at him, feeling the impact of his personality. It had an impact, but the impact was so ambiguous that it was extremely confusing. There was, to begin with, a sort of formless and yielding softness that you felt, as though he were made of ectoplasm, as though if you shoved him in a corner or squeezed him in one place he'd merely bulge out somewhere else; there was also a feeling of hidden sensuality, a kind of boudoir air; and on top of all this there was the surface, the urbanity. "Yes," he agreed, "it was a very tragic day for me." He let all that go by with a shrug. It was over, he implied; over and done with. "Mr. Cameron was seeking information, and I shouldn't hold that against him. I have often sought information myself, although in a somewhat different way." This was got off smoothly enough, admitting me offhand into the companionship of rogues—and, as he implied, the inferior sort of rogues. He smiled again, and went on: "But won't you come in? You have arrived at a rather fortunate time. Lady Irene Wrexford-Bond has done me the honor of promising to be my wife, and we were having a little champagne." He didn't look in the least like a joyful bridegroom as he got this off; he looked vaguely depressed.

MacMasters grinned slightly and nodded; Azarin turned and led the way into the drawing room. The curtains were drawn against the sun; they were green, and gave to the room and the masks a sort of sinister and funereal glow. The room was full of cigarette smoke and all the ashtrays seemed full of stubs with lipstick on them; at the far end of the room, beside the divan beneath the tall mask and the book-cases, there was a table with two champagne buckets beside it. The table was covered with empty bottles, glasses, a tray of sandwiches and a tray of *hors d'oeuvres*, all messed about. Azarin waited to let us enter first, and when he followed, the green light made him look like a corpse.

"I hope," he said, "that your regulations will not prevent your having a little refreshment? I—"

He paused, for Helga had come in. She was still dressed in severe dark blue. It accentuated her heroic size and her pale hair; her hands, as before, caught my attention and held it until Azarin said: "This is Miss Lindstrom, Mr. Cameron. I don't believe you've met before."

I bowed; that secretive face turned toward me, the blue eyes looked coldly at me; then she turned to MacMasters. "You haven't found Miss Azarin's body, Inspector?" she asked.

"Yes," MacMasters remarked. "As a matter of fact, we have. That's what I wanted to talk about. Lady Irene is here, I take it?"

Azarin turned quickly, and for a second he and Helga looked at each other. Helga's expression didn't change in the slightest, and it seemed to me that Azarin's was one of relief.

"You've found her?" he asked. "You've found her? Where? I—"

"I would prefer that Lady Irene be here," MacMasters said.

"Yes," Azarin said. "Of course." He seemed to be a little agitated. "Helga, can't you get her?"

"I think she went upstairs several minutes before the Inspector came in," Helga said coolly. "There was a man here, who talked with her earlier this morning. He seemed to excite her a great deal. She went up for a sedative. I'll call if you wish, but I think she'll be down shortly."

"Yes," Azarin said again. He moved closer to MacMasters. "Shortly. I must know, however, about Marie. I have worried myself half to death. The poor girl . . ."

He paused; Helga was standing quite still, watching him with a sort of detached interest, and at that moment she seemed taller than any of us, taller than MacMasters—who was watching with a sort of detached interest himself. His bushy eyebrows were drawn down; the Tar Baby look was on him. Suddenly he moved, jamming his hands into his pockets and rocking back a bit on his heels. "Oh, quite a Christian burial," he said. "By a representative of the Spanish Loyalist Government."

Helga didn't move at that either; she might have been carved out of wood on the prow of one of the old Norse dragon boats. Azarin swallowed; I could see his Adam's apple rise and fall, but outside of that he was steady too. "A representative of the Loyalist government?" he asked, in a muffled tone.

"Tomayo was the name," MacMasters said.

"Ah!" Azarin said. His upper lip jerked up in a strange way, spasmodically, showing his teeth. They were yellow near the gums. "I was afraid of that," he went on, surprisingly enough. He fell back a step. "Hadn't we better sit down?" he asked. "I wasn't quite frank about that, Inspector. But how can such a thing be talked about? The man was blackmailing—"

He stopped suddenly, with his mouth open; his head slewed around, toward the door. Helga's head slewed around too; everybody's did. For there was a strange noise in the hall, muffled, scraping, seeming to come from the top of the stairs. Everyone stood very still for a second or so; then, after a sort of dull threshing sound, there came a thump, another thump, then a horrible pause and a crash. Everything in the house rattled. We all rushed into the hall, getting into each other's way, then we stopped.

Lady Irene, doubled up, with the blood running from a long gash in her forehead, was lying at the foot of the stairs. Her head was twisted and a crooked, fixed smile was on her face. She didn't move; she had the look of never moving again.

CHAPTER THIRTEEN

MacMasters was the first to move; he moved swiftly, with a great economy of motion, and seemed to be stooping over her before the scrape of his shoe had died out in my ears. The Sergeant stood where he was, watching Helga and Azarin; Azarin was staring, shocked, and Helga performed as one would expect. That is to say she did nothing for an instant except look, her head forward a little; then, coolly, she moved forward and stooped beside MacMasters. He waved her back with one hand; the other was at Lady Irene's pulse. Next he pulled out his watch and held it before her mouth, turning her head a little, then raised the watch and looked at the face of it. He stood up.

One of the maids had run from the kitchen, and stood staring at Lady Irene's face with wide-eyed horror. "Get a doctor," MacMasters told her. "As quick as you can. The rest of you will please go into the living room. Sergeant, take them in and keep them there."

The maid, cutting wide around the body, ran out the front door, and the Sergeant herded us into the living room and took up his post at the door. "Don't sit together, please," he said, and we moved apart and took widely separated chairs around the wall. Helga sat nearest the table where the champagne glasses were; she looked like some Norse effigy, made of ice and colored after the semblance of a woman; Azarin dropped his head into his hands, and didn't move any more. We seemed to sit there for a long time in silence, then there was a noise at the door and the maid and the doctor came in.

"Allow no one upstairs," I heard MacMasters say. "Is anyone up there now?"

"No, sir," the maid said, and her footsteps retreated down the hall.

There were sounds from the hall, stirrings and a few low-voiced remarks, then the doctor went out again and Mac-Masters ran up the stairs. We could hear him moving about. He took a long time; then he came down. He was whistling silently as he came into the room, one eyebrow cocked a little, and there was a sort of padding quality in his gait. He looked around, and about that time the maid walked past in the hall and came back with a constable. Apparently Mac-Masters had had the doctor send him in. "Morning," Mac-Masters said. "Will you please entertain Miss Lindstrom in another room?"

"Is this necessary, Inspector?" she asked, without moving. Azarin looked up, but didn't speak. "Are we looked upon as murderers?"

"It's customary, Ma'am," MacMasters said, skirting sarcasm. "And in the best tradition. If you please."

She stood up and walked out, followed by the constable. The Sergeant sat down and took out his little black book; MacMasters sat down too, and crossed his long legs. Azarin had folded his arms across his breast. His face was once more sleepy and sly, his heavy-lidded eyes were half closed, and his air of being made of ectoplasm was emphasized by the greenish light.

"Could you assign any cause," MacMasters asked, "to Lady Irene's seizure, Mr. Azarin? Has she been ill?"

"Ill?" Azarin asked. "No. Not to my knowledge, Inspector. It is I who will be ill after this. My nerves cannot stand a great deal more. First my protégé, of whom I had great hopes, and now my *fiancée* . . . I would prefer that this examination be deferred, if it were possible."

"I understand thoroughly," MacMasters said. "However, I don't see how it can be done. For a lady who is not ill to have what sounded like convulsions at the top of a flight of stairs, and then to fall down and kill herself, isn't conducive to a deferment of an examination into the causes. Miss Lindstrom spoke of a sedative."

"Yes," Azarin said. "Don't you think, however, that Mr. Cameron might be excused from this? His presence is embarrassing."

"I like Mr. Cameron," MacMasters said, skirting sarcasm again. "So let's not worry about him. He's old enough not to be embarrassed, and he brings me luck."

"Ah," Azarin said. "But I have certain rights, have I not? Mr. Cameron placed himself in a most ambiguous position some time ago; I have reason to think that he does not wish me well."

"So," MacMasters said. "Did Lady Irene, by any chance, strengthen that opinion?" His voice was getting a slight edge on it. "And is it not true that you made the first advances to Mr. Cameron yourself?"

"Lady Irene never spoke to him that I know of. I spoke to Mr. Cameron first because I thought some information might be got out of him."

"And did you speak to Mr. Andrews first also?" MacMasters asked.

"I met Mr. Andrews through Lady Irene."

"Really?" MacMasters asked.

Azarin's eyes opened slightly. "You doubt me, Inspector?" he asked.

"Somewhat," MacMasters said. "I have been laboring for some time under the impression that he came to your cabin on the *Princess Victoria*."

Azarin's lids dropped again. "He did, for the matter of that," he said. "Although I am not sure that you are within your rights in that question. It is something that, possibly, should come out in testimony if there is any. However, I wish to co-operate. He came to my cabin to ask me to engage in a business matter with him. A matter that had nothing to do with tennis. It was a crackbrained affair, but I encouraged him because he had talked a good deal with Miss Dwight."

"I see," MacMasters said. "However, this isn't getting us forward much. You still think that Lady Irene wasn't ill?"

"She was not ill," Azarin said. "But she was very nervous. I don't know what about. A man was here this afternoon and they were in conversation together for a time; when the man left she showed every evidence of worry. She had to take a sedative."

"And that sedative was . . . what?"

"Morphine," Azarin said.

"Do you know where she obtained this morphine?"

"No," Azarin said. "I only know that her source of supply dried up shortly before we arrived in England. She was, of course, badly in need of it. Fortunately, I had some and could help her out until she found more."

"You gave her some the evening Mr. Cameron was here?" MacMasters asked. They both seemed to take Azarin's possession of the morphine as a matter of course.

Azarin's heavy-lidded eyes swung toward me and back again. "Yes," he said, and added: "Possibly Mr. Cameron could have told you that."

"You don't know her new source of supply?"

"No. But it was very uncertain. I kept a little for her here. She has often used it and suffered no ill effects. We kept a solution of it and a hypo needle in the bathroom."

He was becoming very detailed; MacMasters' remark about the *Princess Victoria* had helped, indicating, purposely, what sort of information they had on him; but at the same time he wasn't going to be pushed into anything. He had become a little more bland, if that were possible.

"Were you greatly interested in Mr. Andrews' maneuvers?" MacMasters asked. "Do you have any idea where I could find him?"

"I wasn't greatly interested," Azarin said, "and where he is I have no idea."

"You never heard of a man named Gasden?"

"Gasden? No."

"Detail Lady Irene's movements this afternoon," MacMasters said. "After her interview with her visitor."

"We were having champagne when the man was announced. He came in here and we talked for a few minutes, then Lady Irene asked that they be excused. They went into the next room down the hall, which I use as a . . . ah . . . study. Miss Lindstrom and I waited in here. Presently the man left, and Lady Irene returned, drank two glasses of champagne in quick succession and tried to talk very vivaciously. She did not succeed, and presently went upstairs."

"What was the man's name?" MacMasters asked. "Did you know him?"

"I didn't know him. As I recall, his name was Saunders."

"Very good," MacMasters said, in an indeterminate tone. "Now, as to this Tomayo. You can help me there, if you will. Have you any idea why he would steal the corpse of Miss Azarin?"

"Inspector," Azarin said, "I am sorry that I endeavored to keep it from you before. But, in my opinion, it was a private matter; he claimed to have been her uncle. Whether he was or not is beside the point. I saw her playing tennis in a public playground in Los Angeles. I was passing in a car and was stopped by a traffic light. I know tennis, Inspector. I'd watched Suzanne Lenglen play many times in the south of France. I realized at once that Marie was a natural player, an extraordinary natural player, and I saw an opportunity to make something of her. I adopted her, as her legal uncle. This was done in Mexico. Since then, this Tomayo—who had more or less lived off what money she made as a singer and dancer in cantinas—began to blackmail me. Marie was extremely sensitive as to her origin; her mother was an Indian or a mestizo; if this had got out I would have had a very difficult time with her. This Tomayo, being all mixed up with his Indian gods and his Catholic beliefs, had a very superstitious horror of a post-mortem. That is the way I interpret his action." He paused for a moment, looking very glum. "Tell me," he said, "was there evidence . . . ah . . . that she died from other than natural causes?"

"Tell me instead," MacMasters said blandly, "did Lady Irene ever speak to you of this Saunders? Did you know what there was between them? Do you know why she was nervous after he called?"

Azarin moved forward, waving the question irritably aside. "The thing I want to know is," he snapped, "was my niece poisoned?"

"You have a great number of rights," MacMasters said, "as you pointed out awhile ago. Do you wish her body delivered to the undertaking parlor, or here? Now, as to Saunders—"

"To the parlor," Azarin said sulkily. "I know nothing about him. Lady Irene did not confide entirely in me."

"Is there anyone else, in your opinion, who would wish grievous ill to Marie? Grievous, take note. A noticeable word. Any of her opponents?"

That was a gentle way of putting it. "All of her opponents were afraid of her," Azarin said. "The closer to the top they were, the more afraid they became."

"You wouldn't wish to indicate anyone in particular?"

I held my breath for a moment, waiting for Azarin to say something about Betty. He stared at me, licked his lips quickly, and after a long moment said: "No. No one."

"Right," MacMasters said. "Sergeant, conduct Mr. Azarin to the study, and bring Miss Lindstrom in." He watched until Azarin had got to the door, and said suddenly: "Is it true, Mr. Azarin, that you deposited in the bank a largish cheque of Lady Irene's to your order this morning?"

Azarin swung around. "Yes," he said. That was all, and he bit the word off.

"Is it also true that you were surprised—one might even say unpleasantly—when you encountered Lady Irene as you debarked from the *Princess Victoria?*"

Azarin looked at him, and his upper lip went up quickly in that same spasmodic gesture; but he didn't say anything.

"It's still true that you don't know anything about this Saunders?" MacMasters asked, and rubbed his jaw.

Azarin stared steadily at him from under those drooping lids, but he didn't say anything to that either.

"One more thing," MacMasters said. "Do you take morphine?"

"No," Azarin said, and turned away. MacMasters watched them out the door, grinned slightly at me, murmured: "Little lamb, who made thee?" and recrossed his legs. In a moment the Sergeant was back with Helga Lindstrom.

She walked coolly across the room and sat down, with her big hands in her lap, as straight as before; her pale eyes seemed almost without color, and her hair gleamed greenish in the filtered light. "Miss Lindstrom," MacMasters asked affably, "how long has Mr. Azarin been taking morphine?"

"Mr. Azarin never took morphine," she said.

"Do you take it?"

"I?" she asked, leaning back a little. "I do not."

"It is a matter that can be cleared up by examination," MacMasters said, in an offhand manner, as though talking to himself. "Why, then, would you keep morphine in the house?"

"Some of Mr. Azarin's friends find need of it," she said.

"Mr. Azarin had other friends beside Lady Irene who found need of it?"

"Of course," she said. "Otherwise, why would we have it in the house?"

"Why indeed?" MacMasters said. "Did Miss Azarin use it?"

"Of course not."

"Ah," MacMasters said. "You can see what I'm getting at, I'm sure. I'll be frank with you, Miss Lindstrom. It managed to happen that the first meeting of Lady Irene and Miss Azarin was observed. They took what might be termed a dislike to each other. Now, Miss Azarin—for a healthy girl—died most strangely. There was nothing the matter with her. It looked as though she might be the next Singles Champion; and as the next Singles Champion she would be in a most enviable position. Mr. Azarin had perfected her tennis, and she looked up to him. She practically worshipped him. This," he said, somewhat parenthetically, "was told me by a gentleman named Tomayo. Now, Lady Irene, obviously, also admired Mr. Azarin; this is evidenced by the fact that she intended to marry him. I talked at great length to Lady Irene—whose nerves, as the talk progressed, seemed to bother her a little. When she saw us come to the house awhile ago, she might have thought . . ." He waved one hand, and left the sentence hanging in the air.

Helga said nothing. She was very good at saying nothing.

"Just a little notion of mine," MacMasters said. "Of course, the man who called might have said something to her to upset her. Men who call are sometimes very disturbing. Can you detail for me the movements of this disturbing man?"

"Yes," Helga said, looking at him with those pale eyes. "We were having champagne when he came in, and talked for a few minutes. I did not pay much attention to him, Inspector. I was not concerned with him, but his presence made some awkwardness. Lady Irene did not seem in the least glad to see him. After a few minutes they went into the little room down the hall, and I waited in here with Mr. Azarin. He was upset too, he did not like Lady Irene to be disturbed on such an . . . an occasion. Then the man left and Lady Irene returned here. She was very much troubled, but tried to be vivacious and conceal it. Then she went upstairs."

"Did she drink any champagne?"

"Yes."

"You didn't notice how much? Enough to cause her to fall downstairs?"

"Several glasses, I think."

"She had a good head for champagne?" MacMasters asked.

"Excellent."

"I daresay," MacMasters said. "Did you notice what the man was wearing, what he looked like? It's most important."

"He was a tall man," Helga said. Her position hadn't changed a hair; if she was under any strain, if she was guessing at Azarin's answers, she didn't show it. "A tall, dark man, clean-shaven. That is my impression, Inspector. As I said, I paid very little attention to him."

"He seemed overbearing at all? As though he was in a position to dictate terms? Did he force Lady Irene into going into the other room with him?"

Helga's pale eyes never left his face; her big hands, strong enough to strangle an average man, didn't even twitch. She surely belonged where I'd put her before—on the prow of a dragon boat. "I didn't notice which of them made the first move," she said. MacMasters had come around to it gradually, but she was ready for him.

I felt depressed all at once by this; for MacMasters had caught them at the right moment, before they had had time to speak to each other, and their stories seemed to agree too well to be anything but the truth. His innuendos about suicide didn't cheer me any, because there was no reason for Lady Irene to commit suicide, unless a lot had gone on that I didn't know about. I didn't think so; I thought the answer to Lady Irene's death lay somewhere in the house, but I doubted if he'd get it. Neither Helga nor Azarin were going to incriminate anyone else, if they had killed Lady Irene; they were too clever for that. And yet, I didn't believe that those pale eyes of hers had missed a single thing about the visitor. She would not have seen Lady Irene discomfited and not observed it closely.

"Let's go a little farther back," MacMasters said. "This affair might have had its inception some time ago, and had people mixed up in it that no one would suspect. Have you ever been approached, by any of the other contestants, their emissaries or, even possibly, enemies, regarding the matches at Wimbledon?"

"No," Helga said.

There was a short silence, and I didn't like it. She had denied meeting Betty or Cynthia Blythe. I wondered if MacMasters would ask her next about the scene in the dining salon on the Princess Victoria, but he didn't. She knew what he was up to, with me sitting in front of her. She was taking the indirect way of accusing Betty—chancing, at the same time, incriminating herself. Of course, there would be no testimony but mine as to the business on the *Princess Victoria*, and by going to Azarin's and crawling out the window I had acted in a way to prejudice that badly. She knew exactly what she was doing; she had a brain like a very delicate pair of balances; she might be protecting Betty to protect herself. . . .

"You always got on well with Miss Azarin?" MacMasters asked.

"No," she said. "I did not. She was an overbearing, spiteful girl. As you know, she was very ambitious. She had a streak of savage cruelty in her, and did not hesitate to vent it upon me."

"So," MacMasters said. "Did you hear either Lady Irene or the visitor go upstairs?"

"I cannot say definitely," she said. "I was concerned with Mr. Azarin, who, as I have mentioned, was much disturbed by the man coming in."

Another indirect statement; she wouldn't accuse the man of anything, and she wouldn't clear him. As for MacMasters, he was now looking fresh as a daisy. He had started out by being affable, and he was still that way. "You don't know where Lady Irene got her morphine?" he asked.

"No," she said. "Her source of supply had been cut off a short time before we landed. We had to give her some. Then she found another, but it has, apparently, been very uncertain."

MacMasters stood up. "Thank you," he said. "I think that will do for the time. Sergeant, escort Miss Lindstrom back to Mr. Azarin, and bring in the maids." He gave Helga a bow—I couldn't tell whether it was ironic or not—and watched them go out.

"Will you, won't you, will you, won't you, will you, won't you join the dance?" he asked, as their footsteps died down the hall.

"You're getting very literary," I said.

"Captain Brererton told me, when I checked Andrews with him, that there wasn't another marten jacket on the ship. He checked pretty thoroughly, too. At the customs. It's an evil world. Here's comes the Sergeant."

The Sergeant came in with the maid and the cook; they both looked very unhappy. MacMasters grinned amiably at them, and turned to the Sergeant. "Run next door," he said, "and do a little telephoning for me, will you, Sergeant? Tell them to keep in touch with Mr. Batt, at the Ritz. I have a sudden desire to see him."

The Sergeant went out; MacMasters turned to the two women. "Now, ladies," he said, "your names, please."

"Mrs. Geechings, sir," the cook said. "And Pomfret." She indicated the maid. They looked at each other in a sort of genteelly horrified fashion; apparently they had been talking about Lady Irene as Pomfret had seen her in the hall.

"Pomfret," MacMasters said, "you clean upstairs, don't you?"

"Yes, sir."

"Is this little bottle usually in the bathroom?" He took a squat bottle with a rubber top, thin in the center for hypodermic needles to go through, out of his coat pocket and held it up. The bottle was about half full of colorless liquid.

"Yes, sir," Pomfret said. "It's kept in the cabinet with one of those needles, sir."

"Do you know who uses it?"

"Lady Irene, I think, sir. I often find it after she's left, sir. Standing about. Then I put it back, sir."

"Good," MacMasters said. "Were you upstairs after luncheon today?"

"No, sir."

"You don't know, then, whether the bottle and the needle were out of the cabinet when Lady Irene went upstairs?"

"No, sir."

"How long have you worked for Mr. Azarin?"

"Only since he came, sir."

"You didn't know him before? Be sure of your answer."

"Neither Mrs. Geechings nor I, sir. We came from an agency, sir."

About this time there was a knock at the door, and Mac-Masters went out. There were three or four masculine voices in the hall, and I heard MacMasters say: "Photograph now, and take her with you. You have a hearse, or an ambulance? Good. Take this too, and get me a report on it. Call Doctor Grant before you start. He was here."

When he came back the Sergeant was with him; the Sergeant sat down, made several entries in his book, and looked up. "This is correct, Mrs. Geechings?" MacMasters said.

"Yes, sir."

"Now tell me what happened when the tall, dark man came in, Pomfret."

"He wanted to see Lady Irene, sir. He waited in the library. Then I took him into the drawing room and went back to the scullery."

"Did he seem an unpleasant person?"

"No, sir. He seemed a bit perturbed, if I may say so, sir."

"You may," MacMasters said. "How did they receive him?"

"I couldn't say, sir."

"What was his name?"

"Saunders, sir."

"Did anyone recognize him?"

"I didn't stop, sir."

"After he came, did you hear anyone moving about?"

"I didn't notice, sir. It's hard to hear from the scullery, sir."

"Did you hear anything, Mrs. Geechings?"

"I didn't notice either, sir."

"You didn't hear anyone go upstairs?"

"Before the man came, sir?"

"From the time Lady Irene arrived until now."

"Before she got here we received orders to make the sandwiches and cool the wine, sir. Pomfret took them in."

"Take up the song, Pomfret."

"Yes, sir. I took the things in, and Miss Lindstrom showed me where to arrange them. Mr. Azarin wasn't in the room at the moment, sir. After Lady Irene came in I wasn't back again."

"After Lady Irene came did you hear anyone upstairs before she did?"

"I couldn't say, sir."

"Come, come," MacMasters said, with a sudden—and I think assumed—sharpness. "Think again. Didn't you hear water running?"

The two women looked at each other in a vaguely frightened way, then stared at him. They looked ridiculously like
two fishes for a moment. Finally the cook said hesitantly: "I
. . . I fancy I might have heard water running, sir."

"What did the tall man say when you opened the door?"

"He said: 'Is Lady Irene here?' I told him she was, sir.
He half turned away, then came in. He said: 'Mr. Saunders.'
I went in and announced him, sir. They all looked a bit
blank. I said: 'He's asking for Lady Irene.' Mr. Azarin said:
'See him in the library, Irene,' but she said: 'I'll see him in
here.' I didn't go in again, sir."

"Right," MacMasters said. "Did Miss Azarin and Miss
Lindstrom get along well together?" They both looked at
one another and didn't speak. "Pomfret, speak up."

"No, sir. Miss Azarin, if I may say so, sir, was an unpleasant person. She was most unkind to Miss Lindstrom and to
us, sir."

"Miss Lindstrom is unkind also?"

"No, sir. She is cold, sir, but fair to us."

"And who hangs the laundry out?"

"I do, sir," Pomfret said.

"Do they tell you how to hang it? Handkerchiefs next to
shirts, and all that?"

"No, sir. I hang it any way, sir."

"O. K.," MacMasters said. "No code there. You may
both go." They went out, and MacMasters turned to the
Sergeant. "I'll go back and thank our host, then we can get
on with it. Meet me in the hall."

The Sergeant snapped his book shut and stood up; he
fell in behind me and we went into the hall. The men out
there had gone, and in a moment MacMasters returned and
we went out to the car.

CHAPTER FOURTEEN

We sped recklessly towards town, and MacMasters began to sing, loudly and untunefully, about John Peel. He kept it up until we were almost at the Bridge, then ceased and said: "The old game of questions and answers. Did you enjoy yourself, my fine fellow?"

"No," I said. "Did you?"

"Well, as I'm being literary at the moment, I may say that I heard the ripple lapping at the crag. Fine old fellow, Tennyson. Wonderful fellow for the last generation to quote at us. Sergeant, wasn't Lady Irene at that beauty parlor yesterday?"

"Yes, sir," the Sergeant said. "I was about to remark on it, sir."

"The fresh air's doing you no end of good. Thither we will go, horse, foot and guns. Did you happen to notice anything strange while I knelt by the corpse?"

"The Lindstrom woman failed to look in the least self-congratulatory, sir."

"You haven't conceived an affection for her, have you?" MacMasters asked. "It would be a mistake. She has a private woodpile, all full of n—rs."

"Quite, sir."

"Me, I don't like her at all. Nor does Mr. Cameron. Nor is Mr. Cameron's lady friend going to."

"Oh, for God's sake!" I said.

"What did the doctor find, sir?"

"Boardlike rigidity of the abdomen," MacMasters said. "It's getting to be a common complaint in Wimbledon. I only wonder why good old Gasden didn't go that way, but maybe Mr. Batt, alias Mr. Saunders, can tell us." He mimicked Helga's faint accent: "'I didn't notice which of them made the first move.' If you believe that, Sergeant, I'll demote you to the gasworks beat. We work like hell to find Marie's corpse, and then we don't get anywhere with it. They murder each other under our noses, and there's not a thing to put the finger on. I went over the bathroom and the head of the stairs like a model detec-a-tive, and those two domestics sit in the kitchen and don't hear anyone go upstairs. The British lower classes are entirely empty of bile and deserve to be forever held in economic bondage. Am I right, Sergeant?"

"I daresay, sir."

"Ah!" MacMasters said. The Sergeant had at last stopped him. He came down on the accelerator; the motor began to growl and the Sergeant transferred his gaze to his shoes and steadfastly kept it there. We sailed along until we came to Sloane Street, turned into it, skirted the corner of Hyde Park and wheeled into Piccadilly, endangered a few lives, and turned into Dover Street. We all got out and went into a building and up to the second floor. It was a glittering beauty parlor, full of modern decoration and up-stage young ladies, but MacMasters was in a hurry and cut short all attempts at a somewhat languid formality; in a very short time we were in the manager's office, seated in chairs while the manager, morning coat and all, looked askance at us.

"Lady Irene Wrexford-Bond?" the manager asked, after MacMasters had introduced himself and asked if she was one of his clients. "Yes, Inspector. One of our most valued ones."

"Does she have a particular operator?"

"Yes. Most of our clients do, you know. In fact, I think Lady Irene first recommended the young lady in question. We were fully staffed at the time, but of course. . . . Such distinguished patronage. This is all rather confidential, really."

"I see," MacMasters said. "Bit of a squeeze play, eh?" The manager looked uncomprehendingly at him, and he suddenly raised his eyebrows. "Can you tell me when her lunch hour comes?"

"At one, Inspector."

"And was she out yesterday before her regular hour? About twelve or so? Twelve-thirty, maybe, or twelve forty-five?" The manager started to reach for his phone. "Find out, while you're at it," MacMasters said, "what time Lady Irene was here."

The manager picked up his phone and asked for a Mrs. Gervaise. "Are you there?" he inquired. "I would like to know if Miss Fox was out yesterday morning for any reason?" He listened. "Yes," he said. "Headache, what? Yes. The time?" He listened again. "What time was Lady Irene here?" More listening. "Thank you, that will be all." He hung up, and turned to MacMasters again. "Miss Fox had a headache after her appointment with Lady Irene and went out about 12:35 for medicine. She was back at 12:55. Lady Irene's appointment was from 11:15 until 12:15."

"Lady Irene had appointments here two days in succession. Is that her usual practice?"

"It has never happened before, Inspector."

"Thanks," MacMasters said. "I wonder, now, if we could see Miss Fox in here for a little conversation."

The manager looked indecisive. "Lady Irene, you know—"

"Lady Irene," MacMasters said, "will never hear about it."

The manager stared at him. "Yes," he said, in a voice that reminded me of someone shrinking from a sudden and horrid suspicion. "Of course, Inspector. I . . . I hope it will not be necessary for me . . . ah . . . to be about."

"Not in the least."

The manager stood up and went out. In several minutes a tall, beautifully made-up girl came in. She was, I think, a little nervous, but carried it very well. She glanced quickly at the Sergeant and me, then her regard fixed on MacMasters.

"Sit down, Miss Fox," MacMasters said. "I'm Inspector MacMasters." She didn't say anything. "Where did you meet Lady Irene?"

Miss Fox dropped her glance and a slight frown appeared between her eyebrows. "On the Riviera," she said, after a minute.

"You spent some time at her villa?"

Miss Fox's fingers twitched, very slightly. "Hadn't you better ask Lady Irene?" she asked, after another pause. There was a suspicion of sullenness in her tone, and maybe a little fright.

"Perhaps I'd better," MacMasters said tartly, "ask the French Sûreté. They're rather broadminded, but they don't keep their eyes shut on that account. Let's not have any foolishness, Miss Fox. I'm not interested in what you did on the Riviera."

"I haven't seen her for some time," the girl said defiantly, "except here in the shop."

"Good," MacMasters said imperturbably.

"I don't care what she's told you," Miss Fox said. "I can prove it. I can prove what I say."

"Good again," MacMasters said. "She kept fresh in your mind, I take it, that you owed her a certain amount of respect?"

"She's a devil!" the girl burst out. "I didn't have any money then and no job, and she's been holding something over me ever since. She's threatened to turn me in. . . . What could I do?" she demanded, almost tearfully. "I haven't any influence."

"She made you get morphine for her?" MacMasters asked.

For an instant Miss Fox looked extremely surprised, and then chagrined. "Oh!" she said. "I thought she'd talked about something else . . . Something else." She took a deep breath. "Yes," she said. "She made me get morphine. I couldn't get much of it. I had a friend who's a doctor, but he wouldn't give me much. I couldn't tell him, could I? I told him that Mrs. . . . Mrs. Gervaise wanted it, or I wouldn't have my job here. And when I couldn't get as much as Lady Irene wanted, she began to threaten again. She was in here yesterday and today too, but I didn't have any. I can't get any more. I might as well have said so at the beginning."

"A pretty picture all around," MacMasters said. "If you don't handle any more of it you'll be all right, but if you do it'll be Wormwood Scrubs or some other dank and dismal place."

Miss Fox looked up quickly. "Do you mean you're not going to arrest me?" she asked.

"I don't want you. I've got—"

"But I'll have to be a witness if she's in trouble, won't I?" she interrupted.

"Please," MacMasters said, "avert your mind from catastrophe. We've got other things to bother us. Now, then: did you make a telephone call for Lady Irene yesterday when you went out with your headache?"

"Yes," she said quickly. Her relief had speeded up her answers. "Yes, she made me do it because I hadn't the morphine. She made me ring up the Dorchester and leave a message for Miss Dwight, the tennis player. I didn't want to do it. I've read about Miss Dwight and the Wimbledon match in the papers. I didn't want anything to do with her."

"What was the message?"

"I was to leave a message that I'd call again. I was to say that I was Cynthia Blythe."

"Did you ever see Miss Dwight?"

"No, Inspector."

"Lady Irene never sent you to the Dorchester to see her?"

"No."

"How tall are you?"

"Five feet ten, nearly."

"You never heard anything about Cynthia Blythe until yesterday? I'd recommend that you give the correct answer."

"No, Inspector."

"How long have you worked here, steadily?"

"Nearly two months. It wasn't really bad about the morphine until three weeks ago, although she made me get a little before that."

"Do you know where Lady Irene got it before making you get it for her?"

"No."

"Have you ever talked to Lady Irene, or anyone connected with her, about anything except the morphine?"

"I never talked to anyone connected with her, Inspector. And I never talked to her about anything except what she wanted me to do for her—about the morphine and the phone call, I mean."

"That will be all," MacMasters said. "Try Brighton for your next vacation. Heaven seems to protect a little better at Brighton."

"Yes, Inspector. Thank you so much." She went out, looking slightly dazed and more than slightly relieved.

"Such capers!" MacMasters said. "And we haven't got Cynthia yet. Lady Irene must have heard all of that little confab of yours with Andrews, and taken a chance on Cynthia. She gathered that you were a stool pigeon, and felt sure that Miss Dwight's line was tapped. She wanted to confuse things a little."

"How do you explain the telephone call and the man with the mirror, sir?" the Sergeant asked. "They coordinated."

"I don't explain them, yet. This girl doesn't know anything about Lady Irene. All we've found out is that Lady Irene probably set this girl up in here several months ago because she saw that Garcia in Limehouse was slipping; the girl couldn't deliver as often as necessary when Garcia finally quit handling it, so she had to count pretty heavily on Azarin. She made that last call purportedly coming from Cynthia Blythe, because she thought it would help Azarin. If she hadn't been knocked over we wouldn't have known that much. Wait for me in the street; I want to say a word or two to the manager."

We went out, down the stairs, and waited before the building. It was getting on towards dinner time. There were a lot of things I wanted to ask the Sergeant but a sort of inertia had taken hold of me; I'd hoped that Lady Irene's death would have brought something out, something more, narrowing things down to shut Betty out. It hadn't, I was sure of that; Lady Irene had merely been another event like Tomayo, accidental and, basically, unimportant. She'd had an ax to grind. Like Tomayo, she had got into the mess long after it started, and her call, the last call coming from Cynthia, had been the only one she had made. MacMasters came out, and we walked to his car. He gestured for us to get in.

"You might as well come to my place for a bite of food," he said. "I've called Nick." He was grinning slightly, as though he had something up his sleeve; the Sergeant looked at him and settled back into his seat. For once MacMasters drove like a civilized man. He said: "I called up the A. C. and gave him a polite wigging about Cynthia, Sergeant. I think she's got out of London."

He didn't say any more until we got to his place. We went in, followed him into the back room—and there was Andrews. He was sitting between two plain-clothes men, with a black eye and his tie under one ear, in a brown sack suit and spats; a false moustache he held in one hand and eyed ruefully. He looked very strange in that pleasant room. He glanced up as we came in and recognized me and started to rise; but the two plain-clothes men took hold of him from either side and held him down.

"Where did you get him?" MacMasters asked.

"He stopped in to talk to Mr. Wilfred Ballantine, sir," one of the men said. "It's a pleasure he's turned up. It takes a number of men to watch every good art dealer in London, sir."

"Ballantine!" Andrews said suddenly, in a scornful voice. "He never heard of it."

"Never heard of what?" MacMasters asked. He motioned the two men away, and moved over and sat down next to Andrews. His tone was most confidential; he had suddenly taken on an air of great good-fellowship, with a touch of respect; it was all laid on pretty thick. "Heard of what, sir? After all, Ballantine's only British, and the British are a little slow in these matters."

Andrews nodded, and studied him for a moment. "Why, the da Vinci, of course. I can tell you. You seem to be a man of some perception. You are right about the British, sir, particularly British art dealers. The stupidest race God

ever saw fit to create. I talked to them! I talked to hundreds
of them!"

"It must have been very trying," MacMasters said sym-
pathetically.

"Trying? Trying indeed. It is here. I know it is here. It
was brought from Italy, smuggled in, even with the frame
on it. A couple of simple mouldings, gilded, and between
them a flat band of inlaid wood . . . dark and light squares,
you know, in a geometrical pattern."

"Yes, yes," MacMasters said. "Intarsia, eh?"

"By George!" Andrews said. "You know! Cesare Borgia
gave it to Lucrezia. History says he was in a rage with her
for marrying the Duke, but I think he was glad to get rid
of her." He was quiet for a moment, then suddenly took
MacMasters by the lapels and fairly screeched at him: "The
greatest masterpiece in the world, the companion piece to
the Mona Lisa, and they hide it from me, then grin like asses
and say I must be mistaken!" He stood up and fairly danced
about; the two plain-clothes men stirred near the door, but
MacMasters waved them back. "Cesare Borgia as the opposite of Mona Lisa! That Christ-like face, with the cruel eyes
and bull neck, that man of blood and betrayals and murders!
Not only one picture did da Vinci do, not only the Mona
Lisa, but a pair of them! Complementing each other. I can
see it now, that face with its close-set eyes and long curls,
the white silk shirt showing a little at the neck, the furred
jacket, the flat cap! And behind him a landscape with fantastic cliffs, with dark blue and green shadows, and behind
it all a cold flaring light!" As suddenly as he had jumped up
he sat down again and grabbed MacMasters' lapels again.

"It's worth a million dollars!" he said, suddenly dropping
his voice almost to a whisper. "That's why Azarin was so
interested in it. He pretended there was no such thing, then

had me shadowed to take it away from me if I found it. I looked everywhere, I looked in Limehouse where that Spanish thief had already promised it to Gasden. He didn't have it. He never had his hands on it. He only deals in poisons and drugs and smuggled things from everywhere, and that bitch of an Irene sent me there to get rid of me so she could go to Wimbledon. When she saw that Azarin crook she had no more time for me, she was so gone on him. And he, like a damned cold-blooded spider, he was working them all against each other. He pretended he'd marry Marie if she won the matches, he pretended he'd marry Irene to get her money after he lost his own, he pretended he'd marry that Norwegian she-wolf just to keep her where he wanted her."

He fell silent again for a moment. "And he pretended to think there was no portrait of Cesare," he said, in a reasonable tone, which suddenly changed to a screech again: "They were all in cahoots with him, every damned art dealer! I took enough of their slack. I began to knock them down. When Irene sneaked into the hall and heard me talk to Cameron I knew the pair of them would be after me, they'd knock me out like they knocked out Marie. When that Dwight girl asked me on the boat where she could get . . ." He suddenly closed his mouth like a rat trap, and his eyes flicked slyly toward me. "I told her to phone Irene," he said, in a mumble. "She did it, too. The day after she landed."

"Get what?" MacMasters said, leaning forward. "What did she want to get? When did she ask you that?"

"Just before it stormed," Andrews said.

"What did she want?"

"Something she couldn't get anywhere else, of course," Andrews said, and his face took on a mulish expression. "I won't be mixed up in it."

"Very sound," MacMasters said.

"I thought there might be some difficulty about the picture," Andrews said. "That's why I got Azarin. We were going to divide on it. Sell it, of course. It was too valuable for my modest collection. I knew Azarin could get it if anybody could. Then he got mixed up in that other business. One villainy at a time wasn't enough for him."

"You think he did away with Marie? What makes you think that?"

"He'll get well paid for it. There was a tall, dark man always after him. I saw them together a couple of times before the match, and I saw the same man talking with Miss Dwight in the lobby of the Dorchester. Didn't I say tennis had taken a sad fall?" he asked, turning to me. "I expressed myself to you very thoroughly. *Sic transit,* and so on. Where's my moustache?"

"If I told you where that painting was," MacMasters said, "would you tell me what Miss Dwight wanted to get?"

Andrews moved toward him by a series of little side jumps. "Would I?" he asked. "Would I?" His eyes narrowed. "I wouldn't!" he shouted, jumping up. "I wouldn't! You can't get me into anything else, you . . ." He moved into the middle of the room; MacMasters stood up. "You damned, deceitful, double-crossing low baboon! You're another thief. I see it all! I see every bit of it. Cameron wanted it too, he got you in with him, you send men after me to catch me and bring me here and try to get over me with smooth words—" He suddenly made a dive at MacMasters, who sidestepped and tripped him; the plain-clothes men, saying "There now!" got him by the arms and straightened him up. He stopped struggling, and stood glowering at us.

"Take him along," MacMasters said, and reached into his pocket. He brought out a folded sheet of yellow paper, evidently a radiogram, and handed it to one of the men. "It's a report from Bellevue Hospital, in New York. Give them that."

The man took it, pocketed it, and turning Andrews between them, they led him out. MacMasters sat down.

"For sheer *opera bouffe* this is the greatest case I've ever struck," he remarked. "Nick!" Nick came in, and was told to serve drinks. "He wasn't far wrong at that. If there had been another Leonardo, a companion piece to the Mona Lisa, it would be worth any price. Cesare would have been a wonderful type for it." He took out a cigarette and lit it. "The savage of every age; the ruthless conqueror. It's too bad, Cameron, you talked Andrews into that first drink. He seems to suffer from cyclic changes of personality, and alcohol touches him off. A single drink, according to Bellevue. Probably when he retired from business the change unsettled him a little, too. I hope he doesn't go into paranoia. How much of his ranting do you think's credible, Sergeant?"

"All the parts except about the picture sounded credible to me, sir. He seemed to know quite rationally what went on about him. I mean about Azarin and Lady Irene and all that, sir."

"Amen," MacMasters said. "He was right about Garcia, for the boys have turned up a few more details, such as smuggling raw opium, atropine and some stolen stones, mostly from India. And how else would Andrews know about Saunders if he hadn't seen him with Miss Dwight and Azarin? When Saunders was shadowing him, Saunders wasn't Saunders; he was the man with the limp. As to Azarin playing off the women against each other, I think he's got something there, too. When Lady Irene's will is probated, we'll find out if she'd been talked into changing the beneficiary before she fell down the steps. He must be right about Miss Dwight's phone call to Lady Irene."

I couldn't stand any more of it. "Rubbish!" I said. "You aren't going to pretend to believe any of his crazy maunderings, are you? He knew Betty was friendly with Gasden, and he's got his insane mind twisted around to where he thinks she's after him."

MacMasters' shoulders rose to his ears, and he threw up his hands like a second-hand clothes man. "He checks pretty well," he said. "But then, all our help in this has come from crackpots. One by one we listen to them, and they all add a stitch. You were the first; you wanted us to protect Miss Dwight from the morphine they had for Lady Irene, and we saw Miss Dwight go into Garcia's and not come out. Gasden was the second; he put us on to Cynthia Blythe. Andrews was the third, for he saw Miss Dwight talking to Batt-Saunders before any of us did. Maybe we'll catch another crackpot who'll put in the buttonholes, then the garment will be ready to try on somebody. There was Tomayo, too, and I've found out, through a long but mild career, that a man's always lying when he gets his hands near his mouth while he talks. Tomayo got his hand near his mouth when I asked him about there being a capsule under Marie's bandage. That would indicate that there was a capsule, or the remains of one; if so, it's gone. I've checked it up in all sorts of cases, in court and out, and talked to psychologists about it." MacMasters moved restlessly, then said abruptly, "Sergeant, call the Yard and see what goes on. Shove them again about Cynthia Blythe; tell them to look around all places of egress from England. If she hasn't showed up for a few days the chances are she's skipped, or tried to. Tell them to check up Lady Irene's solicitors and find out about her will. Tell them we'll be at the Ritz this evening, seeing Brother Saunders. And don't waste any time." "Cameron," he said, turning to me, "Nick says he has a good dinner tonight and you've got to eat some of it. I can't have Nick's feelings hurt."

The Sergeant went out. "Something to drink?" MacMasters asked. "Sherry? Cocktail? I'm having sherry myself."

"No, thanks," I said. I was thinking about Cynthia Blythe. Ever since he'd started things had been narrowing down to her.

CHAPTER FIFTEEN

Although I had small appetite for it, I had to admit Nick's dinner was superb. While we were having coffee and brandy, MacMasters broke into one of his rare moments of complaint. "This is beginning to irritate me, all this rushing around and not enough results. I need a holiday; a good trip somewhere. Just now, I'd choose California. Ever been there?" he asked, staring into his glass.

"Two years ago, on some engine business," I said. "Southern California's become a big aviation center."

"It's a big center for quite a number of things, seems to me—movies, oil, lemons. . . ."

"And don't forget the black widow spiders!" I added. "There's a scourge of them."

"You speak feelingly."

"I ought to, one of them bit me in a beach cabaña at Santa Monica. My leg swelled up like a house—I had to stay in bed for three days. Of course one spider can't kill you, but it can make you pretty sick."

"They sound like violent little beasts. Well," he said, getting up suddenly, "time to get going on the old grind again. I have to make a couple of phone calls, then we'll go over to the Ritz." He went out, closing the door behind him.

I sat waiting for about three-quarters of an hour, and became pretty impatient. "Come on, Cameron, sorry to have
been so slow," he called from the hall. "Come on, Sergeant!"
he called in another direction; the Sergeant was evidently
somewhere talking to Nick.

We drove to the Ritz. MacMasters spoke for a moment
with the clerk in the lobby; then we were ushered into the
manager's office. Evidently he was expecting us.

"I'll have the information in a moment, Inspector," he
said. The phone rang; he listened, writing down a string of
dates and numbers. "Right," he said, and hung up. "This
lame man named Conover you want to know about checked
out this afternoon. He had a room next to Mr. Batt. According to the records, he made no phone calls. Mr. Batt,
however, has a list of phone calls to Wimbledon. He's rung
up Wimbledon rather consistently."

"Let's have the phone," MacMasters said. He asked for
Central. "MacMasters, Scotland Yard," he said. "Please give
me the name and address of the subscriber to whom the
following calls were made. . . ." He read the list of the calls
and their dates and hung up. "What's the Dorchester number?" he asked, and when the manager told him he shook his
head. "Not on this list." Then, to me, "If it was a plant the
man would have called her up." Turning to the manager he
asked, "Did any of your clerks ever speak of this lame man,
this Conover? Did they comment on his scar? Or, maybe it
would be handier if one of the clerks could come in here."

The manager rang a buzzer, and a clerk came in. In answer to the manager's questions he said, "I can't say that
we paid particular attention to Mr. Conover. He came in
during the Wimbledon rush, a day or so before the matches.
A good many of the Ascot people were here too."

"A man named Batt stayed for several weeks too, didn't he?" MacMasters asked.

"Yes, sir."

"You never noticed any resemblance between them, by any chance?"

"No, I can't say that we did."

"Did Batt ask for any particular room? For that room he was in?"

"I had better go back and check the correspondence," the clerk said, after thinking for a moment. He went out, and the manager said, deferentially to MacMasters, "Is all this something I shouldn't know, Inspector?"

"It's a dead secret," MacMasters said. "We're going to lug off half your guests to the hoosegow. This lame man came here at the wrong time for somebody's innocence. If he'd arrived a week sooner . . ." The manager looked disturbed; the clerk returned and handed a letter to MacMasters.

"Sentimental reasons, eh?" he said, when he'd read it. "Not many people go to the trouble to justify their reasons for wanting a particular room, do they?"

"Sometimes," the clerk said, "but not often."

The phone rang, the manager answered it, and handed it to MacMasters—who grunted out a "Hello!" listened carefully, said "Thank you," and hung up.

"Not it," he said, and tearing a page off the memorandum pad, he wrote down an address and put it in his pocket. "Looks like another ride, Sergeant!"

The Sergeant manfully repressed a shudder; MacMasters handed the letter back to the clerk, who went out. MacMasters sat staring at us, whistling quietly between his teeth. "More n—rs," he said. "It's a pretty crowded woodpile, eh?" I could see the manager was worried.

"Give me the phone again," said MacMasters. He called the Yard, told them to get the Wimbledon police station or the closest thing to it, rout out the constable on the beat, and find out from him how long the house immediately in back of Azarin's had been occupied, and call back. "Right away," he said. "And don't forget Cynthia Blythe. I pant after her as the hart after the water brooks. Also find out if Azarin's place can be seen from this other house. 'Bye."

"This is beginning to annoy me!" he said. In a few moments the phone rang again; the manager didn't bother to answer it this time. "Hello?" MacMasters said. "Yes. About a month ago? And the houses are perfectly visible to each other? Good. Call me here or at my place if Cynthia Blythe shows up." He replaced the receiver and stood up. "Might as well keep 'em in harness," he said. "Let's go upstairs and talk to this Batt."

"Is he in his room, sir?" the Sergeant asked.

"He's been there ever since dinner. I checked at the desk when we came in. Come along. Thanks," he said to the manager and we went out. In the lobby MacMasters stopped, raised his right wrist with the watch on it, put his left index finger on the nine and slowly ran the finger counter-clockwise until he came to the four. Then he dropped his wrist again. "Just right," he said. "Sergeant, entertain the gentleman with epigrams until I telephone a man."

He went off somewhere, and the Sergeant looked at me rather at a loss. "Maybe you'd better sit down, sir. If I may say so, it looks as if the Inspector is going to spend the evening on the telephone," he said. "What did he mean by epigrams, I wonder?"

"An epigram?" I asked. "Oh, he meant . . ." I stood staring at him, totally unable to define an epigram, and my voice died out. "We'll skip the epigrams," I said finally. "What do you think he's up to?" I asked. "Did he start anything five hours ago?"

"Not that I know of, sir," the Sergeant said. "We were talking to that misguided girl in the hairdressing parlor about that time."

Conversation languished for a space; the clock crawled around to quarter past nine, people went past, and I finally said: "Is there anything else, anything I haven't heard, about Miss Dwight, Sergeant? I'm not asking for any tales out of school, of course, but . . ."

He appeared to be embarrassed. "You've heard about all of it, sir," he said finally, avoiding my eye. There was a look on him as though I'd put him at a nasty disadvantage, as though I'd called something emotional into the conversation; suddenly I felt that he liked me. I don't know why I felt it. "I'd try not to worry about her. If I were you, sir," he said, still not looking at me, "I would indeed. The Inspector's a hard man, if I may say so, sir, without offense."

It was an expert opinion, and I swallowed it. I didn't say any more, and neither did he. We both sat there staring at nothing, for an indeterminate length of time, when MacMasters' voice suddenly made us both jump.

"What?" he asked. "No epigrams? Gloom all over everything? Sergeant, you failed me. I've brought you something." He had three gardenias, one in his buttonhole, one in each hand. "You've each got to put one of these stinking things on. Make Mr. Batt open his eyes."

The Sergeant turned a slightly deeper hue as he took his gardenia and put it woodenly into his buttonhole; we got into an elevator, smelling like a funeral, got out, marched solemnly down the hall, and watched MacMasters knock on Batt's door. He did it with a grin; when Batt opened it and saw the three of us standing there with gardenias on he stared as though bereft of sense.

"Mr. Saunders?" MacMasters asked.

Batt's eyes rolled toward him, with the expression of a rabbit's as it lay in a form with the hounds near it. "Saunders?" he asked. "Some mistake, I think." He started to close the door, but MacMasters had his foot in it. "I *beg* your pardon," Batt said.

"No, no," MacMasters said. "I beg *yours*. Scotland Yard, sir, is always polite. You might ask us in."

Batt considered a moment, then swung the door open with an ill and nervous grace; we all went in.

"Sit down, please," MacMasters said. "You must excuse our funereal decorations, but there has been a death."

Batt sat down at that one; he looked agitated. "A death?" he asked, his voice going up.

"Yes," MacMasters said. "But let us introduce ourselves. I am Inspector MacMasters; this is Sergeant Portrush; this other gentleman you know."

"How would I know him?" Batt asked. "I've never—"

"Come, now," MacMasters said. "If you hadn't seen him with Lady Irene Wrexford-Bond you wouldn't have followed Lady Irene. You wouldn't even have gone to Wimbledon. Am I right?"

I couldn't see his reason for this gambit; the Sergeant, apparently, couldn't either. Batt, however, seemed to find a certain amount of logic in it. His head drew down a little and he sat staring at MacMasters with a sort of somber fascination.

"You wanted to find out what was going on, eh?" MacMasters asked, and added: "My boy, you'll be sold down the river if you're not careful. It's a question of trading horses from now on, and I'd advise you to pick the right horse."

Batt didn't say anything, but his thought processes must have been distinguished in their intensity. A kind of stillness descended upon him. As for MacMasters, he had got his Tar Baby look, and it was revealed to me that he was bluffing.

"Maybe," MacMasters said, "if we took your fingerprints and circulated them around it might turn out that you were a popular gentleman, and in demand. What, now, for example, would you be doing by following a man named Gasden?"

"Gasden?" Batt asked. His feet moved slightly on the rug, very slightly. "I . . . I don't know a man named Gasden."

MacMasters' fingers played a silent tattoo on his knee; and I realized, later than Batt had realized, that MacMasters had tried to confuse him by filling his mind with apprehension about fingerprints in Gasden's room and then slipping in a question about his other personality, Conover. It had almost been successful, too.

"You would have liked him," MacMasters said. "A very amusing fellow he was. However, he's unimportant at the moment. Did you know that Lady Irene was dead?"

"Dead!" Batt exclaimed. He changed color, but didn't move.

"Yes," MacMasters said. "Dead. You may call your friends in Wimbledon . . . but no. Don't call them. Call a man named Azarin, if you want to be sure. He's in Wimbledon too. He lives near your friends. His house backs up to theirs." He sat back, and canted his head a little. "Strange they didn't let you know, isn't it?"

"She can't be dead!" Batt said. "She—"

"Alas!" MacMasters interrupted him. "She is. After you were there she fell down the stairs and killed herself. It is too bad that you went to the bathroom while you were there."

"I didn't go to the bathroom!" Batt shouted. "I wasn't off the first floor!"

"Azarin was under the impression that you did," Mac-Masters said coolly. His eyes were on Batt with a sort of implacable concentration; even the pupils had narrowed. "I told you they'd sell you down the river. Azarin told me (we were there when Lady Irene died, you know) that after your talk with Lady Irene he heard you go up to the bathroom before you left the house."

Batt jumped up. "I didn't talk with Lady Irene!"

"I didn't think so, really," MacMasters said, "but why were you so damned long getting around to admitting it? You got a message when you returned to check Conover out; but that message didn't say anything about Lady Irene's death, did it?"

Batt stood still; he was sweating, and when his glance went to the Sergeant—who was busy with the little black book—he seemed almost ready to shudder. But there was also a sort of listening, withdrawn and calculating quality about him; he must have caught on to something in what MacMasters had said, some uncertainty, which had got by him for several minutes while the pressure was on, and it had suddenly come back to him. "What's this about someone named Conover?" Batt asked. "What's this about checking him out?"

"I thought you knew him," MacMasters said. "A man named Conover. He had the room next door here." He relaxed a little, then took out one of his American cigarettes, lit it, offered Batt one (which was refused), and recrossed his legs. "Were you ever in Conover's room?" he asked, and gestured. "That one?"

Something went on in Batt's head; the thought of fingerprints, probably. "Once or twice," he said. "A few days ago. He saw me in the hall, and asked me in for a drink. I don't know what his name was. I didn't care. I didn't much like his looks."

"Good," MacMasters said imperturbably. "Now that you've had a minute or two for relaxation, what about this spot you're in? Are you more afraid of Azarin or Scotland Yard? You might tell me about what happened when you went into Azarin's house. Let's have done with this Batt-Saunders business; you can keep Conover for another day or so if it suits you. I'm not quite ready for that yet, anyhow. At the moment—if I were you—I'd be more interested in why they didn't say anything about Lady Irene's death."

This tack disconcerted Batt because he couldn't be sure of it. He thought a moment, his eyes restless, then said: "I don't know this Azarin you're talking about. I went out to see my friends, the Gunnes, and as they weren't there I stopped in at the house backing up to theirs to see—"

"Rubbish!" MacMasters interrupted him, in a disgusted tone. "Don't be a complete ass. Besides that, Azarin's maid said you were worried about Lady Irene being there when you knocked on the door. When you found out she was there you almost left. Come along, don't make a holy show of yourself."

"All right," Batt said, turning sullen. "I was there. I had seen Lady Irene and this man," indicating me, "having lunch, and I didn't like it. I went out to ask Azarin what was going on."

"Why?" MacMasters asked, mildly.

"If you've got to know," Batt said, "I was watching a man named Andrews for him. He and this Andrews had some sort of a deal. Andrews was staying with Lady Irene, and suddenly skipped out. I know Lady Irene; I'm afraid of her. She'll do anything. She's wanted to get Azarin to marry her ever since she saw him, and I thought she and Andrews were working something on Azarin together. After Andrews got out of sight and Lady Irene had such a comfy little talk with this man," indicating me again, "I thought she was selling out Azarin. I wanted to find out if he knew it, and where I stood if anything happened."

"Neat," MacMasters said, "and not in the least gaudy. You didn't follow Andrews down to Limehouse a few nights ago?"

"No," Batt said. "I gathered there was another man working for Azarin on it, but I never met him. I got my orders, and that was all I knew about it." He suddenly looked up and snapped his fingers. "By God!" he said. "Do you think that man in the next room, the one you just talked about, could have been Azarin's other man? If he was, he was watching me too."

MacMasters had leaned back; there was an expression on his face such as a critic gets while watching an actor go through a role. He snapped his fingers too. "By God!" he said, mimicking Batt to perfection. "You deserve a more . . . ah . . . spacious vehicle! Well, everything comes out in the wash, and you might sing a rather different tune when the wringer gets going. You didn't talk to Lady Irene, then?"

"I talked to Azarin and Miss Lindstrom. Lady Irene went out of the room. Into that little den thing, I think."

"You'd never used the name Saunders before, eh?"

"No."

"Did these messages come from Azarin or Miss Lindstrom?"

"I wouldn't know that," Batt said.

MacMasters yawned. Then, looking at Batt, he said in a tone tinged with ironic amusement: "Sergeant, you can leave now. Go past the Yard, and get the routine started on this man. We might need a few memory aids for him later on. Tell them to get going on that house backing up to Azarin's, too. We might as well know a little about that and the people in it."

Batt walked to the window; he stood with his back to us as the Sergeant went out, and turned again as the door closed. He was holding himself very straight, but his face had a sort of haggard shadow on it. He didn't say anything; he just stood there.

MacMasters got up. "It would be better," he said, "if you didn't go rushing here and there, ringing people up. It might be misunderstood. I'm telling you this out of the kindness of my heart, and because you have moments of naiveté. Come on, Cameron."

We went out, down in the elevator, and after MacMasters had spoken a few words to a man sitting in the lobby we went to his car. Neither of us felt talkative; I stood by the side of the car for a moment after he'd got in. I wanted to say something, but nothing would straighten out in my mind. He watched me, a little distantly, a little ironically, then stepped on the starter. The motor caught and began slowly to turn over. "Well," he said. "See you tomorrow. Carry on, my lad, carry on."

I stepped back and the Packard slid away. I walked slowly to the Mayfair and went up to my room. Just as I was getting into bed the phone rang. It was MacMasters. "Dogged perseverance has triumphed," he said. "Get yourself ready early." He hung up, and I sat there staring at the phone.

CHAPTER SIXTEEN

At breakfast next morning as I sat having a couple of extra cups of strong black coffee, I let my mind moved from point to point over the panorama of the case and as I did so it took on the actuality of an unbelievably complex picture. I suspected from what MacMasters said on the phone the night before that he'd got his hands on Cynthia Blythe. An important part of the whole thing had been the hunt for her, with his other endeavors a kind of sideline in which he had been pulling odds and ends together while he waited for the implacable net to spread all over England and entangle her. It almost stopped the imagination to consider the number of men, the sheer amount of effort, that had been required to come up with that one girl.

My imagination, so fertile at picturing people running about, refused to work when it came to that miserable girl: what she would say about Betty, about me, what she would make up in answer to MacMasters' questions. I swallowed the last of the coffee just as there was a knock at the door.

It was MacMasters, and he had another flower in his buttonhole; a blue one this time. "Like it?" he asked, as he came into the room. "It's the color of hope."

"I can stand it, if you don't talk so much!"

"I always talk too much," he said. "It relieves the feeling that I'm no single-handed hero of fiction, but a symbol of efficiency. I'm slip-shod, erratic, a bluffer and impolite to customers. I don't like to get out of bed in the morning; I have a vindictive nature—but fate is kind and finds Cynthia Blythe for me in Bognor Regis—a wide place in the road down the Channel. Very indicative, eh?"

"What's indicative of what?" I asked. I didn't care.

"The wide place in the road," he said. "But never mind, the Sergeant will be back soon. He went to get her. Let's go."

"I hate to go with you, but I've got to," I said.

"I'll say you've got to! It'll be a handy little object lesson to you if you ever take another transatlantic boat ride. And besides I may need you. I don't want to round up all these people and drag them around to the A. C.'s office for the purpose of a one-act dramatic sketch which will, in the last few minutes of this entertaining affair, unmask the guilty villain—or maybe not. That would be too much of a strain! Did I tell you that the Home Office experts are stalled again? Evidence of morphine in Lady Irene's post-mortem, but not enough to be fatal—no evidence of peritonitis. Lady Irene's heart, outside of being black because of her evil life, was right enough. Nobody seemed to care about the color. Odd, isn't it?"

"Come on, let's go," I said. I couldn't stand him talking anymore; I got my hat and we went downstairs into the bar. I ordered a brandy.

"A very nice poison," he continued. "There are a few that are damned difficult to find. Histamine, toxalbumin from castor oil beans, things like that. Hardly ever used to murder people. They stick to arsenic and prussic acid with an appalling lack of imagination. Toxicology books are easy to get, too."

He lit a cigarette and went on talking. I stood by the bar half listening to him, with my mind on Betty. But I couldn't dismiss him from my mind entirely; he filled the eye. His long frame, his eyebrows, the air of faintly ironic amusement which seldom left him, all added up to the sum of an exterior beneath which there seemed to lurk the capacity for violence. It made an equivocal and puzzling thing out of the first impression I had had of him—I had thought he liked to take his time. Now I knew he did not take his time, once he got into action; he pushed into things, and let the legmen straighten up after him.

My attention came back to what he was saying: ". . . and you look as though you might have enjoyed yourself once upon a time," he was saying, "you shoot, don't you? Freeze in duck blinds, and that sort of thing?"

"I crawl off once in a while," I said. "To the North Woods or after ducks. When I get fed up with tinkering on airplane motors."

"Uh-huh," he said. "So you let the Cosmic Urge mess you up. You're as bad as Andrews. Well, let's get on with it."

He walked along with his glance on the pavement, whistling his damned "John Peel," and I walked by his side in as gloomy a frame of mind as I could ever remember having. When we got to the Dorchester the palms of my hands were wet, and the hollow feeling inside of me was hollower than ever. We walked through the front lobby and into the rear one; there weren't many people about at that time of day, and I saw at once the Sergeant and Cynthia Blythe sitting behind one of the little tea tables. The Sergeant looked very brushed and competent, and stood up; the girl sat where she was, watching us across the room. Her features were coldly expressionless and stony. And under this mask were lines that wouldn't come out; lines of discontent and malice.

"Good morning," MacMasters said. "Good morning, Miss Blythe." Before she could say anything he turned from her and gestured to the Sergeant. "Go up to what's his name's office," he said, "and have him send that elevator boy here." The Sergeant went over to the elevators and vanished from sight; MacMasters sat down. "I'm glad to see you," he said, to Cynthia Blythe.

"Will you tell me," she asked icily, "what this ridiculous procedure is about? Why I should be disturbed at Bognor Regis and brought here by that wooden-headed idiot?"

"It's his heart that's solid British oak," MacMasters said pleasantly. "Not his head. Old Bailey would be in a sad way without him. You've heard of Old Bailey, I take it? It's not very decorative, but it works. You know Mr. Cameron." She looked at me. For an instant her face took on an indescribable expression of dislike tinged with bitterness. We sat down. "Pleasant place, Bognor Regis," MacMasters went on, "but lonely. Did you have money up on the matches?"

"No," she said. She almost bit the syllable in half.

"That," MacMasters said, "is unusual in the circles in which we've been moving." He looked up, and I followed his glance. The Sergeant and an elevator boy were standing about halfway across the lobby, looking at Cynthia Blythe; then they spoke a few words to each other and the boy went back to his elevator. The Sergeant came over.

"Identification is complete, sir," he said. "There is no doubt in the lift boy's mind about his having seen Miss Blythe before."

"Good," MacMasters said, and turned to her. "I'm going to ask you to go upstairs with us, Miss Blythe."

"Why?" she asked.

"To meet Miss Dwight. I—"

She interrupted him. "I won't go," she said. "You cannot make me go. This farce has gone on long enough. I will only act through the advice of an attorney."

MacMasters sighed. "They call them solicitors here," he said. "You're within your rights, but we'll forget about your rights for the moment. What with one thing and another, I've been irritated long enough by people talking about their rights. If you don't come along quietly I'll have the Sergeant carry you, and you can make any sort of scene you like. The management won't mind." He gestured. "However, you can sue afterward if you wish. Gross indignities to the person, coercion, mayhem . . . I'll write you out a list. Sergeant!"

"Yes, sir," the Sergeant said. He looked supremely un-comfortable; he looked as though he wanted to crawl off.

The bluff worked; she turned white with rage but stood up. MacMasters was on his feet at once, beside her; he took her arm courteously, but she shook him off. The four of us walked to the waiting elevator, the boy closed the door, and we went up.

Nobody spoke. There was a strange atmosphere in that elevator, a confusion between fury, tensity and farce. She stood looking straight before her, pale, her eyes hard; and as I watched, she flashed me a look, like the one she had given me downstairs. Then she glanced away and her jaw tight-ened. I could see the muscles quiver. I noticed, as I had on the boat, that she was about the same general build as Betty and not unlike, except her face, which was entirely different. The elevator stopped, we got out and walked down the hall. MacMasters knocked at Betty's door, and there was the sud-den feeling in the air of everyone girding himself for battle.

The door opened suddenly, and Betty stood there. For an instant she was perfectly motionless. "Oh, David!" she

said, surprised. She seemed to want to say something more
to me. Then she looked at MacMasters, and finally at Cynthia Blythe. She stiffened and her face became perfectly expressionless. She asked us in with icy politeness.

"A little symposium," MacMasters said. "To clear the air.
I hope you don't mind all of us coming."

Betty moved back without answering, and we went into
the room. I watched her; I couldn't get my eyes off her.
There ran up my back a sort of prickle. After all, did she
have some serious connection with the crime?

MacMasters pulled a chair over until its back was against
the door, and sat down on it. He crossed his legs and looked
around; his eyebrows had drawn down, and there was a look
on him such as might have been on a cat which had just got
away with a pint of cream.

"Sit down everybody," he said. "As I said, we are going
to clear the air—and incidentally help the Sergeant fill up
his little black book. I would prefer that the truth prevail.
It's much simpler all around. Miss Blythe, you were on the
Princess Victoria?"

"Yes," she said.

"Did you, by any chance, talk to Helga Lindstrom on the
boat deck after dinner on the last night out?"

"No," she said, "why should I? *I* wasn't going to play
against Marie Azarin at Wimbledon!" There, I thought,
she'd begun to try to implicate Betty already.

"A good start," MacMasters said. "Miss Blythe, why did
you engage passage on the *Princess Victoria?*"

"To get to England, of course."

"There are other ships," MacMasters said. "You knew
that Miss Dwight was sailing on her?"

"Yes. I read it by chance in the paper. But it had nothing
to do with my choice of this ship."

"Did you know Miss Dwight?"

"No," she answered.

"Did you know anyone else on the ship?" MacMasters asked.

"Yes, I knew David Cameron," she said, but she did not look at me.

"Well, well! That's interesting!" he said, glancing at me. "Did you meet Miss Dwight on the ship?" He was asking her questions rapidly.

"No, not exactly. She spoke to me on the fifth day of the voyage. She saw that there was some resemblance between us—the same general build, and fair hair, and that it might be easy for people to confuse us under certain circumstances. She wanted me to approach Azarin for her. She was afraid Marie Azarin would beat her at Wimbledon. Everyone knows he is not an honest man. Miss Dwight's aunt is very rich . . ." she implied that she had left much unsaid.

"I did not speak to Miss Blythe, nor did I ask her to approach Azarin for me!" said Betty, looking straight at Mac-Masters before he could ask her the question.

"So," MacMasters continued, addressing Cynthia Blythe, "did you approach Azarin for Miss Dwight?"

"I did not!"

"Why not?"

"Because I didn't want to get mixed up in anything like that. Then she offered me a much larger sum of money, but I wouldn't take it."

There was a short silence. Cynthia Blythe sat back with a glance of dislike at Betty and one of triumph at me. Betty maintained an attitude of scornful aloofness.

Cynthia Blythe went on of her own accord. "She called me on the phone and told me to come to the deck outside her cabin and she would hand out her marten jacket through the porthole; then I was to call the Lindstrom woman and meet her on the boat deck. I was supposed to wear a white frock, like hers—it was all a part of the act—and when I refused, she did it herself. She would have done anything to win the match!"

"How do you account for the disappearance of the marten cape?" MacMasters asked.

"I suppose she threw it overboard, then reported it was stolen, so as to make people think that someone else had worn it during the Lindstrom conversation."

"Rather disillusioning, eh?" MacMasters said. "And what did you come here to the hotel for, that time? Blackmail?"

"Blackmail?" Cynthia Blythe asked with an edge on her voice. "Do you think I want any of her aunt's money? I came here because after Marie Azarin died I began to worry. I could see that I might be one of the people you wanted to find. I warned Betty Dwight to keep my name out of it, or I would go to Scotland Yard and tell them about what I had seen. Do you blame me for being worried?"

"Not in the least," said MacMasters. "And you were quite right in thinking you might be one of the people we wanted to find! However, it seems a little strange that Miss Dwight wanted to get someone who looked like her to talk to Helga Lindstrom. What is your idea about this, Miss Dwight?"

Betty didn't answer; she didn't move.

Cynthia Blythe said quickly, "Her idea was to let me run the risk. I would have been well-paid for it—but I didn't want to be paid for anything underhanded."

"Was there any plan mentioned by Miss Dwight? Did she say what idea she had in mind for interfering with Marie Azarin's game?"

"No, first she wanted to see if Azarin would be interested in money."

"And so, Miss Dwight came twice to your cabin to try to convince you," MacMasters said. "It seems to me she was taking a chance, but the whole thing's so cock-eyed it seems to make sense."

Cynthia Blythe began to laugh hysterically; MacMasters suddenly stood up and walked to the window. "Sergeant," he said, "escort Miss Dwight to her room. I would like to talk to Miss Blythe."

Betty looked at me appealingly. I jumped to my feet. I only knew that I wanted to hold her in my arms, to comfort her. "Betty!" I said.

"Sit down!" MacMasters said sharply.

"To hell with you!" I said and took a step.

He was quick; he moved more quickly than any man I had ever seen, and the Sergeant moved with him. They were in front of me before I even knew they were out of their chairs. Somebody's foot caught my ankle expertly and I went down with a crash that must have rocked the walls. The next thing I knew the Sergeant was sitting calmly on my chest, holding my arms extended.

"There now," he was saying, politely. "There now, sir."

I struggled furiously, but it would have been as easy to dislodge a mountain. MacMasters moved about him, darting in to add his weight where it was needed; and after a moment I saw the futility of it and gave up. I was panting and ready to weep with rage, but MacMasters started to laugh. It was all very ridiculous.

"The Sergeant," MacMasters said, when he stopped laughing, "carries his center of gravity low, so you might as well behave yourself. If you'll go back to your chair I'll let you up."

Cynthia Blythe was staring at me, and I felt like a fool. "All right," I said crossly. "I'll go back."

The Sergeant got up and went after Betty; I went back to my chair, and MacMasters went back to his. He grinned at me and turned to Cynthia Blythe.

"What," he asked, "were you doing in Helga Lindstrom's cabin?" His voice cracked out, clipped and cold, and Cynthia Blythe straightened up spasmodically in her chair. Her jaw dropped, her mouth fell open, her eyes opened widely; she looked as though she was going to scream. "Come out with it!" MacMasters rapped out, on the heels of his question. He half started from his chair. His hands shot out; it was all very melodramatic.

Her face lost the look of surprise and swiftly took one of fear. "I was looking!" she cried out. "Looking!" Her face changed again, as swiftly as before, and disbelief was on it, disbelief and protest; then she squirmed about with a single motion and beat the back of her chair fiercely with both hands. "I was looking!" she said again, now turning on him, showing her teeth in a snarl. She dropped her head into her hands and began to cry violently.

MacMasters turned to me. "Bluff again," he said in an undertone. "But it worked. Some excuse for it this time, though. She's a rank amateur. Nobody but a rank amateur would get out of London when the heat was on and go to Bognor Regis. If a stray cat comes into Bognor Regis everybody knows about it in half an hour. There was a little confusion, remember? Miss Dwight was seen before Miss Blythe's cabin door once, with her hand on the knob, or knocking. But she didn't go in, because Miss Blythe wasn't there. Miss Blythe was at that moment ransacking Miss Lindstrom's cabin. When Miss Dwight shook Captain Brererton's bloodhounds and got out of sight on that second trip of hers she went to Miss Blythe's cabin again and found her in. And that straightens out who was where—and when. Miss Blythe!"

She raised her head reluctantly and looked at him; her face was smeared with tears and distraught. She looked somehow deranged.

"You might as well tell me the rest of it," MacMaster said. "You *stole* that marten jacket?" She nodded. "And called Miss Lindstrom?" She nodded again. "And she'd have nothing to do with you, eh?"

Cynthia Blythe stiffened a little. "She . . . She . . ."

"Come," MacMasters said. "If she'd listened to you, you wouldn't have ransacked her cabin. You tell me. It's easier."

"I hate Betty Dwight!" Cynthia Blythe said, clenching her hands. "I hate her—she took him away from me . . ." She began to cry again with very disconsolate sounds.

MacMasters said, "Well, I'll be damned!" he said. "Took whom *away?*"

"David!" she cried out woefully.

I couldn't believe my ears; the girl must be crazy.

"I met him in Chicago," she went on, "and I was wild about him, but he paid no attention to me. When I was in New York I called him up, but they said he was going abroad. . . . I found out he was going on the *Princess Victoria*, so I went on it too. I saw him the third night out, he was with Betty Dwight. I could see he was already in love with her. He was very short with me. I began then to hate her—she was famous and beautiful and had everything."

"So then what did you think you would do?" asked Mac-Masters.

"I didn't know exactly. I wished I could find some way of turning David against her. Then I thought of the argument she and Marie Azarin had had in the dining salon. . . ."

"You thought you might be able to do Marie Azarin a good turn, eh?" MacMasters asked.

"I had to—I had to stop him liking Betty Dwight. I knew as everybody does, that Azarin is a dishonest man— that he wouldn't stop at anything. So, I decided to watch Betty Dwight closely and when she left her cabin, pick up something of hers. The idea wasn't clear in my mind, but I thought I might take her marten cape, fix my hair like hers which is about the same color and arrange a meeting with the Lindstrom woman so that if anyone saw me they would think it was Betty Dwight. Or, I thought that if I had something of hers I might then take something from Lindstrom's or Azarin's cabin and leave the thing that belonged to Betty Dwight as a clue, as if she had dropped it by mistake. I wanted to cause trouble for her. I hadn't made up my mind . . ."

"It seems to me you were going to a good deal of unnecessary trouble," said MacMasters.

"Oh, no, I wasn't!

"Well," she went on, "when I was waiting around that evening I saw Betty Dwight leave her cabin. She had on her marten cape. I followed her up to the boat deck. I got behind a lifeboat and watched. She walked up and down a couple of times, and I was just going to run down and take something out of her room when I saw Helga Lindstrom walking down the deck towards her. Betty Dwight moved in a little toward a boat to let her pass, but the Lindstrom woman walked towards her, came even and stopped. They stood talking for a moment. Lindstrom seemed nervous and looked up and down the deck. After a moment or two Betty Dwight crossed the deck quickly and went back to her cabin. Lindstrom walked on around the boat. I was just going to hurry after Betty Dwight when I saw David Cameron. He had evidently been watching them too. He went below as soon as Betty Dwight had got out of sight. I hurried after her, still hoping I could take something out of her cabin, for I saw that there was some kind of a chance to mix things up, and what I had just seen had made me suspicious."

"It would have made anybody suspicious," said MacMasters.

"I went onto the deck outside her cabin and looked through the window—there were windows on that deck, and when I saw her go into the bathroom, I reached in and took the marten cape which she had put on the back of a chair below the window. But she came right out of the bathroom again and I thought she had seen me—so I got frightened and threw the cape overboard. Then I went right back to my own cabin and called up the Lindstrom woman. She wouldn't listen to me—said they were only interested in tennis for the sake of sport. And when I said I had seen her on deck, she only laughed at me and hung up. Then I laughed at her. I decided I would play Azarin, his niece and the Lindstrom woman against Betty Dwight."

"A very nifty idea!" said MacMasters.

"I thought so too," she said. She seemed rather proud of herself for a moment. "So, I telephoned Betty Dwight, and I told her all sorts of things—that I had just seen her talking with the Lindstrom woman on deck and that it had looked pretty mysterious and secretive, that David was writing special articles for the newspapers about behind-the-scenes in tennis, and that I would tell him about her talk with Lindstrom unless she kept away from him. I said I was naturally very upset at seeing her with him, as he and I were really engaged, that I was going to Europe with him—otherwise why was I on this boat, but that we had to keep our engagement secret until later because of some family reasons. I said if she didn't believe me she could ask him, and she said she would never ask him such a question."

"I don't think that Miss Dwight is the kind of girl who would have been likely to question a young man on such matters when she had known him only a few days. You were very clever to see that, Miss Blythe," said MacMasters in a flattering way.

"Then I went to Lindstrom's cabin. She was out and I looked around for anything I could find," she said.

"Miss Blythe," MacMasters said, "you are in a very ticklish position at the moment. You can be arrested for impersonating another person for malicious purposes, for stealing, for all sorts of things; but I'll let you off if you will tell me one thing. Did you find any medicine—powders or capsules or bottles or boxes that attracted your attention? Be careful of your answer."

"I . . . I found only toilet articles, cold cream, and things like that."

"Arrest," MacMasters said, "is very unpleasant."

"Ah," she said. "Yes, I remember. In the bottom of her trunk I found a little glass bottle, wrapped in paper. It had things like commas in it."

"Commas?" MacMasters said. He sat up. "What do you mean, commas?"

"Like the commas a typewriter makes. They were black. There were a lot of them, dried looking things."

I looked at her in astonishment—either she was unbalanced completely or she was trying to get out of the situation with some far-fetched imagining.

"It must have been while I was in Lindstrom's cabin that Betty Dwight came to mine the first time. Oh, I had her badly worried by that time," she said with some satisfaction. "Then she came to my cabin again when I was in, and said I had no right to annoy her, and that I must stop it. I said her conversation with the Lindstrom woman must have been pretty serious, or she wouldn't be so excited now. She got angry then, and I laughed and said she was making a fool of herself and was showing that she was jealous because of David and me. I couldn't help that he loved me. He had just been trying to get a story about her. When I said she was jealous, she controlled herself and got very up-stage—you know the frozen-face act she puts on—and went out. I knew I had caused her to change her mind in some way. . . ."

I saw it now. This miserable Blythe had taken a crazy kind of fancy to me—there was no doubt about that, and had started some doubts in Betty's mind about me. Betty had been more hurt than angry. Then I went away to the Continent just at the time when I could have been of some help to her, Aunt Bea had forgotten to give her my message, I had been stalking around with MacMasters after Marie Azarin's death. Evidently Betty had felt that I shared Mac-Masters' suspicions.

What more was the Blythe girl going to say? I watched her with a kind of fascinated stare. She was looking at me with a sort of despair on her face. She was no longer pleased she had been so clever. She went on in a hurried, shaky sort of way: "I really thought I had changed her feelings about David, so I didn't go near her any more. I wasn't going to, but when Marie Azarin died at Wimbledon, and the papers began to hint at murder, I saw I had a real chance to get even with her. I came to the hotel here and told her I was going to tell the police I had seen her plotting with Lind-strom. I told her I had heard David suspected her too. Then I got thinking that Inspector MacMasters would suspect me, perhaps; I had heard about his reputation as a detective so I got frightened and went to Bognor Regis."

I groaned.

"How do we know that you didn't steal Miss Dwight's fur cape earlier in the evening and wear it yourself? Perhaps it was you on the boat deck talking with Helga Lindstrom!" MacMasters said. "You have no real proof that it was not yourself on deck that last night. Could you swear, Cameron, that the woman you saw in the white dress and marten cape was Betty Dwight?"

"No, I could not swear to it," I said.

"Of course he wouldn't say! He's in love with her!" she cried. Then she was quiet for a space. Her ever-present dissatisfaction was like an active thing—it was there in spite of her being haggard and tired. She twisted her hands. "I didn't do anything really, except take the cape, and I didn't intend to throw it overboard. And I didn't intend telling you anything, Inspector MacMasters, but you frightened me into it. You have no right to use third degree methods!"

"I did not use third degree methods, Miss Blythe," he said with a smile. "You've even enjoyed telling me some of the things."

"I certainly have not! I got terribly nervous coming here. That man," she indicated the Sergeant, "who brought me here was cruel and unkind. And the other one who found me at Bognor Regis was a brute."

My God! I thought, where had she got the idea that people were trying to persecute *her!*

She stood up. "I hope you are satisfied," she said to us. "You have ruined my life. You have taken David away from me forever. I want to get out of here and not be tortured any more. Will you let me go—you know everything—and you've used brute force to get it. I've told you the truth."

MacMasters said nothing.

She threw back her head, and said, "Don't forget you haven't found out what Betty Dwight said to Helga Lindstrom!"

This gave me a real shock. Things hadn't been cleared up so well, after all. I thought MacMasters was making a mistake when he decided to let Cynthia Blythe go. He said, "You may go, but remember, from now on you leave these people alone, or we'll have you in jail for the theft of that marten cape if for nothing else! And furthermore," he said severely, "don't go around pulling any funny tricks on other people either!"

She stood up and went to the door.

"You can't leave England until I say so, you know," he said. "Where will you be staying?"

"I am at the Warwick Hotel," she said shortly.

"By the way, did you ever know a man named Batt? Or Saunders?"

She shook her head in negation. MacMasters got up and moved his chair, and she went out without looking at us again. "Crackpot number four," he said. "She put in a lot of buttonholes and sewed it up the back." He took a cigarette and lighted it, and grinned mockingly at me. "What a man!" he said to me in a theatrically admiring tone. "They just follow you around!"

"I've never seen anybody like that before," I said.

"Oh, we come across them occasionally in this business," he said. "An unstable, emotional type, with erotic inclinations. Like to get themselves into a situation where they can enjoy the idea that they are being persecuted. It makes them feel important. They feed on mild delusions."

"You call that mild?" I asked. "Well, it was all too much for me."

"Sorry I had to sit on you a while ago," MacMasters said. "Sergeant!" he called.

CHAPTER SEVENTEEN

We both stood up when Betty and the Sergeant came in. As she entered the room Betty glanced swiftly at me. A little color had returned to her face, and a little animation; there was a difference in it, a difference that was very slight but unmistakable. MacMasters watched her curiously; he looked at her as though he were interested in her, not as a suspect, but as a personality. He continued to look at her as she walked to a chair and sat down; then he sat down himself.

"Miss Dwight," he said, after a moment, "will you tell me how Miss Blythe got mixed up in this affair?"

She looked at him steadily and appeared to withdraw a bit. "Didn't she tell you?" she asked. There was a hint of that old appealing timbre in her voice.

"I didn't ask her," MacMasters said with great blandness.

I stirred a little. It was going to be that know-nothing sort of questioning again, and I was going to have to sit through it. The Sergeant looked at me, raising his glance from his book and dropping it again.

"I wouldn't like to go into it, unless it is necessary," she answered.

"Yes, it is necessary to go into it. Don't hesitate to explain things to me—more people have tried to explain things to me than you could count on an abacus."

"She was just a foolish girl," Betty said. "I feel sorry for her."

"You mustn't, Miss Dwight. People like that can do a great deal of harm sometimes—unless they are found out in time," MacMasters said. "Tell me, did you know her before sailing on the *Princess Victoria?*"

"I didn't know Cynthia Blythe," Betty said. "I'd never seen her before I got on the ship."

"But why in the name of common sense didn't you tell me about her before? You can't always go through life without explanations—especially when people fall dead around you!"

She colored a little. "I can't help it," she said. "It's part of me and I can't help it—I've never explained anything. If people like me, they trust me."

"Will you answer this—did you speak to Helga Lindstrom on the boat deck that last night?" MacMasters asked leaning forward.

"Yes," she said, after a visible hesitation.

I hadn't expected this; it gave me a shock. I was sure Cynthia Blythe had been lying.

"How did that happen?" MacMasters asked.

"I slipped up on deck for a little air. The Lindstrom woman spoke to me first. She said she wanted to tell me some things about Marie Azarin's game—that she knew how Azarin had been coaching his niece, and what he had told her to do if she played me," Betty said. "I paid no attention to her at the time because people often try to tell me how to play; but afterwards I thought it strange of her to have done it, since she was with the Azarins."

"You wore your marten cape?" MacMasters asked.

"Yes."

"Did the Lindstrom woman make any other suggestions as to how you might win the match? Drugs or anything?" he asked.

"Why, no," she said, paling. She realized she was in a difficult position.

"You're sure?" he asked.

"Yes."

"Did you know Lady Irene Wrexford-Bond?" he asked.

"No," she said.

"Didn't you telephone her?"

She looked up quickly. "Telephone her?" And after a long moment she answered: "Yes."

"What about?"

Betty didn't say anything; but her face took on a stubborn expression, and there was a subtle change in her bearing. Her head had come up slightly, and the stubborn expression became tinged with impatience.

MacMasters waited for a moment. "Would there be any connection," he asked, "between your call to Lady Irene and your visit to Limehouse?"

"I prefer not to say," she said.

MacMasters raised his eyebrows. "No?" he asked sarcastically. "No, I suppose not. Where did you go when you went out the back door with that Garcia? Why did you write him to come here? Why did you find out about him in the first place? I'll tell you why. You wanted to buy something and didn't know where to buy it, so you asked Andrews and he mentioned Lady Irene. And what did you and that scarred man find to talk about?"

"I didn't talk to him," she said, and the stubborn expression deepened on her face. "He talked to me. First he talked to me in the lobby, and then every time I went out he came and asked me the time. He was harmless. There have been a great number of such people, people who wanted me to help them dig for gold in old castles, and people who sent me flowers, and people with all sorts of crazy notions. They see my name in the papers and bother me."

MacMasters made an irritated gesture. "Forget them," he said. "I would like answers to my questions. Why did you draw eight thousand dollars out of the bank and go to Limehouse with it?"

"I won't answer your questions," she said. Her color had come back to normal; it was even a little higher than usual. She had taken on the appearance of anger, and suddenly let go at him. "I think you are all mad!" she said. "Every one of you! Have I done anything to be followed about in this way? I have hardly seen my Aunt Bea. She is out all of the time, and if I go out she tries to discover where I am going."

MacMasters interrupted her. "And why not?" he asked. He had raised his voice, as she had raised hers. "Good Heavens, do you have to act like a shrinking violet when there's a murder charge hanging over you?" He stood up. "I want information, I—"

It was her turn to interrupt him. She stood up too, and said: "You won't get it from me. What I bought is my own affair, and I intend to keep it my affair. Wasn't it dreadful enough for me to see Marie Azarin fall dead before me without this? I had nothing to do with it, I tell you!" She was so angry—or simulating anger—that she was quivering. It was very strange, it was one of the most confusing scenes I had ever witnessed; but she looked very beautiful like that.

"Will you deny that you came downstairs when the scarred man in the Park flashed a mirror into your window?" MacMasters demanded.

"I will deny nothing," she said. "Although I know of no scarred man flashing mirrors into windows. If I happened to come downstairs while people were flashing mirrors about it was entirely accidental."

MacMasters walked up to her. She moved back from him quickly. Then there was a tremendous rattle at the door. "Oho!" MacMasters said, turning toward it. "Now we'll get somewhere."

He took four rapid strides toward the door, shoved the chair aside and opened it. Mrs. Cosgrove was standing there, looking furious and puzzled at the same time. When she saw him she hastily composed her features and stepped into the room. I looked around then, for Betty; but she had gone into one of the bedrooms and wasn't in sight.

"Why, David Cameron!" Mrs. Cosgrove said. "I've been waiting for you to call for a long time. It's got so that I *simply* can't bear it any more. You've either got to—" She broke off, remembering MacMasters, and looked inquiringly at me. I introduced him. "Glad you've come," MacMasters said. "Will you tell me if you were here the other day—yesterday or the day before—when someone flashed a mirror in the window?"

"Of course I was here," she said. "And I was *most* uncomfortable. My niece and I had been quarrelling, and she had just gone out when this perfectly *horrid* little thing began to dance about on the ceiling, and I looked out. There was a man in the Park doing it and I telephoned down for them to stop him *immediately*. And we were quarrelling, if you must know, about David Cameron, because I told Betty that she knew nothing about him, that one knows nothing about young men one meets on boats, and I told them downstairs if he called up they were positively not to let him talk to her." She paused to take a breath, and I stared at her incredulously. "I decided the other day to put a large sum of money in the bank in Betty's name, thinking it would be a good idea to keep some money in England—you know how it is in America now—you can't tell what the Government will do next. What did she do first thing but go to a perfectly *horrid* place and pay a simply *enormous* price for a star sapphire—I suspect it had been smuggled in from India. So we quarreled again. It was to be a present for this young man," she indicated me. "Why should she buy such extravagant presents for some person whom she scarcely knew? After all, he had come here only once, and she was so upset, then, she wouldn't go anywhere. I had to go about with Charley Gasden to the theatre and dancing, and then Charley vanished, positively *vanished*. He was always talking about suicide, said he carried a gun, but I don't believe it. Where the poor boy is now I can't imagine. He was so nice. And of course he adored Betty. . . ."

MacMasters stood looking at her with his head on one side; the Sergeant had dropped his little black book on the floor and was staring at her. She looked at both of them helplessly, then burst into tears, put her hands out, and came blindly towards me. I took a step towards her; her arms went around me with surprising strength.

"Oh, David!" she blubbered. "Oh, David! You and Inspector MacMasters look so respectable that I am sure you are to be trusted. I like you very much, after all, David. Oh! Oh! I've been so unhappy! Betty is all I have in the world. I've been so worried about her. . . ."

It was all so incoherent, I was completely confounded. I looked at MacMasters, who suddenly started to laugh. He laughed until the tears ran down his face. Then he walked over and disengaged Mrs. Cosgrove from me, led her to a divan, and sat her down on it. She continued to cry, with abandon, paying attention to no one.

"Come on," MacMasters said.

I realized he was talking to me. "Come on?" I asked. "Come where? I'm not going anywhere. Did you hear what Mrs. Cosgrove said? Betty . . ."

He interrupted me by putting my hat on my head. "Do you want me to laugh myself to death," he asked, "over the girlish pranks in this whole asinine affair? You'll have plenty of time later to explain to Betty. You saw the start of this and you'll see the end of it. And besides we need strength in numbers now. Get his arm, Sergeant!"

The Sergeant, looking thoroughly bewildered, came over quickly and took me under one arm. Simultaneously they were upon me. What a team! I dug my feet into the rug, but they won by superior weight. I said if they would let me go, I'd go with them. We went out the side entrance and got into a cab.

"I've got to get back as soon as possible," I said. I didn't know whether to be furious or whether to cheer. "Betty bought the star sapphire because we talked about them on the boat," I said. "She bought it for me. It is as clear as day now." My spirits had risen a hundred per cent.

"Yes," said MacMasters, "it was her little secret. A very coy interlude, I'd call it. On the ridiculous side if you ask me—but I don't mind."

"I don't think it was ridiculous," I said.

"Cheer up, everybody," MacMasters said. "We've got a day's work ahead of us yet. It just goes to show that you mustn't hold it against a girl because she refuses to explain herself or propose to young men, when they are so backward as not to do it themselves."

"I thought she was mad at me," I said, "and besides you would never let me get near her except once and then I put my foot in it." Then two nasty suspicions crossed my mind. I turned on MacMasters. "I want you to answer just two questions: did you think I had something to do with the murder, and did you tell the Dorchester operator not to let me speak over the phone to Betty?"

"Well, I won't say yes or no to those two questions—you will have to think the answers out for yourself," he said with a grin. "I must say, though, that I rather like the idea of Betty's making up her mind that she wouldn't admit she cared for you, or that she had bought that sapphire for you. She has her pride, that girl! You haven't got a very good understanding of women, I'm afraid."

"Well, you didn't understand so very much either until Aunt Bea busted in."

"But you did have sharp eyes when you picked out Saunders-Batt-Conover so handily." He was thinking out loud. "On the whole, however, I feel I would have gotten along faster with the case without you."

"Well, that makes me feel fine," I said, happy for other reasons, "maybe I can make up for lost time now!"

"Wait and see," he said. "And keep your hands out of your pockets. You too, Sergeant. You might need them in a hurry." He slouched back and closed his eyes; his face seemed to grow leaner and colder. There might even have been a touch of cruelty in it. But then, I reflected, looking at him, he had to have a certain amount of it. After all, it was his business to catch crooks in any way he could—not to waste time wondering what had made them that way. He was a hard man; he had been hard on me; but with his character and method, it seemed to work. It even seemed to amuse him in an ironic fashion.

Presently I stopped studying his still face and fell to looking out the window. We came to Putney Bridge, and the

River had a new shine on it, the air a new brilliance; for the first time since the *Princess Victoria* docked at Southampton I felt an interest in seeing England. We might even see it together, I thought, Betty and I.

The river fell behind, and the streets of Putney; things began to open out. We passed the edge of Putney Heath and the Reservoir, and as we came into Wimbledon MacMasters opened his eyes and sat up.

"I want a constable," he said to the driver. "Stop when you see one. If you can get two of them, so much the better."

The Sergeant stirred a little; an air of tension crept into the cab. It caught me too, and I wondered what MacMasters was going to do. He didn't have much to go on in the way of actual evidence, no solid thing that could be brought out and handed around in a court. The driver saw a constable and stopped for him; MacMasters told him to get in, and we drove on. We picked up another one near Azarin's house. When we came to the house, MacMasters told the driver to wait in the street, and we all got out.

"One of you take the back door," he said to the constables, "and the other take the front. If any particular row starts, come in. If anybody comes out on the run, wing him." We all marched up the walk; one constable halted at the bottom of the steps and the other disappeared around the house. We went up on the porch and rang. Pomfret came to the door; she started slightly when she saw Mac-Masters, then tried to smile at him.

"Morning, Pomfret," he said. "Tell me, do you ever clean the third floor?"

"No, sir," she said. "I'm not to go on the third floor, sir."

"Good," MacMasters said. "We'll come in. Please tell Mr. Azarin I'd like to see him in the drawing room."

She turned away and we went in, along the hall, and into the drawing room. The curtains were drawn again, and the greenish light lay over everything, more sinister than before. It wasn't very long before Azarin came downstairs and into the room. He had on flannels and a white shirt open at the neck, an orange scarf; but he hadn't shaved and his beard, beginning to turn gray, shadowed the faint, oily, greenish shine of his sleepy-looking face.

"Good morning, Inspector," he said. "Won't you sit down? Sorry I have no champagne to offer you this time." There was an edge of insolence in his tone, and he sat down in the nearest chair while the rest of us were still standing. "What can I do for you now?"

MacMasters walked over and backed up to the fireplace. "Indications would point out," he said, "that there is some sort of communication going on between this house and the one behind it. Are you in charge of these communications?"

Azarin didn't move, and he should have moved. He sat perfectly still, as still as a stone; only his eyes swung toward MacMasters. "Communications?" he asked. "What communications?"

"There has to be a headquarters somewhere," MacMasters said, "and you're elected. Just to remove the air of mystery, I'll break down and admit that we've scooped up all in one, a man named Saunders, a man named Batt, and a man named Conover and a make-up kit."

Azarin's eyes narrowed swiftly and opened again to their usual drooping-lidded position. "Really?" he asked. "And what of that?"

"He talked," MacMasters said. "Being full of regret that you didn't tell him of Lady Irene's death, he talked. If he hadn't been worried about Lady Irene—whom nobody, by the way, seems to have trusted—we wouldn't have caught him. He'd done his work for the day and taken his whiskers off; but when he saw Lady Irene and Cameron here lunching together at the Ritz he thought that Lady Irene and Andrews were selling out. It's too bad you ever played tag with Andrews."

"The son of a bitch!" Azarin said. "All right. Can't I have an outside man to give me reports?"

"Yes," MacMasters said. "Yes, indeed. I'm glad you're not going to be tiresome. But why would he kill Gasden?"

"He didn't kill Gasden," Azarin said. "When he saw Andrews go to Limehouse he followed him. I had to know what Andrews was up to. He pitched me such a convincing story, as though he'd actually seen the Da Vinci picture, that I wanted to know what he was up to. It would have been worth about a million dollars. When Gasden talked to Andrews the man thought Gasden was in it too. He didn't kill him. He merely went to the nursing home the next morning and asked what Gasden knew. Maybe he frightened Gasden."

"Of course he did," MacMasters said. "He frightened Gasden into killing himself. Gasden had been on the edge of doing it for a long time, hadn't he? His nerves were gone to the devil."

"So what?" Azarin demanded. "Am I responsible for every damn drunk in London? This Batt kept an eye on Andrews and looked Betty Dwight over for me once in a while, but what's that? You haven't got anything on me. If he disguised himself and was seen with Betty Dwight, can I be given the rap for that? Betty Dwight's opponent died on the courts; if I could hang anything on Betty Dwight so much the better. The heat was on me enough." He paused and licked his lips. "I lost money on that match, more money than suited me. I had to borrow some from Irene—you know that—and I paid a stiff price for it. Do you think I wanted to marry her? Hell! She was a hophead and everything else. I'll tell you straight, Inspector, I've done nothing in England. It's too hard to get away with it. By God, I've lost my money and the best tennis player I ever saw, and you come around with a lot of drivel. Why don't you find out who killed Marie? Why the hell don't you do something?"

"A sound idea," MacMasters said. "You didn't even get any money in Lady Irene's will. But why did you tell me that she talked with Batt?"

"She did talk with Batt."

"She didn't talk with Batt." MacMasters went on. "She didn't even know Batt. Are you trying to tell me that Batt killed her because he was afraid she'd get him mixed up in something? I expected better of you. Batt came here to find out whether you knew what was going on between Lady Irene and Cameron, and when he found out she was here he nearly went away again. He's so afraid of you—like all the rest of them—that he got rattled and came here in broad daylight. You've given the jitters to all of them, but they didn't expect any killings. If there hadn't been any killings you'd have been all right; but there were, and they let you down. Listen: you got out of France because things were getting a little warm, and went to the States. By and large you behaved yourself there. Your income dropped a little, but you found a tennis player who promised to fix that. There's money in tennis these days. But you've lost your tennis player and your money. Think that over for a minute."

Azarin sat very still, staring at him with a sort of abstract, withdrawn coldness. As for MacMasters, he still leaned against the mantel; but he had got a Mephistophelian look on himself. His eyes were narrow and his face seemed to have narrowed along with them; his lean figure was tight as a coiled spring.

"Tomayo," he said. "Tomayo was afraid of you too. At first he wouldn't admit that he found a small piece of gelatin, such as capsules designed to melt at body heat are made of, under the bandage on Marie's arm. The doctors at Wimbledon didn't take it off because things were in such a scramble, and it had nothing to do with what appeared to be peritonitis, anyway. Everybody was too flustered to think about poison then. But what's that to you?" His voice, slow and incisive and prodding, went on. "What's it to you that you promised to marry her if she won the match? And what's it to you that you promised to marry Irene Wrexford-Bond if she pulled you out of a hole? They're both dead now. All the women you promise to marry die, don't they?"

Azarin still stared at him. He seemed to have sunk into his chair a little. "Go on," he said. His voice was hoarse. "Go on, damn you."

"And what's it to you," MacMasters' voice kept at him, "that one black widow spider rarely kills anyone? But if you get a lot of them, a hundred or so, and pull out their fangs and poison sacs and dry them, the potency remains unimpaired. And you can take eighty or so pairs of sacs, dried and potent, and extract them in one centimeter of water; and in that one cubic centimeter of water you have a poison unrivalled for power and quickness, with the further advantage that it acts like an acute peritonitis and leaves nothing for the Home Office experts to find. It can be put into capsules over an open wound or into a syringe full of morphine left lying where anyone could find it. One cubic centimeter isn't much. Several drops. And then where's your money, where's your tennis player?"

Azarin had got to his feet, slowly, in a sort of crouching fashion. He took a step, into the filtered green glow falling through the curtain, and immediately seemed to expand, to get larger than his usual size. His face had become suffused with blood, and his eyes glared greenishly. His arms hung down in a slight curve, like an ape's, and his mouth worked. He stared at MacMasters for a long minute, a crazy stare, then began to move, still in crouching fashion, toward the door. MacMasters moved alongside of him; the Sergeant was on his feet and took the other side. At the door they stopped him.

"Call her," MacMasters said. "Call her down."

Azarin made a strangled noise in his throat. "Helga!" he said. I wouldn't have recognized his voice, but the tone of it sent a chill up my spine. "Helga, come here!" He was cursing under his breath.

There was a stir over my head, a few rapid steps, then silence. It seemed to stretch on forever, it was the most horrible period of time I had ever experienced. I turned my glance from the door, from the three figures; it stopped on the great gray African mask, washed over with green light and grinning, at the other end of the room. As I stared at it the time went on, a crawling thing; the Sergeant made a move toward the hall, but MacMasters checked him. The silence held, and my hair stirred; then there was a gun's crash above our heads and the ceiling shook as a body fell to the floor. We knew it was Helga. There was no further sound. Azarin, turned loose by MacMasters and the Sergeant, almost fell down too. He pushed himself up again, like a half-conscious fighter trying to come back, and with a crablike scuttle moved across the hall and started up the stairs.

"Go along, Sergeant," MacMasters said. "I'll be up in a minute."

My knees felt suddenly funny, and I started for the porch. I didn't like the green light in the room, or anything that had happened there. I pushed open the door, and the air tasted good. MacMasters came out.

"You see?" he said. "Helga was too smart to keep the stuff around anymore. She even emptied the makings down the drain, so I wouldn't have any of it to produce in court. I didn't have anything on her."

"You mean to tell me you haven't got a thing to show that Helga murdered Marie Azarin? After all this?" I asked incredulously.

"I didn't have anything on her," he repeated. "But she must have thought I had or she wouldn't have shot herself. She knew murderers don't have much chance in England. Anyone has to be a pretty queer fish to poison another person in cold blood the way she poisoned Marie Azarin. Helga was at least consistent in her cold-bloodedness. I think we'll find when we go upstairs that she did a good job of the suicide too." He lit a cigarette. "Tomayo, Marie's uncle, might have found something, but he would never have admitted it; they found nothing in the hypodermic syringe and nothing in the bottle but morphine solution. On the day Lady Irene died, Helga had gone upstairs, filled the syringe, added the poison to it, and left it where Lady Irene would pick it up."

"Black widows," I said. "You knew a lot about them? Was that a bluff too?"

"Oh, no," he said. "That's about the only thing I didn't have to bluff on. I telephoned to a place in California where they make the anti-venom and they gave me the works. Remember when I made that telephone call that evening in my house just before we went over to the Ritz? I just got curious at that moment about various 'natural' poisons—I suppose our conversation about your black widow bite in California brought it up."

"Well," I said to MacMasters, "I've got to hand it to you!"

MacMasters' eyes took on a far-away look. "There's a recurrent line in some of the old Norse sagas, it goes: '. . . And the feeder of wolves was fed to the ravens.' I suppose it means gals like Helga."

I took a step. "I don't think I want to see Helga—again—otherwise is there anything I can do for you?"

"Nothing more today—but drop in and see me sometime before you go back to New York."

"I will," I said. "Well, I'm glad this is all over."

"Every man to his own choice," he said, and grinned. "And don't ever start any arguments, my lad. You'll have to do all the making up yourself! That girl never explains anything. She just sits and waits for the fullness of time to prove she was right. Maybe she always is, at that. Well . . ." He let the word hang on the air, and turned back into the house.

ABOUT THE AUTHORS

Helen Wills (1905-1998) held the top position in women's tennis for nine years (1927-1933, 1935, and 1938). She won 31 Grand Slam tournament titles, had eight wins at Wimbledon, and won two Olympic gold medals (Paris, 1924). She has been called 'arguably the most dominant tennis player of the 20th century,' and one of the greatest female players in history. Nicknamed 'Little Miss Poker Face,' she was driven and focused, rarely displaying emotion in her matches. She didn't just want to win, claiming: 'I know I would hate life if I were deprived of trying, hunting, working for some objective within which there lies the beauty of perfection.'

Born in California, Helen graduated from Anna Head School in Berkeley, then attended the University of California, Berkeley. An introvert, she often had difficulty making friends with other players or interacting with the crowds. She did gain many admirers and celebrity friends throughout here career, and married twice. She wrote a coaching manual in 1928, her autobiography in 1937, and co-authored *Death Serves an Ace* in 1938. She retired in tennis after her last Wimbledon title in 1938.

A fine new photograph of Helen Wills, whose tennis-mystery story, "Death Serves an Ace," written in collaboration with Robert Murphy, was published recently by Charles Schribner's Sons.

Robert William Murphy (1902-1971) was a naturalist and author, writing numerous nature books. He was senior editor at *The Saturday Evening Post* from 1942 to 1962. Besides co-authoring *Death Serves an Ace*, he wrote *Murder in Waiting* (1938).

REFERENCES:

Fein, Paul. 2005. Who is the greatest female player ever? *Inside Tennis.com* https://web.archive.org/web/20110103135840/http://www.insidetennis.com/archive/0405_bestfemale.html

Obituary. 1971. Robert Murphy, a nature writer. *New York Times* https://www.nytimes.com/1971/07/14/archives/robert-murphy-a-nature-writer-exeditor-and-an-author-of-many-books.html

Wikipedia. 2018. Helen Wills. https://en.wikipedia.org/wiki/Helen_Wills

COACHWHIP PUBLICATIONS
CoachwhipBooks.com

MURDER
IN THE
ROUGH

LESLIE
ALLEN

COACHWHIP PUBLICATIONS
CoachwhipBooks.com

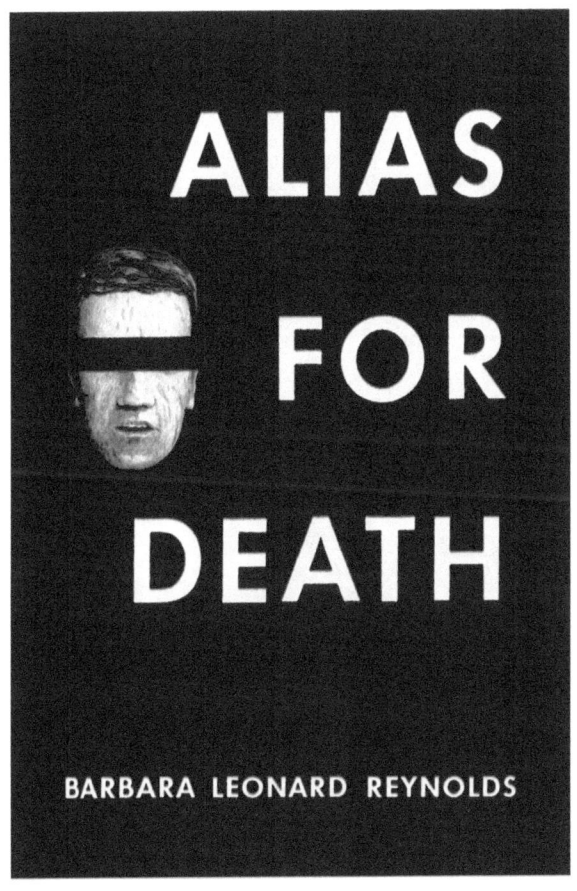

ALIAS
FOR
DEATH

BARBARA LEONARD REYNOLDS

COACHWHIP PUBLICATIONS
CoachwhipBooks.com

THE
RUMBLE
MURDERS

Henry Ware Eliot, Jr.

COACHWHIP PUBLICATIONS
CoachwhipBooks.com

THE
SARA ELIZABETH
MASON
MYSTERIES

MURDER RENTS A ROOM

⫸ ⫷

THE CRIMSON FEATHER

COACHWHIP PUBLICATIONS
COACHWHIPBOOKS.COM

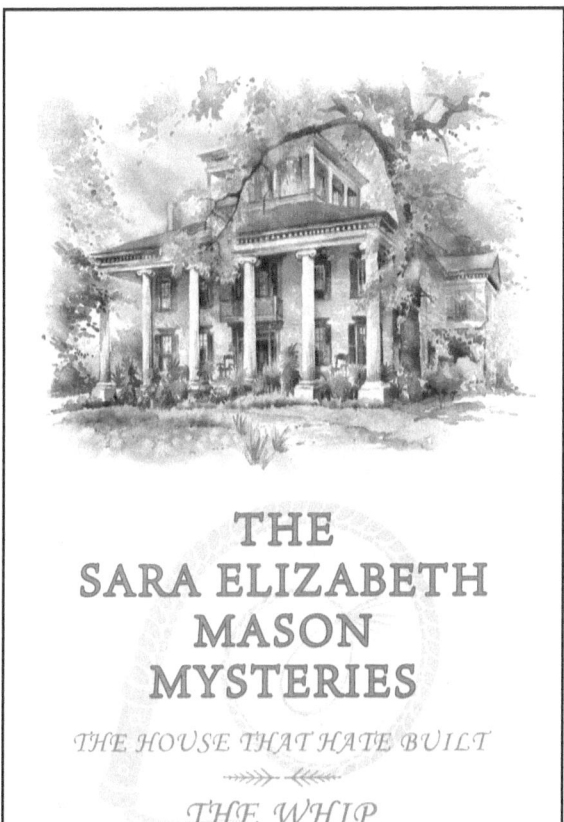

THE
SARA ELIZABETH
MASON
MYSTERIES

THE HOUSE THAT HATE BUILT

>>> <<<

THE WHIP

COACHWHIP PUBLICATIONS
COACHWHIPBOOKS.COM

NARROW
GAUGE TO
MURDER

CAROLYN THOMAS

MURDER TAKES
THE VEIL

MURDER AT
ST. DENNIS

SISTER SIMON'S
MURDER CASE

THE MARGARET ANN HUBBARD
MYSTERY OMNIBUS